The
Curmudgeon
and the
Wormhole

J.F. WIEGAND

Copyright © 2020 J.F. Wiegand

All rights reserved.

No portion of this book may be reproduced in any form without permission from the author.

Visit the author's website at www.jfwiegand.com

Background art by Andrei Bordeianu, Benguhan Ipekoz, and Ryhor Bruyeu – Depositphotos.com.

Full cover by the author.

CHAPTER 1

The man sitting across from me is clean-shaven, wearing a shirt and tie, and smells like he's had a shower and a cup of coffee. Not something I'm used to. I've spent the last few months on Bomba, and there the men are unshaven and shirtless, with brands on their sunburned arms, and smelling like complete ass; which is how I'd describe myself right now.

"You lived in Henderson, right? Nevada?" the man asks.

I nod.

"Is that where you were ... when it happened?"

"Yes," I say, my voice groggy.

"That was June 2nd?"

I'm tired of his questions, which he's been asking for the past hour. I'd get up and leave, but my legs won't support me yet—a side effect of having gone through.

He straightens his tie. "June 2nd?"

As I open my mouth to answer, a wave of nausea fills

my stomach. I hunch over the table and hold back what will eventually come out.

"Are you okay?" the man asks. Although calling him a man is generous. He's in his mid-thirties, maybe. With his ballpoint pen, he writes something on a clean pad of paper—an improvement from that charcoal and parchment shit I'd been using.

"I'm going to read off some names," he says. "When you hear one that's familiar—and not one you heard on the news, but someone you actually met on Bomba—let me know. That's what you called the planet, right? Bomba?"

Clutching my stomach, I nod. Then I set my elbow on the table and rest my throbbing head against my palm.

"Brian Pindell … Julio Sanchez … Lucy Tasker … Rodrigo Flores …"

"Yes," I say, nodding.

"Rodrigo?"

I nod.

"Is he still alive?" the man asks.

I hesitate for a moment, picking dirt from under my fingernails. "No."

The man writes something, then wipes sweat from his temple. It must be ninety-five degrees in here, so I know he's hot. Not me. There are goosebumps on my arms, and a chill runs down my spine. I glance up, taking in the plain, wooden structure. We're in an outdoor FBI training facility close to where they found me. I can't imagine being in an air-controlled location. I'd be fucking freezing.

He continues. "Teresa Acevedo … Andrew Tessmer …

Jose Alto … Shauna Kingswood …"

I hold up my hand. "I knew a Shauna, but—" I wince, tasting vomit in my throat. "I didn't know her last name."

"We're only aware of one Shauna that's gone missing, so it's probably her," the man says.

"Well, now I know her last name."

"Is she alive?" he asks.

"The last time I saw her, she was."

Again, he writes.

I cross my arms against my bare chest. "Are you going to skip Jennifer?"

The man rolls his pen back and forth between his fingers, which are clean, with neatly trimmed nails. "If you want me to."

I exhale.

"I'm sorry, Norman, but like I said, you were the only one we found." He shifts in his chair. "So my assumption is that she's still there, still on Bomba."

I hold back tears as Jennifer's face fills my mind.

"Do you want to tell me what happened?" he asks, setting down his pen.

"I'm on Earth now," I say. "How am I supposed to know?"

"I meant there," he says. "What happened before you went through? Before you came back."

I stare down at the table. "I was arranging for her to get to Santuario. That's Spanish for sanctuary." I rub my head. "It's apparently some human-only island. Away from the goddamn sponges."

"Have you been there?" he asks. "To Santuario?"

As he lifts his pad of paper, turning over a fresh sheet, his sleeve rides up, revealing a mark on his bicep.

Was that a brand?

My chest tightens. "What is that?"

"Excuse me?" he says.

"On your arm."

The man looks down, confused. "What do you mean?"

I point, my eyes locked on his bicep. "You have a brand." I suck in a breath as my heart begins to thump. "You have a brand on your arm."

His eyes drift to his left arm. He reaches down and lifts his sleeve, revealing a tattoo of a cross. "It's a tattoo."

I stare at it for a long moment, then say, "Can you lift your other sleeve?"

The man sighs, then lifts his right sleeve. Another tattoo, this one an intertwined crown of thorns, wrapping around his bicep.

"Jesus' crown?" I ask.

He nods.

The tension in my shoulders ease; for a moment I thought I was still on Bomba. Although honestly that's where I'd rather be right now. Not because I liked it there—it sucked, but to reach her. To get to Santuario.

My gaze returns to his tattoos. I shake my head. *Typical millennial.* They can't just go to church every Sunday and be fine with that. They need to show everyone how religious they are. So damn pretentious.

"You were mentioning," he says, letting his sleeve fall.

"Santuario."

I ignore his question. "What's your name again?"

"I'm Special Agent Maryson," he says.

"No, what's your first name?"

"It's Joshua." He swallows. "Why?"

"We didn't use last names on Bomba. I'm not used to it." I dig gook from of my eyes. "I'd rather call you by your first name."

"Okay." He thinks, tapping his finger against the table. "Wait, but you knew Rodrigo's last name."

"That's because I saw his father's grave."

"On Bomba?"

I nod.

"Was that," he says, scanning his list. "Mateo? Mateo Flores?"

"Yes, but like I said, we didn't go by last names. It was Norman from house six or … Joshua from house four."

"Did you know a Joshua on Bomba?" he asks.

"No," I say, shaking my head. "Although I did hear that name a few days ago."

He picks up his pen and uses it to find his place on the list. "I'm going to read a few more names."

"No, no, please," I say. "I'm done with the names."

"Well, then can you tell me what happened to you?" he says. "That's what I really want to know. And while it's still fresh in your mind." He leans forward. "I know you're tired, I know you don't feel well, but this is important."

I drop my head and close my eyes. I sit there, motionless for a minute.

Finally, I say, "Can I see my wife?"

"Like I mentioned, Mr. Dohring, we've sent agents to your house," he says. "But even when your wife arrives, it'll be a while before you can see her."

I open my eyes. "Why?"

"Because there are still tests we need to run on you." He looks me over. "For your safety and for ours."

"What about you?" I ask. "It's not like you're wearing a hazmat suit. Aren't you worried about catching some weird Bomba disease?"

"I thought it was worth the risk to get your story quickly." He interlocks his hands together, as if preparing to pray. "I need to know why it brought you back."

"It?"

"The wormhole," he says, straightening in his chair.

I stay quiet. My eyes feel heavy. My body aches.

"Mr. Dohring—"

"Stop." I clear my throat. "I'll tell you what happened." I grip the sides of the table and scoot closer. "But I feel like shit, so don't interrupt me. I don't know how long I'll last."

"I won't," he says, preparing to write. "But start from your last day on Earth, when you woke up. And I want details, everything you can remember, no matter how minor you think it is."

I swallow down more vomit and lick sweat from above my lip. "Fine." I blow out a long breath, thinking back to June 2nd. "My last day on Earth started with a heat advisory, which is ironic considering where I went."

CHAPTER 2

"The heat advisory will go into effect at ten-thirty," the weatherman said. And he emphasized the time, as if we only had a few hours to live. For me, it was sort of true; I just didn't realize it at the time. Then he pressed his hands together, pleading with us. "If you need to leave the house—and only do so if it's an absolute emergency—wear lightweight clothing, drink plenty of water, and use a buddy system. Go with someone."

I could have summarized his forecast in one sentence. *It's going to be hot.* Not to mention, if I want to know the weather, I just go outside. The only reason I was even listening to that idiot was because my wife had fallen asleep on the couch again, and turning off the television would have woken her up. So as much as it pained me to run an appliance unnecessarily, I kept the shitbox on.

My breakfast that morning was the same as the previous day—two eggs, toast, and a cup of black coffee. When I finished, I washed my dishes by hand, and then packed my lunch, which included a roast beef sandwich. And I don't buy lunchmeat, it's shit. I buy a full prime rib roast, cook it, store it in the fridge, and cut off slices each morning, which I stack between two pieces of seeded rye bread. Then I add red peppers, onions, spinach, and horseradish. Now that's a sandwich. Unfortunately, the knife slipped out my hand, and as soon as it clanged against the kitchen floor, my wife stirred.

"You haven't left yet?" Amy asked, rolling over.

Fucking great.

I shook my head, even though her question didn't warrant a response. I mean, I was standing right in front of her.

Amy rose from the couch, leaving an indentation in the cushions, and made her way to the refrigerator. She stood there with the door open, something she did a lot. My eyes drifted to her ass, which had exploded over the past few months; it had morphed into something that no longer looked human.

Don't call me a hypocrite. I'm fair.

When comparing body weight between a man and a woman, I compare the size of a woman's ass to the size of a man's belly. And in this case, I would have won and won handily. I walked three miles a day, every day. It didn't make me look like some pretty boy, but I was respectable, which was more than I could have said for my wife. She looked sloppy, wearing old, ripped pajamas until the middle of the afternoon, and rarely did she take a brush to her hair.

I was up at 5:45 every morning, and showered, shaved, and dressed by 6:00. I didn't dress fancy, but I tucked in my shirt, wore a belt, and kept my hair high and tight—the same haircut I had since joining the Navy thirty-four years ago.

Amy returned to the couch with a piece of pecan pie. I don't care what kind of organic nuts you shove into a pie, it's still a pie, and that shit's unhealthy.

After swallowing down a bite, Amy's gaze drifted outside. "Norman, look," she said, pointing out the window with her fork. Her lips curled up, and for a moment I thought she was going to smile. That would have been a rare sight. "I love watching them in the morning."

A group of high school kids were gathered on the corner of our street, waiting for their bus. I don't know why she liked watching them. They spent most of their time staring down at their cell phones. What a sad generation. Although their parents, with their coddling and lack of discipline, are as much to blame.

And don't get me started on those fucking smartphones. I don't own one and never will. If I need directions, I look at a map, and a real map, one I can spread out. If I want the news, I watch the local newscast or read a newspaper. And if I need to make a call, I use my house phone or flip phone, both of which handle the task flawlessly.

"I wonder if we should have tried again," she said, continuing to stare at the little bastards.

Twice was enough. I was surprised we even tried after Frederick. But there was no way at fifty-two that I was going to try again.

"I have to go to work," I said.

With the windows down, I drove my Ford F-150 along Interstate 515. Despite the warning from the weatherman, I kept the AC off and windows down. I prefer the fresh air, even in the summer. My truck has a 5-speed manual transmission, which they no longer offer on the F-150s. But I like changing the gears myself. I like the extra work it takes. Nowadays, everyone wants things easier, but that's a terrible approach to life if you ask me.

Part of my morning drive routine included counting the number of missing person signs. That day, I counted eleven, one more than the previous. According to the media, the disappearances were the work of a serial kidnapper. They wouldn't say 'killer' because no bodies were ever found. They called this person the Heat Miser, you know, because it's hot in Nevada. Why miser? Well, because they think the guy is well-educated, possibly wealthy. Idiots. If only the Heat Miser had kidnapped the media.

It was 6:45 a.m. when I reached the office. As usual, I was the first to arrive. I own Dohring Landscaping, a company I started after leaving the Navy. Dohring is my last name, pronounced *Door-ing*. Most of my employees called me Mr. D., which I was fine with. The ones who attempted to pronounce my name usually got it wrong. They'd say *Doe-ring* or *Dah-ring*.

My secretary, Camila, arrived a few minutes later. That's

right, *secretary*. She wasn't an administrative assistant, she wasn't an office manager, and she wasn't a support specialist. Camila was my secretary and a good one. The only issue I had with her was the music she played from her desk. She called it *top 40*, but nothing that came out of her phone should have ever been at the top of any list. All of the songs had the same stupid beat; they sounded so hollow, so lacking of any substance. What happened to rock 'n' roll—Stevie Ray Vaughan, Blue Oyster Cult, The Clash, Thin Lizzy, Ted Nugent? Those were musicians, who actually played instruments. Crazy thought, I know.

But despite her crappy music, Camila was respectful, worked hard, and had only missed one day—when her son knocked her unconscious during breakfast. Leonardo was autistic. But he wasn't the high-functioning kind that could do math equations and shit like that. He needed constant care, which she had to juggle between special needs schools and family members.

Hell, Camila would even go out on jobs with me, weed-whacking, aerating, whatever I needed. So I just ignored the shit that came out of her speaker.

Camila printed out the work schedule, and I looked it over as my crew trickled in. We had four jobs that day. The first two were at a business park in Henderson, trimming bushes and cutting grass. The third job was in south Vegas, dropping mulch at a casino; easy work, but good money. The final job, which we'd start after lunch, was in Boulder City, where we'd be installing a large patio. That one would take a few days.

Most of my employees were Hispanic, but all legit, no illegals. Still, I did get irritated when they spoke Spanish—not because I couldn't understand them—but because we weren't in Mexico or Cuba or Argentina or any other country where they speak Spanish. We were in the United States of America, and here, we speak English.

That evening I watched the news, which was delivered by a cast that included four different ethnicities. Yay for diversity! Anyway, the news that day was very political. This Democratic Senator was making an impassioned speech about how 'dreamers' should be allowed to become citizens, even though they're here illegally. And he had this sad looking Hispanic family on stage with him. What a show. The Senator, who lives in an upscale white neighborhood, is a hypocrite, and the Hispanics standing by his side are nothing more than puppets.

Then they sent it over to the storm team, where I was warned again about going outside. With that, I decided to go for my evening walk. I slipped on my Navy shirt and laced up my shoes. As I stood, Amy came out of our bedroom, her bathrobe dragging against the floor as she walked.

"Did you hear? There's another missing person." She pushed her matted hair out of her face. "A girl from Goodsprings."

I nodded.

"I can't stop thinking about it," she said.

My head began to ache and I rubbed my temples.

"Maybe they'll find her," I said, though I knew they wouldn't.

Her bloodshot eyes fell to my shoes. "You're walking?" she said. "I think it's too hot."

"I'll be fine," I said, moving toward the door. I wound my mechanical watch and slid it onto my wrist. "I'll be back in about an hour."

I took my usual route that evening, walking by Heritage Bark Park, past the water treatment facility, and then up to River Mountains Loop Trail. Most people drive to the trail, but that's stupid. Why drive somewhere to go walking? If you want to walk, just walk. Anyway, from there, I scaled the first ridge and rested for a few minutes.

That's when I saw it.

Although it looked more like a giant bubble than a wormhole. Not that I knew what a wormhole looked like, but still, it was just kind of floating there on the other side of the ridge. Initially I thought a pipe had burst at the water facility, but after I eased down the hill and got within twenty feet of it, I knew it was something else. I stood for a minute, staring, my eyes wide. It was as big as a house and inside were trees—I could see trees and a huge sun. But the sun wasn't above me, it was inside the bubble. I rubbed my eyes and refocused. Nothing changed.

I took a few steps closer, and a wave of heat rushed over me. Sweat beaded on my forehead, then rolled down my face. I tried to take a step back, but my feet wouldn't move. Instead, they began skidding across the ground as if the bubble was reaching out and pulling me toward it. And the closer I got, the hotter I became. Maybe they were right about the heat advisory.

My heart pounded. I raised my hands in front of my face as I stumbled toward it, bracing myself. I expected to bounce off or burst the fucking thing. Instead, it swallowed me. I could hear the suction as it took me in. For the first few seconds, I flailed my arms and legs, expecting to fall through it and crash to the ground. But when that didn't happen, I pulled my legs up to my chest and curled my arms over my head.

There were flashes of light as the bubble turned into a tunnel. It was like being inside a wave, surfing, but instead of water around me, it was space—blackness and stars zipping the hell by. Thumping and moaning blasted my eardrums. My eyes were slits, my body shook. Up and down I went, like a roller coaster through space.

The last thing I saw was that giant sun.

CHAPTER 3

A spatter of rain against my face woke me. My arms and legs were numb, my throat dry, and nausea filled my chest. I forced my eyes open, but the rain came again, and I squeezed them shut.

Cracking my mouth, I let the water trickle down my throat. I swallowed and took a shallow breath. Bursts of rain continued, and as the numbness began to fade, I could feel the water soak my body. I moved my hands along my chest, and then onto my legs.

I was naked and on my back.

My vision was blurry when I opened my eyes again. Eventually, the shape of a head materialized above me. I blinked hard and for the first time saw those wide, white eyes; only the pupil was dark, everything else a cloudy white. I stared into them for a long while, but not once—even when the rain washed over them—did those eyes blink. They were gentle though, searching.

As the head pulled back, I began to study its face, which looked, well, squishy. It had a small mouth, strangely so, compared to the size of its face. Its skin was as white as its eyes and covered in tiny pores, which glistened with water, like some bright sea sponge. I raised my hand to touch it, but my arm was eased back down and tucked against my side.

Still groggy, I continued to stare, my chest rising with each breath. The head shifted out of sight, revealing the sun, which pierced my eyes. I winced and slammed them shut. Even with my eyes closed, I could feel the heat against them, the brightness seeping through.

Then I heard a muffled, high-pitched voice, followed by loud footsteps. A shadow fell over me and I was able to crack open my eyelids. Another set of white eyes stared down at me, but these were different, harder. The texture of the face was the same, although this one had a square jaw and dark creases running under its eyes.

"Fohp," it said as its head moved closer. "Fohp."

I tried to push it back, but my hand was slammed back down. That was followed by a swift slap to my head, which made me recoil and curl into a ball. I watched him as he walked away. He was huge, standing almost eight feet tall, but lean and muscular. After rummaging through my shorts, he pulled out my flip phone. He studied it for a moment, set it aside, then continued going through my pockets.

Another burst of rain fell, but that seemed to wake me, and as the grogginess wore off, the more anxious I became.

What the fuck is happening?

I wanted to get up, get my shit back, and run the hell out of there, but my legs felt weak and still too numb.

The smaller one returned. And when I say smaller, I mean smaller than the other one, not me. She was over seven feet, and I think she was female, mostly because of what she didn't have that the larger one did, which was one big-ass penis that flopped around between his two giant thighs. Although the woman didn't have breasts, there were other things that convinced me she was female, such as a heart-shaped face, wider hips, and generally more curves than muscles.

She rolled me onto my left side, then my right, her white eyes moving up and down my body, which shook nervously. That's when I caught a glimpse of her hand, which had six fingers, all covered with pores; her whole body was.

Then I saw another stream of water, but this one was going up. A few seconds later, I realized I was pissing myself. It was about this time that the larger one, the guy, went fucking berserk. He threw my clothes, kicked the wall, and squealed in that high-pitched voice.

"Mo! Mo! Fohp!"

The female crossed to the other side of the room. A moment later, I heard the clanging of metal, and then smoke filled my nostrils. When the female returned, she was holding an iron bar, the tip red and smoldering. She set her free hand on my shoulder, her six fingers spreading onto my chest, and said, "hhut."

The male shouted at her, then yanked the iron bar from her hand. He pinned my left arm down and, without hesitation, pressed the tip of the bar against my bicep. My back arched. I wailed in pain, so loudly that the female covered her ears. I guess she meant *hurt*. And it fucking did.

She passed him another bar, and again he jabbed me with it, using his weight to drive it against my arm. I clenched my teeth and squeezed my hands into balls, screaming. The smell of burning flesh made me gag, and with it came another smack to the head.

Again and again they burned me, and again and again I howled like fucking hell. When they were finally done, I forced my glassy eyes onto my arm and stared at it with an open mouth. The wound was still bubbling, a horrible pink, a combination of dashes and wiggly lines.

Then I gasped as I was yanked off the table. The male carried me, clutched under his arm like a screaming child. Facedown, I could see his feet as we moved, water seeping through his pores with each step. A walking sponge. Suddenly, the ground came rushing toward me. The male had dropped my ass, and I'm pretty sure it was on purpose. I crashed down with a grunt. Then, using one of his spongy feet, the male kicked me between the eyes. I shrieked and covered my nose, which began to bleed, a red stream running onto my palms.

I lay there, breathing haggardly, a mess of piss, blood, sweat, and burning flesh. I heard footsteps and through narrowed eyes saw the female set my clothes down. She reached up and yanked on a rope. A bell clanged.

Crouching next to me, she held up one of her six fingers. "Wai ..."

It sounded like she was trying to say "wait," so I did. I mean, I couldn't really move anyway.

I either fell asleep or passed out because the next thing I remembered was someone shaking me. And I could tell from the grip that the hand wasn't spongy. It was human. I looked up, squinting through the sunlight. A thin, shirtless man stood above me, his arm outstretched.

"I'm Rodrigo," he said in a Spanish accent.

Grimacing, I sat up and shook his bony hand.

"Do you need help putting on your clothes?" Rodrigo asked.

Still disoriented, and hot as shit, I hadn't realized I was naked. "Oh ... uhhh ... no," I mumbled.

I wiggled on my shorts, wincing as I stretched my body. The numbness had almost faded, and in it its place was pain, lots and lots of pain.

"You can put on your shirt," he said, "but you'll just end up taking it off." His accent was thick, but he spoke clearly and methodically.

Staring at my shirt, I tried to process what he was saying. My thoughts were slow, almost dormant.

"You'll want to put on your shoes though," Rodrigo said. "The ground's too hot for bare feet."

After giving a delayed nod, I clumsily slipped on my socks and shoes. I wrapped my arms around my legs and took three long breaths, trying to clear my head. "Where ...

what did I …" Another breath. "Where am I?"

"Let's chat later." Rodrigo crouched down, and I could see streaks of grey on his temples and in his beard. He continued in his slow, deliberate tone. "Are you well enough to walk?"

I shrugged, giving a slight nod.

"Then let's move," he said, glancing around. "We shouldn't hang around here longer than we need to." He slid his hands under my armpits. "I'm going to lift you."

Rodrigo raised me to my feet and then held me as I wobbled in place. I could feel his ribs against my side. His sweaty, sticky skin clung to mine, but it was his breath—or maybe the stench billowing off him—that made my head turn. Then I flinched as a sharp stream of water pelted my face. The male stood a few feet to our left, his hands pressed together and pointed at me. Water dripped from his fingertips. He screamed at us in that high-pitched voice.

"Papa," Rodrigo said to him, then nudged me. "We should go. They tend to get violent when you piss on them."

I was going to ask how he knew, but I didn't have the energy.

We began to walk.

"Don't worry about urinating," he said, wrapping his arm around my back for support. "It happens to a lot of us. Just be happy you didn't crap yourself. Things wouldn't have ended as well."

The sun beat down as we plodded along. My eyes were slits as I adjusted to the brightness.

"It's going take a few days for this to sink in," Rodrigo said, "but you're no longer on Earth. You went through a wormhole—at least that's what we think it is—and ended up here. The locals call it Bomba. They refer to their species as 'mops' although they don't say the 's' because they don't have tongues, which is also why their vocabulary is so limited and why they sound the way they do."

I kept my head down as he talked. With my legs feeling heavy, I concentrated on each step.

"The missing persons list back in Nevada is essentially the human manifest for this place, which, if you haven't noticed, is hot."

With my arm, I wiped sweat from my forehead and cracked my eyes open a little further. We were walking along a wide, dirt path. Wooden structures stood on each side. There were people moving past us in both directions as if this was some type of central corridor; but when I say people, I don't mean human people. I'm talking about those spongy looking things.

"Can we stop?" I said, sucking in a breath.

We stepped to the edge of the path, where he lowered me into a sitting position. Even with my shorts on, I could feel the heat from the ground burning my ass like a piece of meat. Rodrigo stood over me, blocking the sun as I continued taking shallow breaths.

I held up my hand as a thank you, too tired to say the words.

"It's not just the sun," Rodrigo said. "The air's thinner too. It'll take some time to adjust."

My eyes were hazy. I picked gook from the corners. "And ... and where am I?"

"Bomba," he said.

"No, I mean ..." I dropped my head, panting. "I don't know ... I don't know what I mean."

The sky darkened slightly and more rain came. A moment later, Rodrigo held out a cup—one that looked like a five-year-old had formed it out of clay—and let it fill with water. When the shower passed, he handed it to me.

"Please," he said, his accent strong.

The cup was in the shape of a vase, with a wide opening at the top and narrow in the middle. I gulped the water down, let out a sigh, and handed it back to him. He tied the cup to his belt loop, then sat next to me.

"What's your name?" he asked.

I blew out a breath. "Norman."

"Hang in there, Norman," he said with a pat on the back.

"Why did they burn me?" I asked, wincing as I stared at my bicep.

"Technically they branded you." Rodrigo turned slightly, revealing his left arm. "I have one too—it's an ID. It lets them know when you arrived."

"Why does that matter?" I asked.

"So they know when to start collecting taxes," he said.

My gaze drifted to his right bicep, which had a *K* on it. "What's that?"

"That," he said, his eyes settling on the *K*, "would be strike one."

"Fohp."

We looked up and saw another male, shaking his head as he stared at us.

Rodrigo calmly held up his hand. "Papa." He got to his feet. "Let's go."

"What does 'fohp' mean?" I asked.

"Weak ... lazy ... *human*," he said, and pulled me up.

More of those spongy things—the mops—hollered at us as we walked. I heard a few more 'fohps,' but everything else they said was gibberish. At least to me. My wormhole hangover was fading, which was good because I could feel my limbs, but bad for the same reason. My arm burned and my body ached.

Eventually we reached a town that had more humans than mops. The humans were mostly Hispanic, with the men looking a lot like Rodrigo, thin with unkempt beards. Many of the women wore only shorts, and some not even that. But there was nothing sexual about it. These women may have been topless, but like all the humans I saw, kids included, they were filthy, bony, and reeked like sewage.

"This is where I live," Rodrigo said, pointing to a building ahead of us. "And where you'll live too."

A wooden sign, with the number six carved into it, hung out front. Like the other structures I had seen, this was a single-story building and, as best I could tell, didn't have a roof. Two wooden barrels stood at each corner of the house. I watched as a kid ran up to one. He turned the spigot with his grimy hands, filling a cup with water.

We walked inside and up to a counter, where a female mop sat. Rodrigo said something to her I couldn't understand. She scratched her head, sending a trickle of water down her face, and glanced at a faded piece of parchment. A moment later she replied to Rodrigo, and then her white eyes shifted to me. Although she was sitting, I had to look up to meet her gaze.

"Uu paaay weelve daaay," the female said, holding up all twelve of her fingers.

"You'll have to start paying in twelve days," Rodrigo said. "It's their week."

"Pay?" I asked. "What am I ... with what?"

"Coins, once you earn them," he said. "Work isn't hard to find here, even for humans, but you won't be paid much. Enough to live here. Not much more though." He scanned the room, which was bare and dusty. The wooden walls were rotting and uneven. Sunlight sneaked through the gaps. "It's their version of low-cost housing."

The mop extended her long arm over the counter, setting her hand on my shoulder. She shifted my body, moving my left side toward her, and then began to write with what looked like a charcoal stick.

"What—what is she doing?" I asked, staring at the pores on her arm.

"She's writing down your ID," Rodrigo said.

I glanced at the burned flesh. "Why?"

"So she can give it to the cops if you don't pay," he said.

My head started to ache. "But ... where will I get ... where will I work?"

"I'll explain. Come on, I'll show you to your room."

The floor boards squeaked as Rodrigo led me down a hall. We approached two humans who were speaking Spanish. They pressed their bare backs against the wall, giving us room to pass. "Gracias," Rodrigo said, and they nodded back.

Halfway down the hall, we stopped in front of a door. "This is number two, this is you. Two is 'ubu' in mop." Rodrigo pointed to a marking. "Can you remember that?"

I studied the marking, which looked like a curved, upside down V. "Yeah," I said, my voice still groggy.

Rodrigo pushed the door open, and I followed him inside. It didn't take long to tour the place. The room was ten by ten, maybe, with a single bed, table, and chair. I lumbered over and lay on the bed.

"Why isn't there a roof," I asked, staring up through the joists.

"The mops take in water through their skin. They become uneasy when there's too much covering above them." Rodrigo stroked his beard. "They don't consume anything else. That's why there aren't any toilets—they don't need them. Any excess water is dispensed through their pores, which is why they're disgusted when we take a piss or, God forbid, a shit."

There was a knock on the door, and a black woman entered. "I can tell from the look on your face that you're the new guy," she said. "And a Caucasian." A grin spread across her face as she moved toward me. "I hope you know how to speak Spanish." She reached the bed and set down the sack she was carrying. "Can you sit up?"

I leaned up and swung my feet over and onto the ground. "Are you a doctor?"

She shrugged. "A pediatrician. But it's the best you're going to do here."

"This is Shauna," Rodrigo said.

Shauna dropped to a knee and placed her hands on my face. Her fingers were thin and dirty. She wiped beneath my eyes, then shifted my head left and right. "Your symptoms are pretty typical." Her right hand moved to my forehead. "Mucus around the eyes and ears, fever … open your mouth." A few seconds went by and she patted my leg. "Can you open your mouth for me?"

"Oh … sorry," I said, and then stretched it open.

"That's alright, honey. Do you feel light-headed?"

I nodded.

"What's your name?"

"Norman."

"And what's your last name?"

"Dohring."

"No matches that I'm aware of," Rodrigo said to her.

"And how's your stomach, Norman?" Shauna asked.

It was queasy. I shook my head.

"You'll be nauseous for a few days." She reached into her sack and pulled out something that looked like pineapple, though it was more green than yellow. "This is a local fruit. You just suck on it. Don't eat it whole." She dropped it onto my palm. "It's a little messy, but it'll help with your stomach. It'll take time for your body to adjust to this place, so be patient."

My left arm surged with pain, and I tucked it against my body.

"Let me put something on that." Shauna reached into her sack and pulled out a small bowl filled with a light blue gel. "This is similar to aloe." She slid two fingers around the bowl, then gently applied the gel to the brand, which was more orange now than red, but still hurt like fucking hell.

I winced, drawing in a long breath.

"Lo va a hacer?" I heard Rodrigo say.

Shauna nodded.

"Es lo suficientemente fuerte como para ser un transportista?" he said.

"With time," she said.

I was too tired to ask.

Shauna handed me a cup, similar to Rodrigo's. "This is free. Anything else, you'll have to pay for yourself." Using a separate container, which I assumed was hers, she poured water into the cup and motioned for me to drink.

"Your meals are free too," Rodrigo said, "as long as you help with the crops. If not, you're on your own."

I swallowed down the water, then hunched over. "And …" I took another breath, which it seemed like I could never catch. "Where did you say I would work?"

"I didn't," Rodrigo said. "But don't worry about that right now. Just rest. We'll talk more tomorrow."

Rain came down through the joists and doused us. It was like a goddamn rainforest here.

"You might want to put a sheet of wood up there at some point," Shauna said, pointing to the joists. "And probably above your table too. The wood here doesn't rot as quickly as the wood on earth. Although honestly, it's so damn hot here, I really don't mind getting hit every few minutes."

"You can't build a full roof though," Rodrigo said. "The owner won't allow it. They don't want to have to remove it if a mop moves in after you." He shook his head. "But forget all that for now ... you need to focus on paying your rent first."

I took a few more long breaths and closed my eyes. "This can't be happening. How did I even get here?"

Rodrigo cleared his throat. "Like I said, there's a wormhole—"

"I know what you said," I started, and then sucked in another mouthful of air. "But that's it? That's all you can tell me? I'm on a different planet and all you can say is that I went through a wormhole?"

Shauna patted my leg. "That's all we know, Norman. There are a lot of theories on why, where, when, and how ... but you're not in any condition to have a conversation about that right now. And only the man upstairs knows for sure anyway."

I opened my eyes and rubbed my wrist, where my watch used to be. It felt strange not wearing it. The skin was pale compared to the rest of my arm. Then I stared at the ground for a long moment. "Can I get some more water?" More rain splattered down, further soaking me. "But ... like in my cup."

We made our way outside, and Shauna filled my cup from the barrel. "There's a spring nearby too," she said, handing me the water.

I nodded and swallowed it down. "Where are the bathrooms?"

"I thought you already went." Rodrigo said.

"I did. It's not that. I think I'm going to get sick."

"You're going to feel that way for a few days," Shauna said, and then glanced back inside. "But like we said, there aren't bathrooms in any of the buildings."

"So where do I go?"

"In shit town," Shauna said.

"But it's not close," Rodrigo said.

"The mops find our excretion process repulsive," Shauna said, and then pointed past me. "There are latrines about two miles that way, on the outskirts of the desert."

I hunched over. "I'm not sure I'll make it that far."

Rodrigo grabbed my arm and hurried me behind the building.

"What—" I said, stumbling as we walked.

"Behind the bush," he said.

Then I dropped to my knees and threw up.

When I stepped into the bathroom, I found Amy hunched over the toilet. We had just been having dinner. Amy made us Porterhouse steaks, which she hadn't done since our anniversary in March. When I asked if this was a special occasion, she just shrugged.

"Are you okay?" I asked, standing in the doorway. "Should I not eat the steak?"

Clutching her stomach, Amy let out a hardy laugh. She laughed so hard that she began hacking and nearly threw up again.

"What's so funny?" I asked.

She dropped from her knees to her butt, then used her forearm to wipe her mouth. "Your steak is fine. I just couldn't wait any longer."

I slid a towel off the rack and handed it to her. "Wait for what?"

She exhaled. "For you to ask about the extra place setting."

"What—I did. I asked if your mother was coming over. Why?" Her pale face stretched into a grimace. "Can I do something? Do you need help?"

Amy shook her head. A second later she leaned over the bowl, waited, and then settled back onto the floor when nothing had come out. "When I said she wasn't, you should have asked a follow-up."

Taking a step inside, I sat on the edge of the bathtub and faced her. "A follow-up?"

"*Yes*. If the place setting isn't for my mother, then who's it for?" She exhaled. "I also thought about putting a surprise in your dessert … or hiding the test in your work boot … or … or maybe giving you a coupon that read 'redeemable for one baby in nine months.'"

My eyes moved to her belly. Then my lips curled into a smile.

Again, I hurled behind the bush. Rodrigo kicked at the ground, spraying dirt.

"What are you doing?" I asked.

"Hiding it," he said. "Because if the mops see this, you'll get a strike."

"F—For …"

"For throwing up. Or for crapping, if you do it outside of shit town. They're a little more accommodating with pissing. That'll just get you beat up. It's similar to how they dispense water I guess, but they don't like the color of our piss or how it smells." He pulled me to my feet. "Come on, let's get you back to your room. Do you remember the number?"

I hunched over and rubbed my forehead. "Two?"

"And what does a two look like?" he asked.

"Like uhhh …" I spat. "Like an upside-down V, but kind of curved at the top."

"And how do you say two in mop?"

"Ubu?"

"You're going to do great, Norman," Rodrigo said. "Welcome to Bomba."

CHAPTER 4

Even before I opened my eyes the next day, I knew it hadn't been a dream. During those few seconds between sleep and consciousness, I felt the sun beating against my eyelids and the perspiration on my body. The throbbing in my branded arm was a good indicator too, as was the mop tapping on my face.

It didn't really hurt though because his finger, like the rest of his body, was spongy. The harder he tapped, the more water seeped from his pores. I wiped my face dry and stared up at him.

A badge, with a blue insignia, hung around his neck. My eyes drifted past him and caught sight of a second mop, a female, the same one who had examined me the day before.

The male motioned for me to stand. I attempted to lean up in bed but, still woozy, went back down.

"Pob," he said, and gave another upward wave of his hand.

I guess that meant stand, or maybe hurry up, so I exhaled and swung my feet off the bed and onto the floor. Black spots filled my vision. As I blinked and sucked in a breath, the male seized my legs and dragged me from the bed. I landed hard against the wooden floor.

The female, who had a bag slung over her shoulder, squatted next to me as I moaned. The male paced and shook his head, grumbling. Slowly, the female helped me to my feet, then held her hands against my shoulders to steady me. As she stood there, facing me, the male reached down and ran his fingers up her leg and onto her ass.

She casually shuffled to her left, out of his reach. Peering around me, the male hollered at her. I thought it was for moving away from him, but then she reached into her bag. It was a command.

Her hand emerged with my flip phone.

"Wwwhaaa?" she said.

I raised my shoulders. "Huh?"

"Wwwhaaa iiiss?" Each word was long and drawn out.

"What is it?" I asked. "That's what you're asking?"

Her white eyes grew large and she nodded. She was the translator.

"It's a phone," I said.

She shook her head, then pulled an iPhone from her bag. The screen was black and full of scratches. "Hhiss is phooo."

This is phone. No tongue meant no t's and no n's, among other letters.

"Mine's a phone too," I said, rubbing my sore back. "It's

just a little different. I actually like mine better."

Her face scrunched into a confused look.

"It doesn't matter," I said, then pointed at the iPhone. "*Phone.*" I shifted my finger to the flip phone. "*Phone too* ... but different."

I held out my hand, asking for it. She hesitated, then handed it over. After unfolding it, the phone chimed and the small screen lit up. The translator took a cautious step back.

"See, it's kind of the same," I said, showing her the tiny display.

"Eever see phooo liie hhis," she said, then said something to the male.

He yanked it from my hand, yelled, "Huma mo phooo," and handed it to her.

Mo was *no*. Human no phone. Not that it would have been much use on Bomba.

The translator dropped it into her bag, but when her hand slid back holding another object, my heart began to thump. It was my watch. My Timex.

"Can I shake it?" I asked, looking at the wrapped present in my hand.

It was my thirtieth birthday, and the smell of a freshly baked cake lingered in the air. Amy sat next to me on the couch, one hand resting on my thigh and the other resting on her belly, which had filled out over the past seven months.

She shifted to get comfortable. Amy was almost thirty

weeks and moving around had become awkward. Ten weeks prior we learned we were having a boy. We planned to name him Frederick after Amy's brother, who had special needs. He died when she was a teenager.

"I don't really know," she said, staring at the gift. "I guess you can shake it."

I held it to my ear and gave it a light shake. Nothing. Then I sniffed it.

"What would I give you that would smell?" she asked with a grin.

"Prime rib," I said.

"I probably wouldn't wrap prime rib," she said.

Setting the gift on my lap, I began to peel back the wrapping paper. When I was done, I was left with a plain box that was small enough to rest in the palm of my hand. I peeked over at Amy, but she stayed focused on the present. The corners of her mouth creeped further up.

I opened the box, revealing a watch. My eyes drifted to the watch on my wrist, then over to Amy.

"I know you have a watch," she said, then paused. "This one's mechanical."

It was a Timex with a silver dial and leather strap. I held back a smile as I turned it over in my hands. Amy knew. She knew I would like it. She knew because it was mechanical. It didn't have a battery and therefore required more effort, which I liked. It might sound strange, but I liked earning things, even something as trivial as the time.

My first instinct was to grab the Timex, but I figured that

would result in a punch to my face. So, I just followed the second hand as it ticked by, my thoughts still on of Amy.

The male screamed, which startled me. He pointed at the watch face and said something to the female.

"Whhhyyyy wwoowwwwdd?" the translator said, making a circle in the air with her finger.

It took me a moment to realize what she was asking. "Oh, why does it go around? Why does it go in a circle?"

The translator nodded.

"It's a clock … that's how it keeps time," I said.

Again, she made a circle with her finger. "Whhhyyyy?"

I rubbed my eyes, wondering how to explain the fundamentals of a mechanical watch to an alien. As I stood there thinking, the male, who had become restless, rubbed against the translator like a horny dog. She pushed him away.

Blowing out a breath, I said, "It's just the way it works."

As her eyes moved from me to the watch, she translated my answer back to the male. He shouted at me, grabbed the watch, and chucked it into the translator's bag. It clanged against something inside.

I gritted my teeth. *If that fucking mop scratched my watch.*

Then the male shoved a picture into my face. I took a step back so I could make it out. It was a sketch of a human—a man with wrinkles, large ears, and an overgrown beard. If he had been wearing a red and white hat, I'd have thought he was Santa Claus, but thinner.

"Whhooo?" the female said, pointing at the sketch.

"Who is it?" I asked. "You're asking if I know him?"

She nodded.

I wiped the back of my neck, which was covered in sweat. "I don't think so," I said with a shrug. "But it's hard to tell from a drawing."

The confused look returned to the female's face.

"No," I said, giving a slow shake of my head. "I don't know him. *Mo*."

The male blurted something at the translator, then pushed her toward the door. I guess he was done with me. He didn't seem too pleased with her either. Although the way he was looking at her, he sure liked what he saw. He stared at her ass, and I watched his penis—I swear I couldn't help it—swell to the size of a cucumber.

The male licked his white lips and, breathing heavily, strode toward her. As she reached the doorway, his hand closed around the back of her neck. He shoved her into the corner, then bent her slightly, and pressed himself against her.

My mouth fell open.

I rushed toward him, dropped my shoulder, and rammed it against his side. As I bounced off him—probably because he was squishy—he roared in pain; although what came out sounded like a little girly yelp.

He jerked his head toward me, and his spongy face filled with rage. He took two long steps, lifted his huge foot, and stomped down on my chest. I gasped for air. But his foot came again, water squirting from his heel as it impacted against my bare chest.

With his hands on his hips, he stared down at me. Then

he leaned over. "Fohp."

He gave me another kick, this one against my hip, and then walked out of the room, the giant cucumber all but gone now.

As I lay curled up on the floor with my arms tucked against my body, the translator stepped over and offered me her hand. I gaped at it, taking in the hundreds of pores, then extended mine.

"Hhaann uuu," she said.

I grimaced as she pulled me up. "You're welcome."

She tapped her chest. "Ma."

"Your name is Ma?"

The translator nodded.

I set my hand against my own chest. "Norman."

"Orma?" Ma said.

Without the letter N, yes, I guess it was Orma. I smiled.

Bending her long torso, Ma peered into her bag. She pulled out my Timex and handed it to me.

"*Thank you.*" I wound the silver dial and slid it onto my wrist. As soon as I secured the leather strap, the pain in my back began to ease.

Shauna and Rodrigo passed Ma as she left the room.

"Are you okay?" Shauna asked. She wore shorts and sandals, but nothing else. "I thought I heard something."

"I'm okay," I said, rubbing my chest.

She sighed and shook her head. "What did she do to you?"

"It wasn't her," I said. "It was a male. He had a blue badge around his neck."

"That's a cop," she said. "What did he do?"

"A couple kicks to the chest."

"Why?" Rodrigo asked.

"He was being a little frisky with Ma—the translator."

Rodrigo nodded. "From a moralistic standpoint, the males are barely a step up from the cavemen."

With a hand on my lower back, I ambled over to the bed. "So what time do we work?"

"We already worked today," Shauna said.

"What time is it?" I said, glancing at my watch.

"Well, the days are longer here—thirty-one hours." Rodrigo looked up through the joists, shielding the sun with his hand. "We're at about hour twenty-two now." His eyes shifted back to me. "You probably slept all day. That's normal. It'll take a few days to get used to the heat and air. I'd stay in bed for another day or two before you start working."

"And what will I be doing?" I asked.

Rodrigo looked me over. "You look like you're in good enough shape. I take it you don't have an issue with manual labor?"

I shrugged and sat down on the bed. "No, that's fine."

"Good, then you'll work with Shauna and me, and most of the other humans who live in house six."

"Doing what?"

"General construction mostly—houses and businesses. Right now we're helping build a new sports complex. Although we're not doing much of the building. We're just hauling the materials. The humans usually get the grunt jobs." Rodrigo smiled. "It sucks, but it pays the bills."

Shauna walked over and set a hand on my shoulder, gently nudging me back onto the bed. "But like Rodrigo said, you need to rest."

CHAPTER 5

I woke up the next morning, hungry and thirsty. I reached down, grabbed my cup, and drank what was left. My bed was soaked, either from my sweat or it had rained overnight. Maybe both, or maybe I pissed myself again. I covered my face with my hands, mostly to block the sun but also because I still couldn't believe this was happening. I had a business. I had a wife. I had a house. I lay there as negative thoughts filled my mind.

Eventually, I sat up. Rodrigo wanted me to rest today and I think even tomorrow, but I didn't feel like sitting in my room all day. I rolled out of bed and headed outside, where I found Rodrigo, Shauna, and about ten other humans sitting around a table. Everyone stood as I reached them.

"Hey," I said. "What's going on?"

"Eres un novato?" a man asked me, his accent thicker than Rodrigo's.

"He doesn't speak Spanish," Rodrigo said to the group, and then headed for the water barrel. "No habla español."

"What did he say?" I asked.

Rodrigo opened the spigot and filled his water. "He asked if you were the newbie."

"Oh …"

"We're heading to work. We'll see you this evening," Rodrigo said. "If you go out, remember …" He pointed to the wooden sign hanging out front. "We're house six."

"Wait, I want to come," I said.

Shauna shook her head. "You need to rest, Norman. *At least* another day. Maybe two."

"I feel fine," I said, although I only felt better than the day before, and that wasn't saying much.

"It doesn't matter." Shauna stepped toward me and placed her dirty palm against my forehead. "You haven't even eaten anything, and you still have a slight fever."

I shrugged. "Maybe it's just the heat you're feeling."

Her hand moved to my chest, where she gave a light pat. "I can tell the difference, honey."

"The fever's not a big deal," I said. "And I can eat on the way."

Rodrigo and Shauna exchanged glances and then spoke to each other in Spanish. I was on another planet and still couldn't escape that fucking language.

"Come on," I said, interrupting them. "What the hell else am I going to do?"

Rodrigo looked at me. "This is hard work, Norman. Are you sure you're up for it?" He paused. "You might be a little old for this."

My hands moved to my hips. "No older than you, Rodrigo."

Shauna sighed. "Alright, but don't say we didn't warn you," she said, and then pointed to the table. "Fill your pockets with nuts. You can eat them throughout the day."

"Just don't do it in front of them—the mops," Rodrigo said.

"Why?" I asked.

"Because they think eating is disgusting," he said. "And the males tend to get violent when they see humans doing disgusting things."

"Okay," I said, and then stuffed my pockets full. "Let's go."

Shauna let out a long breath. "Go get your cup and fill it to the top."

It felt good to walk, but the sun was strong, beating down hard on my shoulders and face. I wondered if I should have worn a shirt. Most of the humans were shirtless and their skin, which was dark and leathery, seemed to have adjusted, though several did wear hats. The one thing they had in common was their stench. Even outside, they stank like stale sweat.

As far as Bomba, well, it looked a lot like Earth. The sky was blue, and there were plants and trees and shit like that. I'm sure there were differences—the heat and massive sun being two, but I hadn't seen enough to know much more. I guess the nuts in my pockets looked different. I had yet to try them though, but I was getting hungry.

The farther we walked, the fewer humans and more mops we saw. It was hard taking my eyes off them. The mops were so lean and tall, even the kids. Their spongy skin glistened in the light.

About twenty minutes into our walk, I started to lag behind the others. Rodrigo peeked over his shoulder and saw me. He slowed his pace, waiting for me to catch up.

"You're lucky you arrived in winter," he said.

"How hot does it get in the summer?" I asked, drawing even with him.

"About one-twenty-five, one-thirty," he said. "At least we think so. We don't have a thermometer, but a science teacher from house four said he was able to make an estimate … something about how fast the water evaporated in the sun."

I wiped sweat from my brow. "How hot will it get today?"

"About one-fifteen." Without looking up, he motioned toward the sun. "But there's not a big difference between winter and summer here. Apparently Bomba doesn't tilt as much as earth."

Rodrigo explained what we'd be doing for work that day. It was the same job he'd been doing for the past ten weeks, but mop weeks, which were twelve days instead of seven. The most popular sport on Bomba was called Aba, which was a fight to the death. He said it had become so popular they needed a larger arena to meet the demand. I could see it in the distance. Although unfinished, it looked a lot like the Roman Colosseum. Rodrigo said it was humans who recommended the design, specifically using arches for the entranceways.

"So we'll be building the arches?" I asked.

"No. We're haulers. We go to the quarry to get the stones to build the arches."

I raised an eyebrow. "That's it?"

"That plenty," he said. "It's actually easier than when we had to dig out the base. That was hard labor. *Real* hard labor. I was new then, but still." He paused. "But whatever the job, keep your head down, keep your mouth shut, and work hard. If you act aggressive or give them attitude, you're going to get your ass kicked. And I don't care how big or strong you think you are, all mops, even most of the kids, are stronger than humans."

I was already exhausted when we arrived, and my work day had yet to even begin. I wondered if I had made a mistake.

The stadium was loud with activity. Hundreds of mops were inside, working pulleys and manual cranes. The humans, as Rodrigo mentioned, were doing the grunt work—lifting and hauling stones.

One by one, the humans from house six picked up wooden wheelbarrows and started moving east. Well, at least I think it was east; it was early and they were walking toward the rising sun, which gleamed over the horizon like a giant spotlight. The humans kept their heads down as they moved. I grabbed a wheelbarrow, dropped my water container inside, and followed along.

Two mop guards, who were off-duty cops hired by the builders, strolled alongside us. They didn't push anything though. Instead, they carried clubs, which would be used against us in cases of 'poor performance.' Shauna's words, not mine.

My water container clanged inside the wheelbarrow's tray as I pushed.

"How far is it to the quarry?" I asked.

Our group had walked about a mile, and I was hoping we were close.

"About five more miles," she said.

I sighed. *Six miles each way.* If I was this tired after pushing an empty wheelbarrow a single mile, I couldn't imagine how I'd feel after walking twelve, half of which with a full load. But I pushed that thought out of my mind and kept plodding along with my head down.

"You might want to tie off your water," Rodrigo said without turning back. "I think the guards are getting annoyed from it rattling around. And … probably some of the humans too."

My gaze drifted between the others, who had their water containers attached to their wheelbarrow's handles with string or weeds.

"With what?" I asked.

"Use your shoelaces," Rodrigo said.

After another mile, a mop guard yelled something and everyone halted. I glanced around and saw the humans drinking from their cups. So I did the same, finishing about three quarters of it and dumping the rest over my face. As I stood there, looking into my empty container, I began to worry. Should I have rationed my water? Will I be able to get more?

"There's a stream another two miles up," Rodrigo said. "It's okay. You should finish it. And don't forget to eat your nuts."

"Oh, right," I said, and reached into my pocket.

After eating a small handful, I looked around. There were trees on both sides of the dirt path we were walking along. I really wished we had been walking under them though. The sun was a killer, so huge in the sky. It must have been twice the size of Earth's sun.

About thirty yards to my left, I noticed someone lying under one of the trees. I took a few steps toward them, my eyes squinting. Whoever it was, they weren't moving.

A cop poked me with his club, then pointed at my wheelbarrow. The rest of my group had begun moving again.

"Rodrigo," I said, grabbing the handles.

He turned and saw me motion to the body.

"Dead," he said.

"Your wife had a placental abruption."

That was the official explanation. I didn't know what the fuck it meant. All I knew is that I had to leave the room so the doctor could remove the dead fetus from Amy's stomach.

Eight hours earlier, she had slipped on our stairs, which were hardwood. I had installed a carpet runner up the middle of the staircase for that very reason. But on that day, when she stepped down from the top, her sock landed on the outside of the step—the wood.

Amy tumbled twelve steps, landing on our hard, ceramic tile floor. She only ended up with a sprained wrist, a bloody nose, and some bumps and bruises. Those things didn't matter though, not to Amy. The placental abruption, that's what mattered. The placenta supplied Frederick with his oxygen. But when Amy fell, the placenta separated from the wall of her uterus and the flow of oxygen stopped.

I hired someone to clean up the blood—the result of vaginal bleeding. I didn't realize it, but there are people who specialize in blood cleanup. They must have lots of terrible stories to tell. This guy named Drew, an Army vet with a shitload of tattoos, spent five hours cleaning the stairs and floor. The hospital also had to throw out Amy's favorite pair of maternity pants. Not that she needed them anymore.

It was an odd feeling losing Frederick. Maybe not for Amy since she had been carrying him, but it was for me. I had heard his heartbeat and even felt Frederick kick a couple of times, but I had never met him.

I often wondered what kind of man he would have become. Would he have served in the military? Gotten married? Had kids? Would he have called his mother every Sunday? Would he have liked roast beef sandwiches and trucks with manual transmissions?

Hell yeah, he would have.

Amy stayed quiet during the days that followed. She

never cried though. I talked to her, asked her what I could do, but she said very little. The doctor recommended Amy wait six weeks before returning to work, but she was back at New Horizons, the special needs school where she worked, fifteen days later. She spent her evenings on the couch eating and watching TV. The mindlessness of those ridiculous shows was the only thing that helped. I tried to talk to her, tried to engage in conversations, but her responses were short and generic. My words felt useless. They floated aimlessly through the air like the lyrics of one of Camila's favorite pop songs.

So, I decided to use my hands. I built something. I made it using leftover lumber I had in the garage. I cut and chiseled out a section of a 4x4 and then wedged a precut 2x4 into the opening. Then I carved Frederick's name and hammered it into the ground in our backyard.

When I came back inside, Amy asked what I had been doing, having heard the sawing and hammering.

"I built something," I said.

She folded her arms. "What?"

"A cross," I said. "For Frederick."

Amy walked out back to see it for herself. She stared at the cross for a long moment, grabbed my hand, and then began to sob.

I continued to stare at the body.

"Dead," Rodrigo said again. "Let it be. Happened a few days ago."

I nodded and followed him.

A black woman from our house motioned to the path as we pushed our wheelbarrows. "That's why we call this *death road*."

I wasn't sure if she said 'row' or 'road,' but either seemed to fit.

"I can't wait to beat the shit out of one of those sponges," she said.

My stomach growled over the next few miles. I wanted more nuts but decided against it, for two reasons. First, I didn't want to stop. I was already struggling to keep up. Second, I didn't have any water to wash them down. My mouth was dry and felt too pasty to swallow anything.

My group was already filling their containers when I reached the stream, which sat about fifty yards off the trail. They filled and chugged, filled and chugged. I hurried over, dropped to my knees, and splashed two handfuls in my face before swallowing down a third.

"Pob!" a guard yelled.

I was the only one left at the stream. After filling my container, I ran back to my wheelbarrow.

Over the final two miles, there were fewer trees and the ground became harder and hotter. I squeezed my eyes shut as dust and dirt blew along the road, covering my face and chest. When I opened them, I saw my second dead body, a few feet off the path. A couple minutes later, I saw my third.

It was a relief when we finally reached the quarry, mostly for the break; I was able to wait in line for my wheelbarrow to be filled. If it weren't for my fatigue, I might have appreciated their extraction process, which included the use of pulleys and wedges. Mops operated the machines, and humans loaded the wheelbarrows. Once again, the humans were given the grunt jobs.

One by one, our wheelbarrows were filled with rocks and stones. Mine was loaded by an old Hispanic woman who never made eye contact. Her job seemed harder than mine. At least that's what I thought until I began walking.

My first few steps with a full load was slow, and the guard noticed.

"Pob," he said.

At this point, I was pretty sure that 'pob' meant 'hurry the fuck up.'

So I tried, but after only half a mile on death road, I had to stop. With little food, my legs were weak and my hands shook. The energy I did have was sucked dry by the heat. I ate another handful of nuts, washed it down with water, and then after hearing another 'pob,' lifted my wheelbarrow and trudged forward.

The sun was higher in the sky now and its rays stronger, beating against my back and neck. At least I was walking away from the sun and not into it. Not that it helped my vision. With sweat running down my face, my eyes were slits. Grunting, and with my teeth clenched, I forced myself down the road, trying to keep pace with the others. Despite their thin frames, the rest of my crew moved at a surprisingly steady pace, almost machine-like.

Then I hit a bump and my clammy hands slipped from

the handles. The wheelbarrow stopped in its place, but my momentum sent me crashing against my load and then onto the ground. I struggled to my knees, then to my feet. I blew out a breath, lifted my wheelbarrow, and began pushing again.

After another mile, I reached the stream and found the rest of my group waiting.

"Hurry," Rodrigo said, but as usual his voice was calm. "We've already filled up."

I set my wheelbarrow down and hustled to the stream.

"Pob."

Looking over my shoulder, I saw a guard pointing down the path. "Pob!" he said again in that high-pitched, muffled voice. I turned my water container over, trying to show that it was empty, that I needed water.

"Mo!" the guard said, shaking his head. "Mo!"

"Get moving," Rodrigo said to me. "It's too late."

With slumped shoulders, I did. After about a hundred yards, I had caught up with Shauna, who must have slowed to wait for me. "Here, take my water," she said, stopping her wheelbarrow, but keeping her eyes on the guard.

"Are you sur—"

"Take it," she said.

The water helped, and I was able to keep up as we began moving again. The sun though, was relentless—so big in the sky and so goddamn hot. I kept wanting to wipe my face, but with both hands on the handles of the wheelbarrow, I was reduced to quick shakes of my head.

"I'm sweating like crazy," I said.

"At least you won't have to piss as much," Rodrigo said, just ahead of me. "And that's a good thing with the guards around." His eyes drifted to my crotch. "But if you do have to go, I'd recommend going in your pants."

When we reached the four-mile mark, the guards let us drink. I offered the remainder of the water to Shauna, but she shook her head. After taking a few gulps, I ate more nuts, washed them down with the rest of the water, and then handed the empty container back to Shauna.

The sky filled with dark clouds, and when it began to rain, everyone held out their cups while simultaneously tilting their heads back, mouths open. I did the same.

Then the guard said something and we all began moving.

The cloud cover was a relief over the final two miles, as were the frequent bursts of rain. The weather pattern on Bomba was odd; the rain would come in short, heavy bursts every couple of hours. Sometimes it would last a few seconds, sometimes a few minutes, but it was consistent. You could count on being doused at least a dozen times a day. Perfect for the mops, who needed a steady stream to survive. The water tasted different too, thicker almost, as if there were more vitamins and minerals.

The sounds of construction grew louder as we approached the stadium. The number of workers had nearly doubled since the morning. Mops and humans were scattered throughout, but it was the humans who carried the loads and the mops who directed.

Then I noticed something odd—you know, besides the spongy aliens. Just past the stadium, stood a line of poles, about thirty feet high, with cables running between them.

"Are those telephone lines?" I asked Rodrigo as we waited for our wheelbarrows to be emptied.

"Those might be power lines, but both exist." He raised his shoulders. "In parts anyway."

My eyes fell to the load of stones I had just pushed for six miles. "They have power?"

"In certain areas, but it's spotty at best," he said.

"Why?"

"It was before my time, but a group of engineers—humans—explained how they could generate power, taught them about telephone and radio transmissions. The mops were impressed." Rodrigo squinted as he peered back up at the lines. "But it didn't go so well when they tried to build it all out. Because of the moisture they carry, a lot of mops got electrocuted during the construction. They thought we were secretly trying to kill them, so they halted everything."

We continued to scoot forward in line as the humans ahead of us had their wheelbarrows unloaded. It was the only line I had ever been in that I wanted to take a long time.

"But you know what they really love?" Rodrigo said. "Cars. And of course they're all convertibles. Mops don't like shit above their heads."

Again, I glanced down at my wheelbarrow. "They have cars?"

"Some, yes, thanks to the human mechanics who are on

Bomba. But the cars break down a lot ... there's not like standards or checks or anything. But we're in the poorest region, so you won't see many cars here. Partly because there's no gas stations. There are a few in Central Bomba and a few more in South, but even there, it's not like they're on every corner. And even if they were, it'd still be cheaper to pay us to push wheelbarrows than to buy a truck that would probably break down."

It was a relief to walk with an empty wheelbarrow. My grip was loose and my shoulders relaxed. Still, the thought of doing another twelve-mile round-trip made me question my decision to work again. I was glad that I had been wearing running shoes before going through the wormhole. Doing this trek in dress shoes or flip flops—as a few in my group did—would have been a bear.

Too bad I hadn't been driving my truck when I went through. Sure would have been nice to haul my load in my F-150. I'm still not sure I would have turned on the AC though. Well, maybe once to make sure it worked. What I wanted more than anything though was food. But with my nut supply dwindling and no water to wash them down with, I held off eating.

As before, we stopped after two miles to drink. I didn't have water, but I appreciated the break.

"Hey," I said to Rodrigo. "What does 'papa' mean?"

"*Yes, okay, will do*," he said. "There words aren't as specific as ours. It basically means you're agreeing to do something."

The rain continued to come in spurts as we walked. It was refreshing, but it made for soggy socks and shoes. With the heat though, they dried quickly.

The thought of water helped me push through over the next two miles. When we reached the stream, I dropped my wheelbarrow and rushed over. I drank two full containers worth, dumped another over my head, and plopped down against the bank, exhausted.

Shauna stepped past me and dunked her cup into the stream. "I knew this was a bad idea."

Too tired to answer, I just sat there, staring at her.

"No one usually starts this soon," she continued.

I nodded and dropped my head, turning it away from the sun. Then I felt water rush down my neck and over my bare back. I looked up and saw Shauna standing there with her container turned over.

"Come on," she said.

We both refilled, then walked back to our wheelbarrows. Before picking mine up, I tossed a few nuts into my mouth. As I chewed, I made eye contact with the guard, who had a look of disgust on his spongy face. I shrugged my shoulders, then swallowed. The guard grimaced and turned away.

"Try not to eat in front of them," Rodrigo said.

"Why?" I said, and took a drink.

"Remember what I said? They think it's gross. And they also know that eating means shitting, and they hate that even more."

I thought about it for a moment, then nodded.

"And I'd recommend taking the shells off next time," he said. "The shells will make you thirstier, and that'll waste your water."

My eyes grew wide. I pulled out a handful of nuts and stared at them. "I've been eating them with the shells on?"

Rodrigo laughed. "Yeah, there aren't like factories here to remove the shells. You'll need to do it yourself."

"Yeah, I understand ... I just ... I didn't realize."

They didn't look as fragile as traditional peanut shells, but as I squeezed one between my thumb and index finger, it cracked open. I ate the nut inside, which was smaller and lighter in color, and dropped the pieces of shell on the ground.

Being hydrated, and having a few nuts in my stomach, helped me over the final two miles. The same Hispanic woman loaded my wheelbarrow at the quarry, and again she didn't make eye contact. She was thin, but strong and worked with little emotion on her face. She reminded me of Camila. I bet she would have made a good hauler—Camila. Her son Leonardo, however, wouldn't have lasted a day on Bomba. Terrible to think about, but true.

My muscles ached as I watched the woman stack the rocks in my tray, one after the other. When she finally finished, she waved me forward, but our eyes never met. She only looked at the wheelbarrows and the rocks.

Although my load didn't look any bigger than the first I had hauled, it sure felt that way when I lifted it.

"Pob, pob," I heard, and then began moving, following the convoy of wheelbarrows out of the quarry.

The pace of the rest of my group was intimidating. They pushed their wheelbarrows as if they were filled with tennis balls instead of rocks. I grunted, breathing heavily, trying to keep up. My arms shook, straining under the weight. I had only gone about a hundred yards, and I was already spent. It was just too damn hot. And now I had to piss.

The guard yelled something I couldn't understand as I continued to lag behind the others. My legs wobbled with each step. Sweat ran down my face and arms, and I had to constantly stop and wipe my hands against my shorts to keep them dry and avoid losing my load.

Everyone from my group had already returned from the stream when I finished the two miles and reached the stop.

"Get to the stream," Rodrigo said. "And rub your hands in the dirt if you need to dry them. It works better." He lifted his wheelbarrow, preparing to leave.

"Rodrigo," I said, out of breath.

He turned.

"What should I do …" I stopped and took two long breaths. "What should I do if I have to piss?"

"Like I said, you'll have to piss in your pants. Or hold it."

I paused for a moment, thinking about it, and then did just that, shooting a stream of urine down my leg. I turned my foot outward hoping to avoid soaking my shoe. A brown puddle formed on the ground.

Rodrigo noticed. "Do a little at a time, so they can't tell." He shook his head. "But if they see this …"

"And if you're wondering," Shauna said, "it's brown

because you're dehydrated. Keep drinking water."

She lifted her wheelbarrow and followed Rodrigo. I stared down at my rocks. Four more miles until I could unload. I didn't see how I would make it. Not at this pace.

"Pob huma!" the guard yelled as I rushed back from the stream. "Pob!"

I lifted my wheelbarrow and leaned forward, using my weight and legs to build momentum. But with my palms damp, my right hand slipped and the wheelbarrow went over, sending my entire load onto the ground.

The guard screamed. I don't think it was a word; he just screamed. Then the club came down against my back, and I dropped. From the ground, I saw Rodrigo and Shauna hurrying toward me.

When they reached me, Rodrigo said something to the guard, then helped me up. My back stung. I glared at the guard.

Yeah, give me a good whack in the back. That should help.

After I pulled the wheelbarrow upright, Rodrigo and Shauna helped reload my stones. The guard continued to shout, but eventually left us and began yelling at the rest of our group to get moving. At least that's what Shauna told me he said.

With the guard's back to us, Rodrigo and Shauna began moving the rest of my rocks into their wheelbarrows.

"You don't have to do that," I said. "I can manage my own load."

"The hell you can," Shauna said.

I stared at her.

"Well don't just stand there," she said. "Help us."

"I'll help him, Shauna," Rodrigo said. "Why don't you get moving?"

"It'll go quicker with three," she said.

The reduced weight was a relief. My back still throbbed with pain, but the strain on my body had eased. And unless you looked closely, you couldn't tell that I was missing part of my load. I made it to the next stop without issue, arriving only a few minutes after Rodrigo, who was taking his water break. I did the same, but within seconds we were moving again.

The sun bore down as I pushed. It was hard to get used to its size, which made everything else—trees and clouds included—look like miniature versions of themselves.

Despite my smaller load, it wasn't long before I started lagging again. I just couldn't keep up. I couldn't catch my breath. And no matter how much water I drank, it never seemed to be enough to match the heat.

I was the last from my group to reach the stadium. As I stood in line, I could feel my face and shoulders burning. My eyes were slits. Dropping my head, I took long deep breaths.

"Hey," I heard someone say.

When I opened my eyes, I saw that I was ten feet behind Rodrigo. I had fallen asleep.

He motioned with his head for me to catch up. I moved forward, grimacing with each step, and then set my wheelbarrow down.

"Is this it?" I asked.

Rodrigo lifted his shoulders. "Is what it?"

"The day," I said. "Are we done?"

He shook his head.

"We've been out here for like ten hours," I said.

"It's probably been closer to twelve," he said. "But we need to do another run."

I wiped sweat from my eyes. "So we're going to end up working eighteen hours?"

Rodrigo nodded. "That's typical here."

"We'll barely have time to sleep," I said.

"The days are thirty-one hours," Rodrigo said. "You'll have time."

I didn't give a shit how long the day was. I needed to get out of the sun. I felt delirious.

"What if I can't continue?" I felt like a failure even asking.

He shrugged. "Then you won't get paid. The builders don't usually fire anyone—not even humans. They just won't pay you ... and will probably kick your ass."

With weak legs, a throbbing back, and sore arms and shoulders, I followed the caravan for the last time—at least today—to the quarry.

The six-mile stretch was a haze. I remembered the water stop, the stream, and getting screamed at by that fucking sponge, but most of it was a blur.

Although it was a relief again to stand in line at the quarry, I dreaded hauling the stones. Through blurry eyes, I stared down at my empty wheelbarrow and wondered how I could possibly push it another inch.

After the stones were loaded, I rubbed my hands against the ground, picked up the wheelbarrow, and starting walking. Everything hurt. Everything. And my group was already pulling away. Feeling faint, I dropped to a knee, my chest rising and falling. I needed to rest. I needed shade. I needed a damn meal, and a real meal, not alien peanuts.

"Fohp."

I didn't look up, but I could tell from the two long, spongy legs in front of me that it was a mop.

He tapped me with his club to stand, but I didn't feel like getting up.

"Pob," he said.

No. Rest. I needed to rest.

Then the club struck my side. I grimaced and collapsed to the ground, grabbing my hip.

"Pob huma! Pob!"

But I guess what I needed, unless I wanted to get the shit kicked out of me, was to get up and keep moving. The mop raised his club again.

"Papa," I said.

Blowing out a breath, I sat up. Then I grabbed the handles of the wheelbarrow and got to my knees, then to my feet. It's hard to say where I got the energy from—maybe I drew from my experience in boot camp—but I put one foot in front of the other and began pushing.

I knew I wouldn't be able to keep up with the rest of my group, so I just focused on myself. *Just make it to the stream*, I thought. Keep it simple. *Make it to the stream.* I wasn't going to worry about the four miles after that. If I did, I'd end up like the other dead humans, sprawled out on the side of death road.

I made it to the stream, then to the water break, and finally to the stadium. I'm still not sure how I did it.

After my wheelbarrow was unloaded, I let out a long, exhausted breath. I filed past the mop guard, who was handing out coins—two to each person in my group. When I reached him, his white eyes drifted up and down my body. Then he shook his head. "Fohp." He dropped a single coin in my hand and slid the other into the satchel that hung over his shoulder.

"What?" I said. "Why?"

"He's saying you were lazy today," Rodrigo said, waiting a few feet ahead of me.

My shoulders dropped. "But I delivered all of my loads."

"You should be happy you got one," a woman from my group said. "There was a time when humans didn't get paid anything. It was either do the job or die."

"Pob," the guard said.

Even without a wheelbarrow, I had trouble keeping up with the others on the walk home. The sun was setting, but it was still hot. It was always hot.

Shauna waited for me to catch up. She smiled when I reached her. "What do you know. You made it through your first day without dying."

"Well, I haven't made it home yet," I said.

"Do me a favor and eat a big breakfast tomorrow," she said. "And when you have enough money, you may want to consider getting yourself a hat. Your face is burned to hell."

I looked down as we walked. I can't remember ever feeling so fatigued. "We work again tomorrow?"

"Yes, but tomorrow is like a Friday." Shauna grinned. "Just one more day until the weekend. Unfortunately, the weekend is only one day and we usually spend it working on crops."

"So … today's Thursday?"

"Day ten," she said. "The weeks are twelve days long."

I blew out a breath. "Right …"

Shauna told me that most things on Bomba were based on twelve, which she thought stemmed from the number of fingers on a mop's hand. She said working in twelves, instead of tens, made dividing by quarters and thirds actually easier.

Of course, being as exhausted as I was, I didn't really care how much simpler division would be, or how many squishy fingers or toes they had. I just wanted to sleep. But before that, I needed to take a crap.

Shit town was on the edge of the desert. As you'd expect, the closer you got to shit town, the worse it smelled. There were about a half dozen latrines, specifically pit latrines, which were shacks surrounding a hole in the ground. Shauna, who was walking with me, explained that once the latrine's hole overflowed, they built another. Great system.

Shauna went first. There was another latrine fifty yards

further, but I wasn't walking another fucking foot. After crapping out my alien peanuts, I walked with Shauna back to house six. She told me to take a nap, and then come back for dinner.

As I lumbered to my room, I passed a mop in the hall. I think he smelled me.

"Fohp," he said, turning his nose up.

CHAPTER 6

"Are you well enough to walk?" Rodrigo stood in the doorway.

Grimacing, I swung my feet off the bed and onto the floor. I moaned. My entire body ached.

"I think so," I said. "Why?"

"The tax mop is here."

I rubbed my eyes. "The what?"

"Sorry," he said. "Tax man."

When we walked outside—me hobbling—there were already a dozen humans from house six lined up shoulder to shoulder. Two mops, with badges hanging around their necks, strode toward our building. They were both male, one with a red insignia on his badge and the other with blue. Rodrigo explained that the mop with the red badge was a tax collector and the mop with the blue, as I had already found out, was a cop, there to handle humans who couldn't, or wouldn't, pay their taxes. He didn't elaborate on what 'handle' meant, though the cop did have a club in his hand, which swung along his side as he walked.

We slid into line and waited as the tax mop collected coins from each human. After counting the coins, he dropped them into a sack that hung from his shoulder, then wrote something on a piece of parchment.

The mops reached Rodrigo, who held out a handful of coins, his head down. They collected his money, recorded the marking on his arm, and then moved to me.

"Paaayyy huma," the tax mop said.

I've always done my own taxes. I've never hired an accountant or used software. It's not that hard if you follow the instructions.

But it still felt strange the first time I listed a dependent. I remember writing her name in that tiny box on form 1040.

Almost four years to the day that Amy had lost the baby—lost Frederick—we learned she was pregnant again. But there was no extra place setting this time. There was no surprise in my dessert. There was no coupon redeemable for one baby in nine months. I walked in after work one day, and Amy said, "I'm pregnant."

She said it as casually as if she was asking about the weather. There would be no fuss for this pregnancy. In fact, we barely talked about it; except for the few requests she had, which included fully carpeting the stairs, adding a handrail in the shower, installing a water filter to our faucet, and throwing out all our household cleaners, which were apparently toxic. Amy planned to make her own using vinegar and lemon juice.

She also became particular about what she ate. I couldn't just buy apples anymore, they had to be Granny Smith. I couldn't buy canned green beans, they had to be fresh. And I had to get two types of milk—whole milk, which I used, and skim for her. Then there was the hand washing. It's not that it was so frequent, which it was, but it was the way she washed her hands. She'd work up a thick lather, and then start with each fingertip, then the knuckles, then around her rings, and then the folds between her fingers.

Unlike with Frederick, we didn't use a family name this time. Our daughter would be her own person. She would be unique.

She would be *Jennifer Renee Dohring*.

I would be responsible for her wellbeing. It would be my job to teach her right from wrong, to teach her self-reliance and responsibility.

And for seventeen years I did. And for seventeen years, I wrote *Jennifer R. Dohring* on line 6C.

"Paaayyy huma," the tax mop said again. He towered over me.

I turned my palms up and shrugged. "I don't …"

The cop tapped me on the chest with his club. "Paaaayyyyy."

Glancing up, I could see into his mouth, which was pink, but without teeth or a tongue.

Rodrigo, with his head still down, said something I

couldn't understand. Mop language. The cop yanked my arm toward him, his white eyes narrowing on my brand. After reading the markings, he grunted and shoved me back, causing me to stumble and fall.

Then the mops left and headed for the next building. Still on my back, I watched them walk, impressed with how much ground they covered with a single stride.

The rest of the humans from house six began to scatter.

"What did you say to him?" I asked, struggling to my feet.

"I told him to check your ID," Rodrigo said. "You're not supposed to pay yet."

I raised my arm, looking over the marking. To me, it looked like fucking Chinese. "So this is like my social security number for Bomba?"

Rodrigo nodded. "It's two sets of numbers actually, and they go right to left, not left to right." His eyes moved to my brand. "The first number is ninety-four. The second two-eighty-seven. It's the date you arrived."

"So ninety-four is what? The year?"

"No, the day," Rodrigo. "There are three hundred and twelve days in a Bomba year. Today is day ninety-seven. Three days ago was ninety-four, which is when you arrived."

"And the other number is the month and year?"

He shook his head. "They don't have months. Two hundred and eighty-seven is the year."

I glanced over at the tax mop, who was now at house seven. "They've only been around for two hundred and eighty-seven years?"

"That's just when they started counting," he said. "Do you know how there's B.C and A.D. on earth?"

"Yeah."

"It's like that."

My gaze turned to the sky. "Two hundred eighty-seven years … *after death*?"

The corners of his mouth turned up. "No. That's not why they started counting. It was the year of their first games, which they call *Aba*. It's like their Super Bowl." He shrugged. "Although to them, the first winner of Aba is a God."

Rodrigo moved to the water barrel, filled his cup, then drank it down in a few gulps. He leaned against it and looked over at the mops. "We've tried to tell them that there are more efficient ways to collect taxes, but as with most things, they don't listen."

"Are these income taxes they're collecting?" I asked.

"It's everything—income, property, sales tax. It's not exactly fair the way they do it, but it does make it simpler."

I ran the back of my hand across my forehead, then wiped the sweat on my shorts. "What happens if you don't pay?"

Shifting his upper body, Rodrigo moved his right arm toward me, revealing a branded K.

"Why do they use the letter K?" I asked.

"It's a strike," he said.

"As in baseball?"

He nodded and ran his finger over it. "But there are lots

of reasons why humans get K's."

"Why did you get yours?" I asked.

"For stealing."

I looked him up and down, taking in his bony frame. "What did you steal?"

"Nothing," he said. "But I'm human, so I'm guilty."

My eyes moved between the brands on both arms. "Why did they choose K?"

Rodrigo rolled his eyes. "It's our own fault. They actually asked us what we wanted, and some baseball nut gave them that idea."

"So what happens if you get three strikes?"

Rodrigo stared at me. "You're out."

"Out of what?"

"Out of life," he said with a straight face. "If you get three K's, they'll put you into their games—into Aba. But Aba isn't fun. Not for humans anyway."

We heard a scream and both turned. Two cops were kicking a human, who lay curled up on the ground.

A woman stood next to them, her face red, her eyes bulging. "Stop!"

The cops didn't listen, or maybe didn't understand, and continued kicking, their huge feet pounding against the man's ribs. Then they each grabbed a foot and began dragging him away.

He wailed as his bear back slid across the dirt.

"Please!" the woman yelled. "No!"

"Where are they taking him?" I asked.

"To the branding station," Rodrigo said.

"They're giving him a strike?"

Rodrigo nodded calmly, then spoke in a low voice. "Keep your money on you. Or hide it really well. The cops here are corrupt. They'll steal your money, then turn around and ask you to pay your taxes."

"You didn't make it to dinner last night," Shauna said, walking over.

"I slept through it."

"I don't suppose I can convince you to take the day off," she said.

"You said the weekend was tomorrow. I can make it through one more day."

"You'll need a big breakfast then," she said. "Eat as much as you can. You'll burn through it … and then some."

"And make sure you ration your water better," Rodrigo said. "Don't expect Shauna to share hers again. She needs it just as much as you do."

I followed Shauna to a table, where a group of humans—all shirtless, even the women—were gathered around eating. The table was positioned between two trees, which I assumed was on purpose to provide shade. I winced as I sat down. As Shauna made me a plate from the bowls of food, I exchanged 'hellos,' but mostly 'holas,' with the rest of the humans.

Even though the sun had barely broken the horizon, it was already warm.

Shauna slid a plate in front of me. "The best Bomba has to offer."

It wasn't my usual eggs and toast. In fact, nothing on my plate looked like any type of food from Earth, although their textures and shapes seemed similar to cucumbers, peppers, and bananas.

I glanced over at Shauna. "Do I just ... eat it raw?"

She bit into the thing that looked like a cucumber. "Just dig your teeth right in, Norman."

Grabbing the ends of it, like I would a cob of corn, I brought it to my mouth and bit down. Juice dribbled down my chin and onto my chest. It was sweeter than I expected. The skin tasted like a regular cucumber, but the inside was juicier. Within a few minutes it was gone. Then I moved to the two pepper-looking things. They had the width of an Earth pepper but were longer and a light shade of brown.

"For those, you can eat everything but the core. But the inside of these," another woman said, peeling her banana, "aren't going to be what you expect." She turned the peeled section toward me, revealing a line of yellow grapes. They fell into her hand, and then she tossed them into her mouth. "We call them grananas."

"That's my sister, Norman," Shauna said.

The woman held up her hand. "Carla. *Little* sister." And she was, no more than five feet.

"Did you guys ... come together?" I asked.

Carla shook her head. "No, but if it wasn't for Shauna—the good doctor—coming two weeks later, I probably wouldn't have made it." She smiled. "I guess even wormholes target blacks."

I studied Carla's face. "I didn't notice you yesterday. Did

you work with us?"

"I did," she said, chewing. "But don't worry about it. I know you had a rough day."

"Wait, you were the one who told me about death road," I said.

She grinned. "Yep, that was me, honey."

"You said you wanted to beat the shit out of a mop," I said.

"You got it." Her eyes shifted to a mop passing by. "That's right, you fucking sponge. I'm talking about you." Then she nudged the guy to her left. "This is Two Strikes Tomás."

Tomás had two Ks on his right arm, but both were well healed and close to his natural skin color, which was olive-brown.

"We just call him Two Strikes." Carla shrugged. "Well, we usually call him Dos Huelgas, but since you don't speak Spanish, we'll use Two Strikes."

"Get two strike first day," said Two Strikes, who was missing his two front teeth. "No strike since. I be quiet. I work hard."

It didn't take long to finish my first pepper. As I bit into the second one, I noticed a cop staring at me, his nose turned up. I stopped mid-chew and glanced around the table. Everyone had their heads down, eating, loading up on calories for the day. My eyes returned to the mop who stood there, still staring, shaking his head.

"Get used to it," Rodrigo said, sitting down across from me.

I finished chewing, then swallowed down the pepper. "They really don't eat anything?"

"They only drink water," Rodrigo said. "Although they don't actually drink it. They absorb it."

Carla gave the cop the finger. "Hi," she said with an overly friendly smile. "Go fuck yourself."

"We think the water here has more nutrients," Shauna said, "which allows them to survive on it."

Carla pointed at me. Her finger dripped with juice. "Hey, did you hear the story about the first humans? What the mops did to them?"

I shook my head.

"They were sick—the humans—and the mops thought they needed water," Carla said, "but they couldn't figure out how to give it to them since they didn't have pores. So they poked holes in their skin and poured water over them. The humans promptly bled out." She wiped her mouth. "I swear, I'd really love to punch one of those things in the face."

"They like tapeworm," Two Strikes said.

"He's right," Shauna said. "Their texture and coloring are the same too."

As I listened to her, I forced myself to keep my eyes on her face. It was strange talking to the women who didn't wear shirts. They usually wore a bra or shirt when they worked, but around our residence, most were barebreasted.

"Apparently they do have vocal cords though," Shauna continued. "That, along with their lips, does allow them to have a reasonable vocabulary. Of course, without tongues, it is limited. You won't hear many words with Ts, Ks and Ns." She turned to Rodrigo. "Do you want me to make you a plate?"

"No, I got it," he said, and then reached for a bowl.

A man approached our table carrying a stack of papers in his hand. As with most of the men on Bomba, he was unshaven and thin, but unlike everyone else at our table, he was Caucasian.

He put his sun-darkened hand on Rodrigo's shoulder. "Caulquier recien llegado?"

Great, even the white guys speak Spanish.

Rodrigo pointed to me.

"What did he say?" I asked.

"I speak English," the man said. "I'm the messenger. I asked if there were any newcomers."

I rubbed my sticky hands together. "Yeah, I arrived a few days ago. Why?"

"He's one of the few humans who travels between regions," Rodrigo said, swallowing down a bite of food. "Politically and geographically, Bomba has three. And there are humans in each. They call a region a 'Mafa.' We're in Mafa Fah, the northern region. But humans just call it North Bomba."

"Be grateful you ended up here," the messenger said to me. "The mops in South Bomba *really* hate humans."

"So why do you want to know if I'm new?" I asked.

"In case you have family in another region," the messenger said. "It helps with morale to have family around." He glanced at his sheets of parchment. "What's your last name?"

I shrugged. "I can tell you, but I know I don't have any family here."

"What's your name?" he asked again.

"Last name is Dohring," I said, and then spelled it.

"There aren't any Dohrings in our region," Shauna said as the messenger scanned his list.

"Are you sure you don't know anyone that's gone missing?" the messenger asked me, his eyes on the parchment. "There's a Jennifer Dohring in South Bomba."

CHAPTER 7

I felt the color leave my face. I stared at the messenger, my mouth hanging open.

"Are you …" I shook my head. "Are you sure?"

"Yeah," the messenger said. "But let me spell it back to you." He squinted and read. "D-O-H-R-I-N-G."

I gave a slight nod, my heart pounding. "Do you have any other … like … information about her?"

The messenger held the parchment above him. "We usually have city and state, but the rain got to this piece." He brought the sheet closer to his face. "I can only see the state. Of course, most of us here are from Nevada anyway, so that doesn't really help."

I continued to shake my head. "Can't be …"

"You have a daughter that's missing?" Rodrigo asked.

"Since last September," I said. "But … I didn't put the connection together. I … I didn't think …"

"It's okay, Norman, it happens a lot," Shauna said.

"People are just trying to survive when they get here. It's hard to concentrate on anything else."

"How old is she?" Rodrigo asked.

My hands shook. "Seventeen."

"What does she look like?" he asked.

"Uhhh ... she's about five-six ... light brown hair and ... and she's got a scar on the tip of her nose." I bit my lip. "She slipped when she was ... I guess it doesn't matter ..."

Rodrigo looked around the table. "Anyone?"

Everyone shook their heads.

I took a deep breath and stood. "Well, there's got to be a way to verify it's her, right?" I turned to Rodrigo. "Didn't you say there were phone lines here?"

"Yes, but I don't think any are in service. And even if they were, humans wouldn't be allowed to use them."

"Well ..." Shauna started, and then glanced over her shoulder. "There is a mop in town." She kept her voice low. "Apparently he has a phone connection to Central and South Bomba. And he will let humans use it."

"For a price," Rodrigo said, then looked at me. "And you only have one coin. It'll cost you twenty times that. At least. And you'll need to pay your rent soon."

"I don't care about my fucking rent." I folded my arms across my chest. "But I mean, can't I just go to South Bomba?"

"It's not that simple," Shauna said. "The regions are pretty far apart."

"Not to mention, there's a desert separating us from Central Bomba, and then water separating Central and

South," the messenger said. "And you have to pay to enter each region, and for the boat ride to South Bomba." His eyes moved to my right arm. "At least you don't have any strikes."

"What difference does that make?" I asked.

"They no allow criminal in," Two Strikes said, glancing at his arm.

"Humans who have strikes aren't allowed into South Bomba," said Rodrigo. "It's usually not an issue in Central, although I'd still wear a shirt or something to cover it up. But that won't work in South Bomba. You'll never get in there with strikes."

"So what am I supposed to do?" I asked, holding up my hands. "I need to find out if it's her. You tell me—what do I do?"

The messenger sat between Rodrigo and another man, set down his papers, and pulled out a thin piece of charcoal. "Give me some more information about you—your first name, address, other family members' names …"

When I was done, the messenger stood.

"Okay, I'll be back in about two weeks," he said. "I'll let you know for sure then."

"Two weeks?" I asked.

"Yes, and remember, those are mop weeks," Rodrigo said. "So you're looking at about twenty-four days."

I sighed. "Can't I just go with you?"

The messenger folded his papers and slipped them into a satchel. "I'm sorry, no. Like we said, it costs money to travel, and it doesn't sound like you have much."

"Norman, a lot of us have gotten news like this," Shauna said. "You just need to be patient."

Despite the extra food in my stomach, my second day as a hauler—transporting stones from the quarry to the stadium—sucked.

My thoughts were on Jennifer, and because of it, I fell behind often. On my first trip back from the quarry, I lost my stones again, and this time I didn't get help reloading. As bad as my housemates felt for me, they never lent a hand that morning. And I don't blame them. I wouldn't have either. Christ, I would need to do it myself eventually. They all had.

And I needed the money. If the messenger confirmed Jennifer was here, I'd need the coins to travel to South Bomba.

After unloading at the stadium, I was finally able to catch up with my crew as we walked our empty wheelbarrows back to the quarry. But as soon as we loaded up again, I began to fall back. The humans were thin, but incredibly fit and able to get by on much less water. We did three round-trips a day, but I swear, the crew from house six could've done ten.

And now, only five minutes after leaving the quarry, I was already fifty yards behind.

"Norman, come on!" Rodrigo shouted. He motioned with his head as he plowed forward, his hands still on his wheelbarrow.

I gave a pathetic nod as I drew in a breath. Despite the

thick cloud cover, it was sweltering. My head throbbed, my muscles ached, and my heart slammed in my chest. I clung to the handles as my legs began to quiver.

I felt faint and dropped to my ass. A second later I was on my back, staring up at the clouds. I barely felt the first hit to my thigh, but when the guard's club struck my ribs, I screamed. Still, I didn't move. I couldn't. Even if the cop hadn't struck me, I wouldn't have been able to get up.

Through the haze, I saw the guard striding away, following my crew who were still moving. I turned onto my side and rested my sunburned cheek against the dirt road. I stared at a patch of grass, and then my daughter's one-year-old face filled my mind.

Hand over hand, Jennifer crawled toward me through the high grass.

"It might be easier for her if you cut the lawn," Amy said, sitting with her arms wrapped around her legs.

I sat ten feet from her with a glass of freshly squeezed orange juice between my legs. Amy never bought bottled orange juice. If either of us wanted some, she would cut raw oranges in half and squeeze them over a glass with her bare hands. She did this once when we were dating. A lot of guys wouldn't have thought much about it. Some might have even laughed. Not me. I knew right then that I wanted to marry her.

"Well, she should be walking," I said. "And the high grass will help when she falls. More padding."

Amy shrugged.

When Jennifer reached me, I pulled her up from under her arms and set her on her feet. Then I turned her to face Amy, being careful not to spill my orange juice.

"Ma-ma," Jennifer said.

"Yes, that's ma-ma," I said, poking my head around her. "But we're not going to crawl to ma-ma. We're going to *walk* to ma-ma."

I pulled my hands away. Jennifer wobbled in place for a few seconds, then plopped to the ground. She flipped onto her hands and knees, and began crawling.

"No," I said, scooping her up. "*Walk* to ma-ma."

"Ma-ma," Jennifer said. To my dismay, it was the only word she knew.

"Walk," I said, and then let go.

Jennifer began to sway, but then she took a step, and another.

Amy's eyes widened. "Come on, honey. Come to ma-ma."

When she heard Amy's voice, Jennifer hurried, causing her to stumble and fall. Her face turned red and she began to cry. She reached her arms toward Amy, who got to her feet.

"She can get up on her own," I said to Amy, taking a sip of my orange juice.

Amy stopped, frowned at me, then folded her arms.

"Ma-ma," Jennifer called.

"She can do it," I said.

Jennifer continued to cry, and a few seconds later, Amy blew out a breath and walked over.

"She skinned her knee," Amy said, kneeling next to her. She reached down, held up a small rock, and arched an eyebrow. "I guess the high grass camouflages the rocks too."

Amy chucked the rock over the fence, scooped up Jennifer and walked her over. "Stay with da-da. I'm going to get you a Band-Aid."

Jennifer continued to bawl in my lap as Amy went inside. I glanced at the scrape on her knee. "That's not bad," I said to her, standing her back up. "You should be able to walk with that."

Wrapping her arms around me, she leaned into my chest. I could feel her shaking. When Amy came back through the door, I patted Jennifer on her shoulder.

"Ma-ma's here," I said. "And she has a Band-Aid."

No matter what the injury, whenever Amy would apply a Band-Aid, Jennifer would let out a long, exasperated sigh and, magically, be healed.

"Wait there," I said to Amy as she walked toward us through the yard.

"Ma-ma," Jennifer said with wet eyes, her arms extended.

I stood Jennifer up and held the outside of her shoulders to keep her from falling. "If you want ma-ma—if you want your Band-Aid—you'll to have to walk."

"Ma-ma ..."

Amy crouched down and flashed the box of Band-Aids. "We're going to make your boo-boo aaallllll better."

"*Walk*," I said. "Walk to ma-ma."

I lifted my hands from her shoulders and gave her a nudge.

One step ... two steps ... three. She tottered, regained her balance, and took two more. Then three more. Then another step and into her mother's arms.

Still laying on death road, I slid off my Timex. I scraped dirt from its face and wound it. The time was wrong of course. With the longer days, it would never be right in this place, though with adjustments I could keep it close to Bomba time.

Once the second hand started to tick, I propped myself up. I wiped mud from my face, then used the edge of the wheelbarrow bed to get to my feet. I rubbed my eyes and my vision began to clear. In the distance, I could see something.

Moving forward and squinting, I said, "Is that them?"

"It is," a voice said.

I whipped my head around and saw an older man, a human, leaning casually against a tree. He had a long, white beard and his large ears stuck out awkwardly from his wrinkled face.

"But you won't be able to catch them," he said.

I glanced down the road, then back to him.

"Are you from house six?" I asked.

He shook his head. "No."

My eyes drifted to his arms, which we're free of brands.

"You don't have any markings," I said. "You don't have any brands."

"No," he said.

"So … did you just come through the wormhole? Did you just arrive?"

"I've been here awhile," he said.

The man had a presence about him, a calmness that I hadn't seen in humans on Bomba. His responses came slow and easy.

He ran his hand against the trunk of the tree. "Things have grown pretty well over here. I was worried about the heat stunting everything, but the rain has really helped." He gave a casual shrug. "I hear it's still hotter than Earth though."

"Of course," I said, and wiped my forehead dry.

Still leaning against the tree, the old man's gaze turned to the sky. "My son's on Earth."

"Okay …" I peeked down death road again, then turned back to him. "So you don't think I can catch them? My crew?"

The old man shuffled his bare feet. "It'd be easier to walk on water," he said with a smile. "But catching them shouldn't be your goal."

"What … why?"

"Steady plodding brings prosperity," he said. "Have you heard that one?"

"I don't know." Feeling delirious, I rubbed my eyes. When I opened them again, the old man was gone from under the tree. I turned in place but didn't see him. Then I looked back toward my crew. I drew in a long breath, lifted my load, and followed the cloud of dirt and dust.

A mile before the stadium, I passed them as they were heading back to the quarry for their third and final load. Relief filled Shauna's face when she saw me. Then I passed Rodrigo.

"I knew you had it in you, Norman," he said.

Still, they weren't going to stop. They weren't going to wait for me. They'd get beaten if they did. I would have to finish this load, and my third, on my own.

And I did.

I only received one coin, but that was expected. The cop shook his head as he dropped it into my palm, making sure his beautiful, white skin didn't touch my grimy fingers.

As we ate that evening, I noticed that the humans didn't smell as bad as when I first arrived. It didn't take long to realize why. I reeked now as well and just couldn't tell the difference.

After dinner, I hit shit town, and then headed for my room. On the way down the hall, I heard squealing from inside one of the rooms. The door was ajar, so I peeked inside and saw two aliens having sex. It was the standard missionary position, but the sex was rougher, and because of their spongy bodies, water dripped off the bed with each thrust.

Although I was exhausted, I had trouble sleeping that night. Perhaps it was the pain in my ribs, or the thought of Jennifer on this miserable planet, or maybe the sight of two mops fucking. But at least tomorrow would be a rare, and much needed, day off.

CHAPTER 8

The human farm was about two miles from house six. It was roughly the same distance away as shit town, but thankfully in the opposite direction. Shauna suggested that I spend the day recuperating—resting and eating more weird-looking fruit, but I decided to help Rodrigo on the farm instead, at least for a few hours.

The mops cared less about the farm than they did shit town. Harvesting the crops meant they wouldn't fall to the ground and rot, which the mops found repulsive. Of course, the mops also knew that what we ate would eventually come out as feces, but they realized humans—and their cheap labor—wouldn't survive without food, so concessions were made.

Rodrigo and I talked on the way to the farm, but my responses were slow and choppy. I was tired, and my mind kept drifting to my daughter. The more I thought about it, the more certain I was that she was on Bomba. It couldn't be a coincidence. How many Jennifer Dohrings could there be in Nevada? Two or three? Maybe. And of those, how many were missing?

Then another thought washed over me, one I had to consider. One that made me nauseous. Even if Jennifer had ended up on Bomba, there was a reasonable chance she was dead. Horrible to think about, but true considering the conditions. Rodrigo said that most human communities supported the younger kids, only requiring them to work around the residence—farming, tool-making, and hunting, though the latter usually fell to older kids. And when I say older, I'm talking eleven or twelve, but teenagers were required to work. I hoped, *prayed*, that Jennifer's job wasn't too arduous.

"Our crops are over there," Rodrigo said, pointing.

He explained that each house had their own section of farm they worked. There were trades and exchanges between houses, and for the most part, there wasn't a lot of theft. But you could only plant and harvest within your section, which was labeled with a wooden stake. If you wanted to eat a crop from another part of the farm, you either had to trade for it or figure out how to grow it yourself.

Rodrigo set a cloth sack on the ground when we reached our section, which was smaller than I expected. The whole lot was more of a garden than a working farm, which was disappointing because I was hoping there'd be cows. I had only been on Bomba a few days, but I was craving meat. I licked my lips as my stomach rumbled.

"We're going to be planting zanahorias and pepinos."

I stared at him.

"Sorry," he said. "Carrots and cucumbers."

"Was that mop or Spanish?"

"Spanish," he said. "They can't pronounce the letter Z."

"So are the carrots like … actual carrots?" I said, scanning the crops.

He shook his head. "Nothing here is exactly the same, but we thought it'd be easier to use the same names if it was close." He pulled a handful of seeds from the sack. "These have the same color as carrots, and generally the same shape, but they're fatter and not as hard."

Rodrigo moved a few steps to his left, then dropped to his knees and pointed. "Start there," he said, dumping seeds into my hand. "You want to plant them about an inch deep. There's a trowel in the bag."

I tugged on my hat and got to work. A human from our house had lent me his New York Yankees cap. I hated the Yankees, but with my face so fried from the sun, I didn't object when he offered. Fuck, I'd have given anything at that moment to see a Yankees game; and let's go ahead and throw in a beer and a dog as well.

With the trowel, I loosened a ten foot stretch of soil and then began burying the seeds. "You know, I was hoping this was going to be a real farm," I said. "With animals."

"Are you already tired of the vegetables?" he asked.

"They're fine," I said. "I'll eat them."

"We do eat some meat," Rodrigo said. "There's an animal on Bomba that kind of looks like a chicken. It's good. Although its head is closer to a fox."

"Let me guess. You call it a ficken."

Rodrigo turned and grinned. "That's right, Norman." Then his eyes drifted to the ground. "Hey, your seeds are too close together. Those things grow like crazy. Put at least six inches between them."

I sighed. Rodrigo had already gone twice as far down his row, and now I'd have to start over. I began digging up the seeds.

"Leave those," Rodrigo said. "Just do it going forward."

I shook my head and continued to dig. "If I'm going to do it, I might as well do it right."

"I won't argue with that," he said, then continued planting. "The problem with the fickens is that they're really hard to catch. And with this heat, it takes a lot of energy to track one down, so it's not always worth it. In the end, you'll lose more calories than you'll take in." He wiped sweat from his brow. "The mops don't care if we kill them though. They hate those little bastards, although they will use their skins for belts and straps and shit like that." Rodrigo finished his row and started down another. "But the best meat here is pom."

I pulled off my hat and waved it in front of face, fanning myself. "What's pom?"

"They kind of look like a rhino, but they're quicker and have more horns." He took a drink of water. "The mops use the poms for Aba, so they don't like us fucking with them. In fact, it's against the law to kill a pom."

Feeling suddenly dizzy, I shifted from my knees to my

ass. I dropped my head and wrapped my arms around my legs.

"What's wrong?" he asked.

"I don't feel well," I said.

"You'll adjust," he said. "It just takes time."

I let out a breath, then slid off my watch and wound it.

"Your watch works?" Rodrigo asked.

"Well, it's mechanical, so …"

"Good thing you weren't wearing a smart watch," he said. "Ninety percent of the electronics that come through end up fried. We're not sure if it's the trip through the wormhole, or just the heat."

Naturally, my twelve-year-old flip phone was fine; as was my twenty-five-year-old Timex watch. I finished winding it, drank some water—pouring a bit down the back of my neck—and then buried another seed.

"There is industry here," Rodrigo said. "Obviously you know about construction, but they do have a government, as well as banking, paper and cotton production, automotive …"

"If they have banks, why do humans hide their money?" I asked.

His lips curled up. "We don't usually get a good return," he said, and then explained. "It wasn't always easy to get the money back out. And even when we could, it would end up being less than what we put in."

I nodded as I thought about it. "And cars?" I asked. "I haven't seen any."

"You won't here," he said. "Mafa Fah is the poorest

region, and probably the most corrupt." He finished his row, grabbed a handful of seeds, and started down another. As usual, his pace was intimidating. "They have the humans to thank for most of their advances, but we haven't helped with much lately."

Again, I fanned my face with the Yankees hat. "Why?"

"Because they would either use the technology against us or ban us from using it. A lot of us thought they should develop on their own anyway. All I know is that they'd be much farther along if they had just worked with us." Rodrigo spat. "It doesn't help that they find us repulsive." He stared at the ground. "So much sometimes that they'll beat us. Just for being human."

Still on my knees, I put my hands on my hips. My heart began to thump.

Rodrigo looked over, and I think he realized what he had said. "When did your daughter go missing?"

"About nine months ago."

"The first few weeks are the toughest. If she made it through those, she's probably fine."

"Any idea the survival rate during those first couple weeks?" I asked.

He hesitated, brushing dirt from his hands. "It would just be a guess."

I waited.

"Probably forty percent," Rodrigo said. "But it's not just the mops. The heat's the real killer ... sometimes the food ... sometimes just the shock or an infection from the branding."

Thinking about Jennifer, I asked, "Have you ever travelled between the regions?"

"Once. I went through the desert to Central Bomba."

"Why?"

"I received word that my father was there," he said.

I glanced over my shoulder, in the direction of our house. "So your father's here? He lives in our building?"

Rodrigo shook his head. "He didn't make it back." His eyes began to water. It was the first time I had seen any emotion on his face. "He was killed by scavengers in the desert."

"Scavengers?"

"Rogue mops," he said. "They live mostly on the outskirts of town or in the desert. They're anti-government and *very* anti-human." He flexed his hand. "I tried to fight them off, but they were too strong. They knocked me out too—probably thought they had killed me." He paused. "But I woke up. I woke up next to my dead father."

I hesitated for a moment, then said I was sorry.

We sat in silence for a minute, neither of us digging. "How long have you been here?"

Rodrigo began planting. "Four years yesterday."

"Really?" I asked.

He nodded.

"Happy belated anniversary," I said. "When did humans first arrive?"

"About the late fifties."

"Has anyone made it back?" I asked.

"To Earth?"

"Yeah. Like is it possible to take the wormhole the other way?"

"I don't really know," Rodrigo said. "I heard someone from Mafa Ba made it back—that's Central Bomba—but no one knows for sure. Apparently, someone saw the opening, felt the energy, and this guy—whoever it was—was gone." He shrugged. "They never found the guy, so maybe. Or maybe he just ended up on Santuario."

"What's that?" I asked.

"It's Spanish for sanctuary."

Sweat dripped from my nose. "It's a place? Here?"

"Yeah," he said. "Supposedly it's a human-only island."

"No mops?"

"Nope. But the mops have heard the rumors. Luckily for us, they don't like to travel too far out on the water. They'll cross the sea between Central and South Bomba, but that's about it." He squinted as the sun continued to rise. "But the mops don't think Santuario really exists, and frankly I don't either."

After we finished planting, we moved to a different part of the farm and spent an hour pruning and harvesting, filling two sacks worth of cucumbers. On our way back to house six, each with a sack slung over our shoulder, we walked past a river, which Rodrigo said was used for bathing.

Since I hadn't showered for three days and had pissed myself at least once, I thought it was time. So after we dropped off our crops, I went back to the river. Rodrigo lent me a bar soap. At least that's what he called the deformed block, which was crusty and brown, and smelled more like dirt than an Irish spring.

After my bath, I took a long nap, then joined the rest of my group for dinner. As they spoke in Spanish, I sat in silence eating another plate of vegetables. Looking up, I noticed two pale moons in the twilight sky, one a little higher than the other, but both about the same size. I had heard there were three but had yet to see them all at once.

Then a bell chimed and the crew from house six perked up.

"Novato," said Two Strikes.

Rodrigo stood. "I'll go get them."

"Get who?" I asked.

"The novato," he said. "The newbie. Another human came through the wormhole." He took a few steps, then turned back to me. "Do you want to come?"

Having napped earlier, I felt rested and was full from dinner. "Sure."

Shauna glanced at the fading sun. "Just make sure you're back before dark."

I stood and finished my water. "Why?"

"Humans aren't allowed out after dark," said Carla. "And they'll give you a strike for that shit." She grinned. "I've risked it a few times and gotten away with it, but I blend into the night much better than your pale ass."

With that, my pale ass followed Rodrigo as we headed for the branding station.

The walk was longer than I remembered. We moved

through human towns and eventually into those with all mops. There were certain landmarks—trees and buildings—that I remembered, but the towns seemed more active. What stayed the same were the shouts of 'fohp' and other obscenities I couldn't understand. Of course I didn't know they were obscenities until Rodrigo told me, and he said most of them were directed toward me.

"What are they saying?" I asked.

Rodrigo held back a smile. "They're calling you fat."

"What?" I glanced down at my stomach, which I promptly sucked in. "I'm in good shape."

"For Earth maybe," he said.

I let that settle as we walked. Rodrigo was right. On Earth, I'd be considered fit for someone in their early fifties, but here I was a big fatty, even compared to the humans.

"I just hope the novato isn't overweight," Rodrigo said.

"What do you mean? Why?"

"Fat people don't do well here. Most die," he said. "The mops still ring the bell though."

A building to our left provided shade as we passed it. I slowed, extending my time out of the sun, then hurried to catch up to Rodrigo who hadn't broken stride.

"So what do you do if they're dead?" I asked. "Do you still carry them back?"

"I usually get help if that's the case, but yeah," Rodrigo said.

"Where do you take them?"

He motioned over his shoulder. "There's a human

graveyard a few miles from our building."

I hesitated, then asked, "Is your father buried there?"

Rodrigo nodded. "I carried his body through the desert. I thought he deserved a proper burial." He wiped his brow. "The mops don't bury their dead. Not in the ground anyway—they toss them into the river. It takes a while, but their bodies do eventually sink."

We passed a human, a middle-aged man with dirt on his face and hands.

"Will the new person—the uhhh—the novato, be living in our building?" I was curious, but also wanted to change the subject.

He nodded. "Right now house six has the most open rooms. Probably because it's the shittiest building."

"Have you ever considered having people bunk together?" I asked. "It sure would save on rent."

"They won't let us. Not adults anyway," Rodrigo said. "The mops are paranoid, especially the males. They don't like it when we huddle together in closed spaces. They think we'll come up with some devious scheme to wipe them out. Which we probably would." He shrugged. "But a lot of humans think it's more about the money. Just another way for them to take our coins."

More humans passed, and like the man before, they were covered in dirt and sweat.

"So will the new person be working with us?" I asked.

"As long as they fit into the equation," Rodrigo said.

"What equation?"

"Greater than fifteen and less than sixty," he said. "If

they're not in that range, they work in the garden, dig graves, ditches, build tables, make tools ... there are a lot of things to do. We just don't want them doing hard labor."

"Do you have to be a hauler if you live in our building?"

"You don't have to be," Rodrigo said, but it's easier if those that live together, work together. That way, we all leave at the same time and get home at the same time. You don't want to end up alone in a mop town. Bad things will happen." He looked over at me. "But we can move you to a house that speaks more English if you want."

Most of the humans in house six spoke enough English to make it bearable, but it was still a pain in the ass. I thought about it for a long moment but decided to stay with the crew that had helped me through my first few days. "No, I'm good."

The human lay naked on their side as we approached, a pile of clothes next to them. Although the person was pale like me, they were also thinner, and based on the firmness of their skin, younger. In fact, they had such a delicate body I was surprised to see a penis—albeit small—between their legs.

Rodrigo knelt beside him and put a hand on his shoulder. "Are you okay?"

The human groaned. Except for the handful of hairs on his chin, he had a clean face and the hair above his forehead was sticking straight up. Early twenties probably.

"What's your name?" Rodrigo asked.

He let out another moan as he reached for the brand. I could smell his burnt skin. As I stared at his arm, my thoughts drifted to Jennifer. I felt my stomach rise in my throat as I imagined her screaming during the branding.

Rodrigo gave the guy a light shake. "Hey, can you sit up?"

He rolled onto his back and opened his eyes. Then he let out a yelp as the fading sun hit his face.

Still on one knee, Rodrigo shifted, blocking the light. "What's your name?"

"Bran ... Brandon," he said, and then sighed.

"Can you stand up?" Rodrigo asked.

Brandon rolled back onto his side. "I don't feel well."

"What about your clothes?" Rodrigo said. "Can you put them on?"

He shook his head.

"Can you help?" Rodrigo said to me, grabbing Brandon's pants, which looked like they could have fit a twelve-year-old.

We rolled him onto his back and, each grabbing a belt loop, began sliding the pants up his legs. His underwear was still inside, but it took us a full five minutes to get those skinny jeans up to his waist.

Then Rodrigo pulled Brandon into a sitting position. "Can you walk?"

Brandon shook his head and began to gag. "I think I'm going to be sick."

Rodrigo glanced at me and then scanned for mops. "Sorry, but we need to go."

Brandon shook his head.

"We're going to lift you," Rodrigo said.

We got Brandon to his feet, slung his spindly arms around our necks, and began walking. The kid couldn't have weighed more than a buck fifteen.

He groaned. "I'm going to throw up."

"You're okay," Rodrigo said, picking up his pace. "Just keep those legs moving."

Brandon wasn't moving anything. His weight was solely on Rodrigo and me as we hurried him through town.

Shauna was waiting when we entered Brandon's room, which was two down from mine. A sprinkle of rain fell as we sat Brandon on the bed.

"Can you take me inside?" he said.

I peered through the joists above and shrugged. "You are inside."

Brandon craned his neck, looking up. He began to say something, then stopped.

"What's your name, sweetie?" Shauna said, sitting on the bed next to him.

"He gets a *sweetie*?" Rodrigo said.

Shauna tilted her head and smiled at Rodrigo. "That's right. Why, are you jealous? I got plenty of love to go around, even for the old-timers." Her eyes moved back to Brandon. "What's your name?"

Brandon didn't respond. He struggled to keep his eyes open.

"It's Brandon," I said to her.

"Thanks, but I wasn't asking you, Norman," Shauna said. She rubbed Brandon's back. "I know you don't feel well. I'm going to look you over, okay?" She held a cup to his lips. "Can you drink this for me?"

Forcing his eyes open, Brandon stared at the cup for a moment, then took a drink. When he was done, he pursed his lips. "Can I have some ginger ale?"

I laughed. Shauna shot me a look.

"We don't have any ginger ale, honey," Shauna said, continuing to rub his back.

"Could I get two Ibuprofen then?" Brandon said. "And maybe some ice pellets to suck on?"

Again, I laughed.

"How about some more water?" Shauna said, lifting his chin to drink. When he was done, he asked for his glasses, which Shauna retrieved from the inside pocket of his jacket.

"You're lucky they didn't find these." Shauna wiped mucus from the inside of Brandon's eyes, then slid on his glasses. "They usually keep them." She turned to Rodrigo. "I'm guessing you haven't told him anything yet?"

Rodrigo shook his head. "He wasn't coherent enough."

Under a light rain, Shauna finished examining Brandon. Then she gave him some fruit and put him to sleep.

An hour later I was in bed. I removed my watch and wound it, my thoughts moving between Jennifer and Amy. I felt helpless. One was here, but I couldn't get to her. And the other I would never see again. I blew out a long breath. The next day was a work day, and that was just fine with me. I planned to work my ass off.

The tray of food wobbled in Jennifer's hands. She had

already dropped it once. We spent twenty minutes cleaning it up and another twenty making Amy a fresh plate. But Jennifer, only seven-years-old at the time, asked to carry it again. She was a stubborn little girl—I don't know who she got that from.

I agreed she could carry it but explained that I wouldn't help if she dropped it a second time. After leaving the kitchen, Jennifer started down the hallway, her head peeking over the tray, which continued to teeter in her hands.

Amy cracked a smile when Jennifer turned into the bedroom. The sunlight shining through the window reflected off Amy's bald head. She had shaved it the week prior. There had only been patches left anyway. The rest had fallen out after the second treatment of Doxorubicin. Amy's oncologist called it the 'Red Devil.' It wasn't just the color of the medicine. It was the side effects—the nausea, the vomiting, the diarrhea, the mouth sores.

And it didn't leave Amy with much of an appetite. I doubted she would eat much of what we made. I was just happy she let us help. This was one of the rare occasions that Amy had accepted one of our offers.

"No special treatment."

"Only positive comments."

"I'm going to keep working."

"Nothing will change for my family."

She said these things so many times, I grew tired of hearing them. But it worked. In the end, I didn't treat her any differently. I felt helpless, felt like a dick, but that's what she wanted. "Everything should stay exactly the same." So when Amy accepted Jennifer's offer of breakfast in bed, we were happy to oblige.

The tray swayed as Jennifer crossed the room. When she finally reached the bed, Amy sighed. But as Jennifer lifted the tray, the glass of orange juice slid to one side, causing the tray to tilt, and then flip. The fruit, toast, eggs, and juice crashed onto the floor.

Jennifer flopped on the ground and began to cry, her pants soaked with juice. I waited in the doorway with my arms folded.

"Aren't you going to help her clean it up?" Amy asked.

"I already helped her once. I told her she'd have to do it herself if she dropped it again."

"Norman—"

I shook my head. "You said you didn't want me acting any differently. Well, this is me not acting differently."

CHAPTER 9

The sun beat against my face as I pushed my wheelbarrow down death road, heading for the quarry. Having had a big breakfast and almost a pint of water, I felt strong. I kept up with my crew for the first round-trip and, more importantly, wasn't clubbed by the guards.

On the second round-trip, I passed a twenty-something Hispanic woman. It was the first time I had not trailed my group. I felt confident that I would finally earn two coins. But on the final stretch to the stadium, I hit a tree root and lost half my load. I watched with wide eyes as my stones tumbled to the ground. I recovered quickly, but was still last to reach the stadium, and last again when I reached it for the third and final time.

Once again, I received a single coin for my day's work, as well a 'fohp' as I walked away. My spirits rose that evening though. A ten-year-old from our house had caught a ficken while we were at work. That evening I had my first bite of meat on Bomba. It tasted just like chicken.

The next day I woke with a start. I was determined to earn two coins. Part of it was competitiveness, part of it was acceptance from my peers, but mostly I wanted the money. It wasn't so much for my rent or taxes, but for the chance to call my daughter. I couldn't wait for the messenger. I needed to know if Jennifer was on Bomba, and if I could finish the week earning two coins a day, I'd have enough to make the call.

I didn't talk much during breakfast. Instead, I spent that time loading up on food and water, even more than the day before. I also jammed my pockets full of peanuts. They were so stuffed that it looked like I was wearing padded shorts as I walked to the stadium.

That day I paced myself. I didn't try to pass anyone. I rationed my water and peanuts, and was more careful with my loads. Although I stumbled a few times and had to take more breaks than the others, I stuck with them for three round-trips and never lost a single stone.

My heart thumped as I waited in line to get paid. Each human from house six received two coins as they filed past the guard. When I reached him, I held out my shaking hand.

The guard's white eyes drifted up and down my dusty, sunburned body before dropping a single coin onto my palm.

My shoulders slumped as I stared at it. *No.*

Though my hand continued to shake, I didn't pull it back. I titled my head and locked eyes with the guard. I held his gaze as I waited with my arm extended. I *wanted* that second coin. I *earned* that second coin.

"Ubu," I said, which was two.

The guard shook his head.

"Ubu," I said again.

"Mo huma," he said.

"Ubu, ubu," I said, stomping my foot twice against the ground.

The guard waved along. "Mo, mo. Pob."

My pulse raced. I squeezed my other hand into a fist and clenched my teeth.

"*Ubu.*"

The guard flinched. He let out a throaty sigh, rolled his eyes, and then dropped a second coin into my hand.

By the middle of the week—that being day six—I was consistently keeping up with my crew. I had gotten into a routine. Wake, eat, work, eat, sleep. Repeat. And when I ate, *I ate*. And when I slept, I slept *well*, even with the heat and exposed roof. The work tired me out, which is the way it should be. For five straight days I earned two coins.

Brandon, however, had yet to earn anything. After work on that sixth day, Shauna and I stopped by his room. Brandon was on his bed when we walked in. A layer of perspiration covered his hairless chest.

"How are you feeling?" Shauna asked, and then peeked at his cup. "Are you drinking water? You need to drink a lot here, more than you did on Earth."

She leaned down and felt his forehead. I still don't know

how she could check for a fever in this heat; all our bodies were scorching, sick or not. I guess it was all relative though because she said, "You don't seem warm."

Brandon shrugged.

"Did you get breakfast this morning?" Shauna asked.

"Yes" he said, nodding. "I had two of those banana things."

"Grananas," I said.

Shauna's hand moved to his ribs. "It doesn't seem like you lost too much weight. Five pounds maybe."

He didn't respond. Brandon had been on Bomba for seven days, but his eyes were still hazy.

"Do think you'll be able to work tomorrow?" Shauna asked.

"Work?" Brandon said, then rolled onto his side. "Going through that tunnel was like giving birth. I'll need at least a month …"

"A *month*?" I said. "Before you start working?"

Brandon wedged his hands between his knees. "Yeah."

Shauna and I exchanged glances.

"And how do you expect to pay for your room?" I asked.

"They'll need to give me temporary housing," Brandon said with a shrug. "What did you say they were called? Mops?"

I sighed. "The mops aren't going to give you sh—"

"*Norman*," Shauna said, raising her hand.

"Can I get a blanket?" Brandon asked. He curled his knees toward his chest.

Shauna patted his back, then stood. "There aren't many blankets around," she said. "Put on your shirt if you're cold."

I folded my arms and rested my bare back against the wall. "What did you do for work, Brandon?" I asked. "On Earth."

"I was the social media manager for the office of Diversity and Inclusion."

Oh fuck.

"Listen, Brandon," Shauna said. "I know it's a tough adjustment, but you're going to have to earn money if you want to live here. They don't allow vagabonds on Bomba, at least not humans." She moved toward the door. "I suppose you could live in the desert and try to find your own food, but that usually doesn't go well."

Brandon let out a long sigh. "I just need a few more days." He shifted, trying to get comfortable. "I'll start working soon."

"Just give it a good pull," I said to her.

Jennifer ran a hand over her hair, which was straight like her mother's. She also had Amy's slender frame. My contribution was her big, buggy eyes, which shifted from me back to the lawnmower.

"Will it move on its own?" she asked.

I shook my head. "No, you'll need to push it. But you don't need one of those. The self-powered mowers are for weaklings."

She looked out into our yard. "Why don't we just use

one of the riding mowers from your work?"

"They aren't necessary for this job." I squeezed the handle of the mower. "I bought this when we moved into our house twenty years ago, and it works just as well now as it did then. There's no reason to use anything else."

"Okay," she said, moving her hands to her hips. "So do we need a bag, like to catch the grass?"

"That's a good question," I said. "My answer is—it depends. If the grass isn't too long, you don't need a bag because the clippings will help fertilize the lawn."

"How?" Jennifer asked.

I bent down and pulled out a single blade of grass. "When a piece of cut grass decomposes, it releases nutrients back into the lawn, which makes the lawn stronger."

"So why would we ever want a bag?" she asked.

"Because grass needs sunlight to grow. If the grass is too long when you mow, it ends up covering too much of the lawn."

"Which blocks the sunlight?" she asked.

"Right."

I glanced over at Amy, who was sitting on our back porch. She had her feet up, a beer in her hand, and a wide grin on her face as she watched us.

The mower roared to life on its first pull, and a few seconds later my little girl was pushing our twenty-year-old John Deere across the lawn.

After Jennifer had made her first turn, rotating on the back tires like I had taught her, I joined Amy on the porch swing.

"I think you're starting her too late," Amy said, reaching into the cooler. "She's too far behind the other girls. All the neighbors' kids started mowing at like six or seven."

"She'll be fine," I said. "Being female shouldn't stop her from mowing the lawn."

Amy handed me a beer. "No, but I hope she's done by three because she does have Girl Scouts."

I took a swig of my beer and rested the cold bottle against my cheek. "She'll learn just as much mowing the lawn as she would in Girl Scouts."

"Will she have a cigar when she's done? That's what the previous guy used to do," Amy said, nudging me.

"I really liked that guy," I said. "But he's moving into a supervisory role."

Amy swung her legs up, resting them on my thighs. "You did tell her to keep her hands and feet away from the blades, right?"

"It was the very first thing I said to her."

"Will she be doing the weed-whacking too?"

"She'll be doing the full job, just like the previous guy," I said.

A moment later, Amy squeezed my hand. "Do you think she would have been a good sister?"

My gaze shifted to the back of the yard, to the cross I had built for Frederick. I had hammered it into the ground almost fifteen years ago.

I nodded and slid the Timex off my wrist.

House six was back at work the next day, and again I was able to keep up with my crew. I earned two more coins and was closer to having enough money to make my phone call. That was always my motivation. Every time I thought of Jennifer, I gritted my teeth and pushed forward. I needed to hear her voice. I needed to know if she was alive.

By the end of the week, I was leading the push. Several times, Rodrigo told me to slow down. I felt good. I felt like I had adjusted. I was working hard and earning money. Wake, eat, work, eat, sleep. Repeat.

As I pushed my wheelbarrow on the eleventh day that week—which was like a Friday on Earth—I began thinking about the work we did, specifically the process. It was about a four-mile walk from house six to the stadium, where we picked up the wheelbarrows, and then another six miles from the stadium to the quarry. That's ten miles. But it was only seven miles from our residence to the quarry. So why couldn't we take the wheelbarrows home and go directly to the quarry in the morning. It would shorten our day.

"We thought about that," Rodrigo said when I told him my idea. We were waiting to have our wheelbarrows unloaded for the final time that week. "But we decided it wasn't worth the risk."

"What do you mean?" I asked. "What risk?"

"We'd finish earlier if we did that, right? Because we'd be eliminating the time it takes to get to the stadium." He wiped his brow. "And what if they thought we could do a fourth load with that extra time? Are you prepared to do a fourth round-trip?"

"I don't know, but a fourth load would mean more money."

"Nunca," said Two Strikes, waiting behind us. He looked more tired than usual, though it was the end of the week. I'm sure I looked the same. "Sorry ... uhhh ... never," he said. "Mop never give more."

"He's right," Rodrigo said. "They'll never give us more than two coins for a full day. We're lucky to get that. Most human jobs only pay one. Not to mention, we'd have to push our wheelbarrows farther with your plan. They'd be empty during those miles, but still ..."

"But think about the benefits," I said. "Fewer overall miles, less time in the sun, same pay ..."

He shook his head. "I wouldn't risk it, Norman. Like I said, they may ask us to do a fourth round-trip if they notice the time savings."

As I contemplated this, a mop passed us on a bicycle.

"I haven't seen many of those," I said.

"They're probably coming from Central Bomba," Rodrigo said as his load was removed. "Most mops in North Bomba can't afford them."

But that led me to my next idea. Why didn't we convert the wheelbarrows into carts, with four wheels instead of one? It would reduce the strain on our backs and make our work more efficient. The wheelbarrows were good for dumping, which was how the mops first used them, but our loads were too heavy to dump. And although wheelbarrows were more agile over the hills and through the rocky parts of death road, they were also less stable.

After my wheelbarrow was unloaded, I filed in line behind Rodrigo to get paid. I nudged him and explained my idea.

"They give us what they have," Rodrigo responded. "Building the carts you're talking about would take time, effort, and money. And the mops who oversee our operation, don't want to take on any of that. They don't care how much harder it is for us. They just want the job done as cheaply as possible."

I glanced back at Two Strikes, who was well behind us, and waved for him to catch up.

"That's such a government attitude," I said to Rodrigo. "Why don't we just build them ourselves? We could use them for lots of things."

"Because the mops would steal them," Rodrigo said. "If you build what you're talking about, it'll be gone the next day."

I shook my head, then finished my water. As expected, I received two more coins, bringing my total to twenty-two.

"How much will they charge me to make the call?" I asked. "To my daughter in South Bomba."

"The last I heard it was twenty coins," he said.

I brushed dirt from my hands. "And you can take me there?"

"I can," Rodrigo said, "but don't forget about your rent and taxes."

"I did the math," I said. "As long as I continue to get two coins a day, I'll have enough for both."

"Then we'll go tomorrow," he said.

As we waited for Two Strikes, Rodrigo explained that the mops had other denominations of coins, but humans would rarely earn enough to own any.

I turned back and saw that Two Strikes was still ten feet behind us and now hunched over. As I moved toward him, he lifted his head and a grimace spread over his face. He took a step, then stopped, his hands clutching his stomach.

Two Strikes grunted, as if he was holding something back. He balled his hands into fists. Then he wailed as that something came out. A thick, dark stream of nastiness poured down his leg. Diarrhea.

The guard turned his head and let out a disgusted roar, then picked up his club.

"Lo siento. Lo siento," Two Strikes cried, dropping to his knees. "Sorry. I have sorry." He collapsed on his side as the club struck his back.

The guard wanted to swing again but had to shuffle his feet to avoid the brown puddle leaking from under Two Strikes. Then the guard cracked him again, and with it another dark stream gushed from Two Strikes' shorts.

I moved toward them.

"Don't," Rodrigo said, his hand tightening around my arm. "They'll just beat you too."

The guard yelled something, and two other mops came running over. With his club, the guard pointed at the diarrhea and then at Two Strikes. After a brief exchange, they all nodded. The mops grabbed Two Strikes around his wrists and began to haul him away like some dying deer.

Rodrigo gritted his teeth and shook his head. "No … fuck … no …"

The crew from house six gaped as Two Strikes was dragged along the ground. His destination would be the branding station. Two Strikes went three years with two strikes but would receive his third for crapping himself at work.

CHAPTER 10

At breakfast the next morning, we all joined hands and said a prayer for our friend. At least I thought it was a prayer. It was in Spanish, so I couldn't tell for sure, but since everyone had their heads bowed and made a sign of the cross afterward, it seemed likely.

Two Strikes was in a mop jail and would remain there until the start of our region's Aba, which was about a week away. During Aba, he'd be released into the arena, along with other human criminals, to face three mop gladiators, who would slaughter the humans before moving on to face each other. Because of the mops' size and strength, along with their sticks and clubs, humans rarely stood a chance.

We talked about Two Strikes for hours that morning. There was a lot of anger to start. Carla wanted to pummel a few mops as payback. She even talked about trying to break Two Strikes out of jail, build a boat, and try to find Santuario, but Rodrigo and Shauna persuaded her against all of it. They said her first option would only result in strikes, and possibly jail, for the rest of us. And as far as Santuario, well, that was just a myth.

After Carla had stomped away, the mood of the group changed. We smiled and laughed as we talked about Two Strikes' friendly demeanor, his work ethic, and how he earned his nickname, which we considered changing to Three Strikes, but, for whatever reason, decided against it. He would be forever known to the humans from house six as Two Strikes Tomás.

As they continued to tell stories, my mind drifted to Jennifer. I was anxious to make the phone call to South Bomba. Seeing Two Strikes dragged away, made me wonder if I was already too late.

Later that day, Rodrigo, Brandon, Carla, and I began our trek into the city. Although Brandon had yet to work a single day, even though he had been on Bomba for twelve, he perked up when we mentioned where we were going. I suspected he wanted to get a latte and connect to the Wi-Fi.

My shorts sagged with the weight of my coins, which rattled as I walked. Rodrigo recommended I keep my hands in my pockets as well, at least when we got close to mops. The mops knew where humans kept their money and, depending on who and how many you encountered, were likely to steal it. He also said that the cops would be of little help if that happened. They rarely investigated crimes against us, and when they did, it was more for show than anything else—a politician's request to appease the filthy humans.

The mop city was called Fah, which was a shorted version of our region name, Mafa Fah. Though it was mostly populated by mops, one of the first things I saw upon entering Fah was a picture of a human. The person, who had long hair and a scraggily beard, resembled the man they had shown me a sketch of on my second day.

"Who is that?" I asked Carla.

Her eyes followed my finger, which I had pointed at the sign. "They call him Fof."

I slowed, studying his face. He had large ears, droopy eyes, and distinct creases on his forehead. I couldn't tell the color of his eyes though because the mops hadn't progressed to color printing.

"I think I've seen him," I said.

Rodrigo turned. "You've seen Fof?"

"Yeah, I think so. Why? What does Fof mean?"

"First human," Carla said.

I stopped and set my hands on my hips. "He was the first human to arrive on Bomba?"

Everyone else stopped.

"From what we've heard, yeah," Carla said. "Numero uno to go through the wormhole."

"I don't know if he was first, but he did say that he's been here a while," I said.

She titled her head. "You *talked* to him?"

I nodded.

"Where did you see him?" she asked.

"On death road," I said. "Although I was so delirious, I

thought he might have been a mirage."

"He might just be," Rodrigo said. "No one else has ever seen him. At least no one from North Bomba."

Brandon moved toward the sign. "What does it say?" he asked. "Above his name."

"I can't read mop that well," Carla said, "but it's basically a wanted sign."

"As in 'we want to kill you,'" Rodrigo said.

"But why? Why do they want him?" I asked.

"A few reasons," Rodrigo said. "First, they want to talk to him. They want to find out how this whole thing started. How long has he been here? What does he know about the wormhole? He's also been rumored to live on Santuario, so they'd definitely like to ask him about that." His eyes moved to the picture. "Apparently, he's never been branded either, which means he hasn't been paying taxes." He began walking again. "And mops love collecting taxes from humans."

Dark clouds drifted overhead as we traveled further into the city. Of course, calling it a city seemed strange. There were no buildings or skyscrapers; in fact, every structure was one level. Rodrigo said that humans had taught the mops how to build multi-story buildings, but they never constructed a single one. Why? Because the mops didn't want ceilings or roofs. They hated having a cover over their heads. The mops needed a consistent soaking. They didn't want to wake up and have breakfast; they wanted their breakfast to be showered upon them as they slept.

I felt a few raindrops and hoped for more as the sun

shined through an opening in the clouds. Shifting my arm, I slipped off my watch, adjusted the time to match the mop day, and then wound it. I wondered what time it was on Earth. I wondered what Amy was doing right then.

Then I heard the roar of an engine. The crowd on the street began to spread, and in the distance, we saw a convertible rumbling toward us. It sounded like a Harley. Smoke rose from its tailpipe as it sped down the street.

Brandon pushed out a mouthful of air and mumbled something about the environment. We covered our ears as the convertible drove by. It puttered to a stop farther down the road.

After waving a cloud of smoke out of his face, a mop jumped out. He was the biggest one I had seen, standing almost nine-feet-tall with a body to match. Other mops rushed toward him, touching him, screaming, fawning over him like he was a rock star.

"Who is that?" I asked.

Carla used the back of her hand to wipe sweat from her forehead. "He's a Ba," she said. "A gladiator. He fights in the games—in Aba." She shrugged. "If he wins our region's match, he'll move on to the main Aba games."

"So Two Strikes will have to fight that guy?" I asked.

Starring at the Ba, Carla nodded. I could see a vein pulsing on her temple.

With a crowd gathered around him, the Ba raised his arms into the air and yelled, "Pahhva!"

Before I had a chance to ask, Rodrigo said, "It means awesome."

"As in *he is awesome*," Carla said, "which he fucking isn't. He's a worthless sponge."

The Ba licked the neck of a female, who was running her hands over his chest.

"Does he have a brand?" I asked. With the Ba's arm still in the air, I could see a marking on his right shoulder. "I thought only humans were branded."

"It's not a brand," Rodrigo said. "It's a tattoo. But only Bas get them."

"It's kind of like a sports logo," Carla said.

Rodrigo explained that it's difficult to tattoo a mop because of how wet and spongy they are. To prepare for the tattoo, a Ba must fast for several days so that their skin dries up. It's the only way the ink will stick.

"And there's nothing worse than a fasting mop," Rodrigo said.

The Ba pushed through the crowd, heading toward one of the buildings. A statue of a mop stood out of front.

Kneeling before the statue, the Ba yelled, "Bomba!"

"The name of the statue guy is Bomba?" I asked.

Rodrigo nodded. "Yeah. He was the first mop to win Aba."

Brandon scratched his chin. "I thought Bomba was the name of the planet."

"It is," Carla said. "They named it after him."

I laughed. "They named their planet after a sports star?"

"It's even funnier if you speak Spanish," Rodrigo said. "Because Bomba is *bomb*."

"Which is exactly what I'd like to drop on this place,"

Carla said, then began moving again as a light rain fell.

I saw my first NO PISSING and NO SHITTING signs as we moved through the city. There were even stores with NO HUMANS written on the doors. Our region's government had passed a law that forbid that, but it wasn't strongly enforced. Rodrigo said it wasn't enforced at all.

One thing I kept looking for, but never found, was restaurants. Since the mops took in water through their skin, there simply wasn't a need for any. There were stores and shops, but they didn't sell food. They sold things like house furnishings, tools, sports memorabilia—pictures, figurines, and fighting clubs of old Ba's—reading and writing supplies, bags, satchels, and shoes, which a few of the wealthier mops wore.

In the middle of the city was our region's government office. We all stopped, took drinks from our water containers, and watched mops walk in and out.

"Can I go inside?" Brandon asked.

"You *can*," Carla said. "But why would you?"

Brandon adjusted his glasses. "I want to see what provisions are available for humans."

"Provisions?" Rodrigo asked.

"Yes," he said, nodding. "Food stamps, first aid kits, water, that sort of thing."

Rodrigo folded his arms and sighed. "Brandon, they don't offer anything like that."

"Why? It's only right that they supply us with *something*."

Carla shook her head. "They're not going to supply you

with shit."

Brandon stuffed his hands into his skinny jeans and stared at the building. "Well then I'll have to speak to a supervisor," he said, and headed for the door.

Carla called to him, but Brandon kept going.

After blowing out a breath, Rodrigo said, "Wait here," and then hustled after him. "I have to make sure he doesn't get his ass kicked."

I was about to sit down when I heard a faint whining to my left. I took a few steps in that direction and found a baby mop laying on a bench. It was about three feet long, but with the same spongy skin and white eyes. Its voice was faint, but had that distinctive, hollow, high-pitch.

"Christ," I said, reaching for it.

"Norman!" Carla said. "Don't touch it."

I pulled my hands away. "Why? I'm just trying to help it."

"Mops don't like humans touching their kids." Carla scanned the area. "Especially their babies. They think we'll pass on a disease or something."

"You just want to leave it here?" I asked.

Carla moved closer, looking down at the baby mop. "It's normal. Those idiots leave their babies lying around all the time." She pointed up with her thumb. "As long as it rains, they know they'll be fine. It's the mop form of breastfeeding."

A female mop emerged from the building. When she saw me, her eyes narrowed. "Pob!"

I held up my hands.

"Just tell her to fuck off," Carla said.

"Pob! Pob!" the female yelled, glaring down at me.

I stumbled backward. "Papa."

The female scooped up the baby and used her balled hand to rinse it, as if washing away germs. She grumbled at me as she strode away.

"I told you," Rodrigo said, following Brandon out of the building.

Brandon's face was wet and flush. "They weren't very nice."

A quarter mile up the road, we passed a store that had CLOTHES pained above the door.

"There are human stores here?" I asked.

"A few, yeah," Carla said. "They get robbed a lot, but if you can make a profit, it sure beats the hard labor we do."

"Robbed by whom?" I asked.

"Usually by mops," Rodrigo said. "And they don't hide it. They'll walk by the next day wearing the shoes they stole." His eyes shifted to a mop nearby. "Sometimes they'll even get dressed up and pretend to be human—act like they're eating or pissing or any of the other foul things we do."

I took a few steps toward the store. "So this place sells human clothes?"

"Clothes, shoes, hats ... the shit humans need to get by," Carla said. "Although what I wished they sold was tampons. The women here are literally on the rag once every two mops weeks, or as you would say, a month." She glanced down the street. "There are other human stores too—fruit, tool shops … the ones that usually do the best sell to both mops and humans, but those also get robbed the most." She reached into her shorts and slid out a handful of peanuts. "I heard someone from Mafa Bah—that's Central Bomba—is opening a coffee shop." She cracked the shells, then tossed the nuts into her mouth. "That's just what we need, caffeinated mops."

Brandon brushed past me, heading for the clothes store. "I could use a hat. The sun here's terrible for my skin."

"How are you going to pay for it, Brandon?" I asked.

He stopped and thought for a moment. "Right. Can you lend me some money?"

"No."

Brandon looked to Rodrigo and Carla, but they shook their heads. Then he reached for the door handle. "I'll just ask them for store credit."

"Brandon, we're going to keep moving," Rodrigo said. "But don't leave. Stay inside. Don't go anywhere by yourself. We'll come back and get you."

Carla shook her head. "I'm not going to leave him here. I don't care if it's a human store or not." She sat down on the store's front step, which was blocked from the sun, and took a drink of water. "I could use the shade anyway. Just stop by here on your way back."

"Be careful," Rodrigo said. "Don't go mouthing off."

"Yes, da-da," she said, her expression turning innocent.

"This is it," Rodrigo said, pushing the door open.

I followed him inside, where we found mops sleeping on the floor. There was a counter near the back wall with glass bottles and water containers lined across it. Another mop stood behind the counter, his arms folded across his chest.

Rodrigo approached him and began speaking in mop. A few seconds later, he waved me over. As I reached the counter, the store owner left us and tended to a mop who had just walked in.

"What's going on?" I asked. "What is this place?"

"A bar," Rodrigo said.

The mop customer slid a few coins across the counter. "Hop," he said to the bartender.

My eyes moved from the containers on the counter to the mops sleeping on the floor, who I now suspected were passed out. "A mop bar?"

He nodded. "Yeah, although humans come here occasionally. I mean it's alcohol, so it'll get either of us drunk, and the owner doesn't care who the money comes from."

The bartender filled a cup using one of the containers, which I assumed held alcohol and not water. After he grabbed the cup, the customer took a step back, and with a steady hand, poured the liquid over his head. It absorbed into his skin.

"Pahhva!" he yelled.

Awesome. I guess he liked it.

He turned to me, said, "Fohp," then left.

"I thought we were here to make a call," I said to

Rodrigo. "Are you stopping for a drink?"

"We are here to make the call." Rodrigo pointed to the containers on the counter. "They offer two drinks here—a number one, which is 'hop' and a number two, which is 'ubu.' One is like a beer and two is like a shot of whisky." He motioned to the door. "The guy that just left had a number one, and I'm guessing," he said, glancing at the mops on the floor, "those guys had number twos."

"I still don't understand," I said. "What's that have to do—"

"You're going to ask for a number three," Rodrigo said.

I stared at him for a moment and finally realized that 'three' was code for something. "And how do you say three again?"

"Owp," he said.

Facing the bartender, I said, "Could I have a uhhh ... owp. An *Owp*."

The bartender's white eyes locked with mine. He looked past me toward the door. Resting his arms against the counter, the bartender leaned forward and said something to me in mop.

"He's going to let you make the call," Rodrigo said. "But he wants the money."

I reached into my pockets. "How much?"

"Twenty-two," he said.

"I thought you said it was twenty?" I asked.

Rodrigo shrugged. "Well apparently it's gone up. Do you have it?"

"That's all I have, but yeah."

I'd be broke and it would be a struggle to pay my rent on time. With my hands still stuffed in my pockets, I worked my fingers around the coins as I thought about it. I sighed, pulled out all twenty-two, and dropped them on the counter. Before the coins had even stopped rattling, the bartender scooped them away, and then waved for us to follow him, which we did, passing into another room.

Rodrigo, being my translator, explained that even if this didn't work—if I couldn't reach my daughter—I wouldn't receive a refund. I told him I understood as I watched the bartender remove a panel from the wall, revealing a wooden casing with a cord running out the bottom and metal bells attached to the top. The voice transmitter protruded from the center of the box and a separate receiver hung from the side. It looked like an early-twentieth-century telephone.

My heart began to pound. Even before we made the call, I could hear Jennifer's voice in my head.

Please help me. Dad. Dad. Dad.

Rodrigo told the bartender that we wanted to call South Bomba, Mafa Ahh, and speak to a human. The bartender opened the housing and spun the rotary dial. The phone clicked with each stroke.

I nudged Rodrigo, keeping my voice low. "So where in South Bomba is he calling?"

"A mop building close to where the human houses are," Rodrigo said. "Someone will have to go find her."

The bartender finished dialing and held the receiver against his ear, listening. My heart continued thumping in my chest. After waiting about a minute, the bartender shook his head.

"Why's he shaking his head?" I asked.

The bartender spoke to Rodrigo, who translated.

"He said no one answered," Rodrigo said.

I raised my shoulders. "Okay … so what do we do?"

"I'll have him try again," Rodrigo said.

Rodrigo spoke to the bartender, who pushed out a breath, then dialed again. I rubbed my palms against my shorts. Again, the phone began to click.

The bartender's white eyes settled on me as he waited. I stared back, fidgeting with my hands. Another minute went by and again he shook his head.

Rodrigo said something to him, but the bartender simply shrugged and said, "Mo huma."

"No?" I said, feeling my face flush. "I paid to get my daughter on the phone."

"I told you this might not work," Rodrigo said.

"Fuck that. He didn't even try. He waited like a minute."

Then the bartender's eyes widened. He craned his long neck toward the transmitter and spoke. He said something to Rodrigo, then handed the receiver to me.

"Hello?" I said, my voice cracking. "Jennifer?"

No answer.

"He said they would go look for her," Rodrigo said.

"A mop is going to look for my daughter?" I asked.

Rodrigo nodded.

An uneasy feeling rose in my chest. *If they touch her.*

"So I just wait?" I asked, holding up the phone.

"You just wait," Rodrigo said.

The receiver shook in my trembling hand. I stood there, listening as the bartender left the room.

Time ticked by.

"May I ask who's calling?" I said.

The boy's voice cracked. "It's uhhh ... this is ... this is Scott."

"And your last name, Scott?" I asked.

"Murph—Murphy," he said.

I already knew his name. Amy had told me about little Scottie Murphy, who had quite the crush on our daughter.

"One moment, Scott," I said, then called to Jennifer.

Her eyes grew wide when I offered her the phone and gave his name. Jennifer was thirteen, and the blonde hair she had as a child had faded and more closely matched the auburn shade of her mother's.

She grabbed the phone, clutching it with both hands. "Leave," she whispered to me.

I did. Sort of. I picked up my coffee and sat at the kitchen table, facing her. Leaning back in my chair, I smiled.

She pursed her lips and shook her head. "Hello?" Jennifer walked to the corner of the kitchen, stretching the cord.

Most of Jennifer's friends had cordless phones; at least that's what she told me. But the beige corded phone that hung on our kitchen wall worked perfectly fine. There was no need to replace it.

Every few seconds, Jennifer, who talked with her back to me, would turn with a scowl on her face and wave for me to leave. But I just sat there, sipping my coffee, unable to hold back my grin.

Scott and Jennifer talked about movies and songs and kids at school. I discovered that Kenny Clarke had been suspended for bringing a dead ferret to lunch. I assumed it was for show and not what he had packed to eat.

As they continued to chat, Jennifer walked to the other side of the kitchen, stretching the cord, now trying to escape to the living room. But it wouldn't reach. Then she tried to sneak into the hallway but was a few feet short there as well. Funny how that cord was never long enough to reach another room.

I pressed the receiver against my ear. Silence. "How do I know if it's … working?"

"Do you hear anything?" Rodrigo asked.

I raised my shoulders. "Static."

"Then it's working," he said. "It's not like they have clear connections here. You should be able to have a conversation though."

We waited. One minute, then two, then five. At fifteen minutes, the bartender stepped back in. Rodrigo shook his head. The bartender groaned and hollered something at Rodrigo.

"Papa," Rodrigo said, and the bartender left.

I continued to wait. Five more minutes, then ten.

"How do we know if they're even looking for her?" I

asked.

"We don't," Rodrigo said, raising his hands. "I told you this was a risk. I didn't recommend it."

I flinched as a girl's voice echoed in my ear. "Hello," she said.

"*Jennifer*? Hello? Hello?"

"Who is this?" the girl asked.

"It's your father—it's me, Jen. Is that you?"

There was a long pause, and then the girl said, "My father's not on Bomba."

"I am, Jen, it's me."

She didn't answer.

My grip tightened around the receiver. "Jennifer?"

"Who is this?" she said.

"It's—this is your father."

"No. *What's your name?*" she said.

"Norman. Norman Dohring," I said. "Jen, it's me. I'm here on Bomba. North Bomba. Is this Jennifer Dohring?"

I shook the receiver as more static echoed in my ear. The girl said something I couldn't understand.

"Hello?" I said. "Say it again, I couldn't hear you."

"Can you," she said in a muffled voice. Crackling filled the line. "South—"

"What?" I shouted, tapping the receiver. Again—again. Say it again."

The static faded and the girl's voice came through clear. "Can you hear me now?"

As I opened my mouth, the bartender charged into the room, grabbed the receiver, and hung up the phone.

"Hey!" I screamed.

The bartender's fingers closed around the back of my neck, and he shoved me into the bar. Rodrigo followed.

"I was talking to my—" I said, then stopped, seeing three mops standing in the center of the room, two with badges hanging around their necks. Cops.

The third man, the one without a badge, was the tallest and had a pompous air about him. He moved toward us, his chin high. His eyes moved from us to the bartender, who began speaking to him in mop.

But I didn't give a shit about any of them. I needed to get back on the phone.

"I didn't finish the call," I whispered to Rodrigo.

"Not now," he said.

I gritted my teeth. "Rodrigo—"

"*Not now*," he said.

After the mops finished their conversation, the bartender said something to us. Rodrigo turned to me and translated. "The cops wanted to know why we were in the back." Rodrigo paused. "The bartender explained that we were helping with the alcohol production."

Distracted, I gave a slow, uninterested nod. I'll go along with your stupid excuse.

The tall mop stepped closer, said something I couldn't understand, then extended his hand. I shook it and could feel the moisture from his pores.

"This is Bob," Rodrigo said. "He's the leader of North Bomba. Kind of like the governor of a state."

"His name is Bob?" I asked.

"There are a lot of Bob's on Bomba," Rodrigo said, and then also shook his hand. "It's easy to say without a tongue."

Then I noticed Bob wipe his hand—the one he just shook with—against his leg.

Rodrigo and Bob talked for a few minutes. I was impressed with Rodrigo's grasp of their language. When they were done speaking, Bob turned to me, continuing to talk. Rodrigo translated.

"Bob says he's running for president of Bomba. The election is a week after Aba. Although humans aren't allowed to vote, he's asking for your support."

I shrugged.

"You should nod," Rodrigo said, his voice firm.

My eyes moved from Rodrigo to Bob. A moment later, I nodded, causing Bob to flash me a toothless smile.

"He's promising more equality for humans," Rodrigo said. "He feels it's the responsibility of the mop government to provide us with more opportunities."

What a load of shit, I thought.

The door creaked opened behind us. I peeked over my shoulder and saw Ma, the translator, with a camera hanging around her neck. At least that's what it looked like. She stared at me for a moment, then joined Bob and whispered something in his ear.

Bob pointed at me and she nodded. Then Bob said something, which she translated.

"I ell Bob hooww uuu hel meee."

"She told him how you helped her," Rodrigo said. "With

the cop."

Bob looked me up and down, then spoke again. Ma translated.

"How uuu ike hauer?" she asked.

I was beginning to understand more of what Ma said. This time, she wanted to know how I liked being a hauler. I considered sharing my ideas about how to make things more efficient, but Rodrigo had warned me against it.

"It's fine," I said, and then paused. "But I do have a few suggestions …"

Rodrigo snapped his head toward me.

"I think the stadium could be built better … I think a lot of your structures could be built better."

Ma said something to Bob, and then asked, "Hoowww?"

The mops were using a homemade mortar to adhere stones together when building. That was all fine. The problem was the rain. Too much water would make it weaker. I suggested adding a cover when the mortar was being mixed and when the pieces were joined together. I also recommended they use limestone to make their concrete instead of mud and clay. They did use limestone for general building materials, so I knew they had it.

I explained all of this as best I could to Ma, who relayed it on to Bob. He gave me a slow nod as he processed what I was saying.

Listening to our conversation, Rodrigo told me that Bob liked my idea, and liked me; for a human.

Then Ma asked if Rodrigo and I could take a picture with Bob. We both agreed. Bob stood between us, his long, white arms stretched around our backs. He towered over us.

After Ma snapped the picture, Bob wiped his hands against his legs. He talked for a few more minutes, and as I listened, the more I thought the mops sounded like Yoda from Star Wars, with that throaty, squeaky voice. *Mops hate I do.*

After they had left, I asked the bartender to call South Bomba again. He said sure, for another twenty-two coins. I argued until he threatened to call the cops, which is when Rodrigo forced me out of the bar.

"The last thing you need is a strike," he said.

I walked with my head down. Rodrigo had to steer me away from mops as we trudged through the city. I kept replaying the girl's voice on the phone.

"Was it her?" Rodrigo asked.

"I think so. She seemed skeptical."

"Of you?"

"Yeah."

"But it was your daughter?" he asked. "You're sure?"

I shook my head. "I'm not sure, no. I wasn't able to confirm. But it sounded like her."

Rodrigo pushed out a breath. "You're just going to have to go there, Norman."

I had already reached the same conclusion. I needed to get to Mafa Ahh. I needed to get to South Bomba.

As we approached the human store to pick up Carla and Brandon, we heard squeaks and screams. We broke into a jog and as we drew closer, saw a group of mops surrounding something. Only it wasn't something, it was someone.

Carla lay on her back as they punched and kicked her, their faces filled with excited rage.

"Hey!!!" Rodrigo yelled, taking off in a sprint.

They rummaged through Carla's pockets as Rodrigo and I raced toward them. My chest heaved with each stride. The mops scattered when they saw us. As Rodrigo dropped to a knee if front of Carla, who lay motionless, I hurried after one of the mops. He was the smallest of the bunch and probably the only one I had a chance of catching.

He darted down an alleyway between two buildings. He swung his head around, saw me, and then broke into a run, his long arms swinging by his sides. I must have looked pathetic chasing him. My steps were smaller, I stumbled, and my breathing labored as I ran. I squinted as sweat ran down my forehead and into my eyes.

When he reached the end of the alley, the mop took a sharp left, out of sight. I lumbered after him, sucking in breath after breath, digging for the end of the alley. I turned the corner, and my eyes bulged wide as a car roared toward me. I leapt back into the alley, but the car's front end caught my ass, sending me airborne. I crashed to the ground with a thud.

Grimacing in pain, I watched the convertible speed away with the Ba behind the wheel. Mops pointed and laughed as I lay there, clutching my ass. There's probably only one car in North Bomba and I had just been hit by the fucking thing. I glanced the other way, but the mop I had been chasing was gone. At least I thought he was. He could have blended in with the others for all I knew. Those assholes all looked the same.

I limped back to where the mops had attacked Carla, who lay motionless on the ground. Rodrigo and Brandon were beside her, shielding her from the sun.

"Is she okay?" I asked, breathing heavily.

Rodrigo looked up at me. "She's alive," he said, "but they knocked her unconscious."

Carla's face was bloodied and bruised, and her left eye was beginning to swell.

"We need to carry her," Rodrigo said, pouring water over her forehead. Blood washed down her face and onto the ground.

"We need to call the police," Brandon said.

"It's pointless," Rodrigo said. "They won't do shit for this."

Rodrigo, Brandon, and I carried Carla back to house six. It was a tough trek. Carla was petite but carrying anything over twenty pounds in that heat was a chore, even with three men. Rodrigo and I, being in better shape, supported most of Carla's weight. But I'll give Brandon credit, he did try.

Shauna was eating out front when we reached the house. "Another novato?" she asked. "I didn't hear the bell."

"It's Carla," Rodrigo said.

Shauna sprang up. She hurried toward us, her eyes growing large as she caught a glimpse of Carla's face.

"Christ," she said. "What happened?"

"I'm not sure," Rodrigo said. "She got mugged … maybe a fight. I don't know."

Shauna began to tear up. "Let's get her upstairs."

CHAPTER 11

I stared down at Carla, who lay in her bed. Her left eye was puffy and bruised, and she had scrapes on her cheeks and forehead. Her right eye was open, but glassy. When she spoke, her sentences were short and her speech slurred. She kept repeating that she had a headache.

Shauna had stayed with her since we returned. She spent half the time sitting with her in bed and the other half pacing back and forth in her room, which she hadn't left once, not even to eat or go to the bathroom.

"I want to …" Carla began, and then stopped. "I want …"

"You want to stand, I know," Shauna said. She stood at the end of the bed, her arms folded as she looked Carla over. "But the last time we did that, you almost fell over. And we can't have you hitting your head again."

Carla didn't respond, looking blankly at her sister. Then she began to gag. Shauna hustled over and propped her up.

"Can you hand me that bucket?" she asked me. "Quickly."

Just as I passed it to her, Carla began to puke. Shauna caught most of it with the bucket, the rest sliding down Carla's chest. Then Carla heaved again, and again, and again.

A little later, when Carla had finally finished, Shauna returned the bucket.

"Can you go to the river—not the one we bathe in—the other one, and wash this out for me?" Shauna said. "And be discreet. Don't let the mops get a whiff of it because they'll know."

As I walked to the river, I envisioned Jennifer laid up in bed with her eyes swollen shut. Although Carla was more of an instigator than my daughter, it didn't take much to set off the mops. Sometimes it didn't take anything, except for human DNA.

I was convinced that Jennifer was on Bomba. Even with the static, it sounded like her on the phone. She didn't give her name, but did she have to? They went to look for someone named Jennifer Dohring and then a teenage girl answered the phone. It had to be her. It had to be.

Brandon decided to work today. It was about fucking time. We suggested he take another job, one less labor intensive, but he wanted to stay with us and insisted he could handle it. There were a lot of things Brandon wanted to buy and he didn't think he could manage on one coin a day, which was what most human jobs paid. So he decided to give it the old college try.

We encouraged Brandon to have a big breakfast and fill his pockets with peanuts for later. When we reminded him to bring his water container, he declined and said he would just drink water at work. We explained this wasn't an option and ultimately forced him to bring his own.

During the walk to the stadium, Brandon asked repeatedly about public transportation. He couldn't fathom that we had made this walk every day. I also learned that Brandon was twenty-three, which is how old Frederick would have been. But Frederick would have been working for a week already. I'm certain of it.

As we approached our wheelbarrows, it began to drizzle, which was a relief. We had gone nearly two days without rain and the cops were getting cranky; even more so than usual. There were rivers nearby that mops could jump in during droughts, but the rain was so consistent on Bomba that most would wait it out. It's not like they had a five-day forecast. Although when they eventually launch satellites and can better predict the weather, perhaps they could add some diversity to their newscast and include a human. That'd be a good gig for Brandon I think—a member of an alien storm-team.

"I need my fifteen-minute break," Brandon said to the guard as we pushed our wheelbarrows to the quarry. We had completed about half of the six-mile walk.

"He can't understand you, Brandon," I said. "And even if he did, it wouldn't matter."

With pursed lips, Brandon shoved his wheelbarrow forward. After it skidded to a stop a few feet in front of him, he exhaled, then plopped down in the middle of death road.

"Get up, Brandon," I said, stopping. "It's only another mile to the river. You'll get a break there."

He shook his reddening face. "These conditions are horrendous. I want my break now," he said, wiping his brow. "And I'm not doing three trips. Not on my first day. They should work me in gradually."

And he hadn't even picked up his first load.

After setting my wheelbarrow down, I peeked at the cop, who was walking alongside the others. "Don't look too far ahead. You'll never make it that way." I walked back to him. "Just worry about the next mile. You can do one more mile, I know you can."

"I can't," he said. "I'm going to have to take a sick day."

"There aren't any sick days," I said. "You either do the job and get paid, or you don't."

Brandon dropped his head and closed his eyes. I leaned down and poured water down the back of his neck.

He gasped when he felt it. He sucked in a breath and said, "Thanks."

Then I saw the guard moving toward us, his eyes narrowed.

"Get up, Brandon."

"I can't … it's too hot." He began to cry. "I just want to go home."

Now five feet from us, the guard screamed and raised his club. I crouched down and lifted Brandon from the waist of his skinny jeans. "We've got to move."

I left him and hustled to my wheelbarrow. When I looked over my shoulder, I saw that Brandon was back on his ass; not from being hit, but from his refusal to continue. The hits, however, were about to come.

The first one cracked across Brandon's back and the next against his hip. He collapsed on the ground, howling in pain, as his glasses fell from his face. I wanted to help him, wanted to step in, but I knew it would be suicide.

The guard waived his club at me, and I started forward.

"Papa," I said. "I'm sorry, Brandon, but I have to go."

He didn't answer. He moaned and rolled onto his back, his mouth stretched open in pain.

As the guard ran ahead to catch up to the others, I slowed and glanced back.

"Brandon," I called. "Are you okay?"

He was silent.

"Brandon!"

Nothing.

I glanced at the cop, let out a breath, then dropped my wheelbarrow and hurried back to him.

He squinted up at me, his chest rising and falling.

"Are you okay?" I asked.

Brandon let out a groan, then wiped his eyes. "I don't know …" He reached for his glasses. The frames were bent and one of the spectacles cracked.

"Can you manage without those?"

"My vision's fine," he said.

"What?"

He took a moment to respond, breathing heavily.

"They're just for style."

My wheelbarrow wobbled as I pushed. It wasn't heavy, but the position of my load made it awkward. Brandon's wheelbarrow was lying sideways inside mine, with the right tire against the tray and the handles hanging over the side.

Brandon trailed behind me, his head down, his shoulders slumped. Rodrigo folded his arms across his chest when he saw us. He had just returned from the stream and stood there shaking his head.

"Well that's a first," he said. "But it's not going to work too well when he's got a full load."

With Brandon being young and thin, I was hoping he would struggle through. Rodrigo wasn't so sure.

"We should consider moving him to a different house," he said. "I'm not sure he's ready for this."

We both watched Brandon as a woman from our crew walked him to the stream. His steps were sluggish, even without his wheelbarrow, which still lay inside mine.

"He can push it from here," I said, lifting it out.

Rodrigo helped me set it on the ground. That's when I saw my first pom.

It roamed through the forest, on the other side of death road. From a distance, it looked a lot like a rhino. It was a big motherfucker. It had a large horn on the bridge of its nose like traditional rhinos, but two others jutting out from the top of its head. Although its skin was a cloudy white, it wasn't covered in pores. It was just another disgusting animal that ate and shit.

"They're tasty," Rodrigo said, peering at it.

"You've eaten one?" I asked.

He nodded. "A couple guys from house five killed one. We had a bonfire out in the desert."

"I thought it was against the law to kill a pom?" I asked. "Don't the mops use them for Aba?"

"Yes and yes," Rodrigo said. "I probably wouldn't take that risk now. If I were you, I'd stick to ficken."

Brandon returned from the stream. "I'm hungry."

"Then eat your nuts," Rodrigo said.

"I didn't pack any."

"*What?*" I asked. "Why?"

"I can't eat them," he said. "I have a slight peanut allergy."

I reached into my pocket, grabbed a handful of nuts, and forced them into Brandon's palm. "They're alien nuts. You'll be fine."

Brandon stared at them. After removing the shell as I suggested, he bit into one. His face contorted into a grimace. "They taste weird," he said, and spat it out.

The pom stopped and looked over at us. It tilted its head and squeaked like a donkey. The cop said something, then pointed down death road.

"He wants us to go," said Rodrigo. "The poms are territorial, and they'll charge if we're here too long."

"Pob, pob," the cop said.

So we all did, except for Brandon. He didn't last another five minutes. Rodrigo sacrificed his day's pay and walked Brandon back to house six.

On the walk home, I noticed the two moons again, both pale against the dusk sky. I still hadn't seen the third. A Hispanic man told me that I'd never see them all together because of their position and orbit. The three moons did make for some dramatic tides though, as well as a few more solar eclipses. He said the moons were also the reason for the longer days. At least that's what an astronomy hobbyist from house nine had told him.

I checked on Carla when I got home. It was strange calling it that—*home*—but that's how it was beginning to feel. And the crew from house six was becoming my family. The closer I became with them, the more I yearned to bring Jennifer back. Her being on Bomba, but still so far away, constantly festered inside me.

"Is she any better?" I asked Shauna, who lay next to her in bed.

"You ... you can just ask me ... asshole," Carla said. Her eyes were closed and her voice faint, but she was obviously conscious.

"Wrong," Shauna said patting her sister's forearm. "You should be resting, not talking."

Carla cracked her eyes open. "I need to get back ... need to ... need to get back to work."

"You can't even stand without my help. So you can forget about pushing a wheelbarrow."

"I feel tingly," Carla said.

Using a cloth, Shauna wiped sweat from Carla's cheeks. "I know, honey. Drink some water."

With Shauna's help, Carla drank. Then she let out a long sigh and rolled onto her side. Shauna did the same, wrapping her arms around her.

I wasn't sure if it was Shauna or Carla, but the room was beginning to stink; even worse than usual.

"I can watch her for a few hours if you want to get something to eat ... or ..." I said.

Shauna stroked Carla's hair. "Thanks Norman. I'm good for now."

"Okay."

"I do need to talk to Rodrigo though," she said. "Can you tell him to come up?"

Using parchment and charcoal that Rodrigo had lent me—it wasn't free he said, he'd want money for it eventually—I made a list of mop words I knew, adding a definition next to each. Below those, I made a second list of words I had heard but didn't know their meaning. I planned to ask Rodrigo about those later.

At breakfast, I loaded up on fruits and vegetables, though I sure could have gone for my usual eggs, toast, and black coffee. I wondered if the fickens laid eggs. I saw pans for sale in town, and I knew how to start a fire. It'd be nice to have a meal that reminded me of Earth.

Amy used to cook breakfast on Saturday mornings, back when Jennifer was around and we were a family. I would do the same on Sundays, but Amy's always seemed better. Maybe it was the presentation, the way she set the table with flowers and cloth napkins. Maybe it was the extra side she would add—a bowl of fruit, a glass of her freshly squeezed orange juice, a plate of bacon. Maybe it was how she made us join hands and pray before we ate.

But she didn't have anyone to joins hands with now. Amy had lost Jennifer in the Fall and me the following Spring. She had gone from a happy household of three, to a miserable family of two, to a devasted widow. Or maybe she was happy again—happy to be rid of me. She had been so content just nine months prior.

Three weeks before Jennifer went missing, we took our annual trip to McKee Ranch to pick up Halloween pumpkins. Amy thought Jennifer would eventually scoff at the idea of going with her parents to a pumpkin patch, but there she was, just having turned seventeen, squeezed between us in the front seat of my truck.

We took a hay ride, fed the goats and horses, and picked out pumpkins. It was corny and cliché, and I loved every fucking second of it. It didn't hurt that I could toss the pumpkins into the back of my truck. I don't know why, but I love hauling shit in my truck. Even pumpkins.

When we arrived home, we sat on the back porch, drank apple cider, and carved our pumpkins. I finished first. Mine had square eyes, a square nose, and a rectangle shaped mouth. Jennifer and Amy's pumpkins were much more elaborate, and they forced me to choose whose was best. I picked Jennifer's, not because she was our daughter, but because she had designed her pumpkin after me, high and tight haircut, and all.

As I was swallowing down my last bite of granana, I saw a car approach, although I think I may have heard it first. The mops still hadn't figured out mufflers.

Inside was Bob, the leader of North Bomba, the mop I had met in the bar. He climbed out of the convertible and began talking with the humans from house one. Cops flanked him as he moved from house to house, shaking hands and patting backs. The translator followed behind, there to help humans who couldn't speak mop.

We all stood as he approached our house. Bob gave a long, slow wave when he reached us. The wave was more of a human gesture and still awkward for mops. Behind Bob, stood the two cops, who had badges hanging around their necks.

Ma relayed Bob's words as he spoke. "Hewwoo I happeee see huma. Uuu wor harrrr."

The house six crew smiled and nodded.

"If I wimm, mor momie for huma. Mor powee for huma. Huma happeee. Huma …"

My forehead wrinkled as Ma continued to talk. Because of her lack of a tongue, sometimes you needed a translator for the translator—a role Rodrigo filled after Bob had given us another exaggerated wave and left.

"Basically, Bob is promising better pay for humans, police accountability, representation in government, and closer bathrooms."

Brandon began to clap. "You got my vote, Bob."

"You can't vote, Brandon," I said.

"Why not?"

I shook my head. "Humans aren't allowed to vote."

Brandon stared at Bob, who was returning to his car. "Well, with his leadership, maybe one day we will."

"It'll never happen," Rodrigo said. "And he'll never do any of the shit he promised. Even if he is elected."

Despite our pleas, Brandon joined us for work again even though house three had offered to take him onboard. They were building the arches inside the stadium—hot, hard work, but nothing like hauling. Brandon thought he deserved more than a single coin though and turned his nose up when we suggested another job.

"I have a college degree," he said.

I walked behind him as we pushed our wheelbarrows to the quarry. His neck and shoulders were badly burned, and for whatever reason, he had yet to cut his skinny jeans into shorts.

My skin had adjusted. I was more tan now than red. And because of my drop in weight, I had to pull up my shorts, which hung loosely on my hips.

"They really need to post heat advisories when it's this hot," Brandon said, his face covered in sweat.

"Let the sun be your heat advisory," Rodrigo said. "Whenever you see it, assume it's going to be hot."

With still a mile to go before reaching the quarry, Brandon dropped his wheelbarrow and put his hands on his knees, gasping for breath. "How far is the quarry?"

"Another mile or so," I said, still pushing, although slower so I wouldn't pass him.

Brandon had pushed the wheelbarrow all five miles but considering he had yet to push it with a full load, I wondered why we let him come. He was never going to make. I'm sure Rodrigo thought the same.

"Pob!"

I turned and saw the guard standing fifty feet ahead of us, a scowl on his white, cushy face.

"Papa," I yelled back, and then picked up my pace. "Come on, Brandon."

I'm not sure why I felt the need to hang back with him. Maybe because Frederick would have been the same age, or maybe because I was a novato too. Those first few days for me seemed like a year ago, but it had only been a few weeks. Mop weeks though, which makes a difference.

"Pob!" the guard yelled.

Brandon didn't move. He was upright, but staring at his wheelbarrow, his hands on his hips.

The guard rounded on him. "Pob! Pob huma!"

I kept moving. I didn't want the club. Perhaps it was selfish, but I couldn't afford it, physically or financially. I knew if the guard beat me, if he had to expend energy yelling at me, I wouldn't get two coins.

The guard brushed past me, moving toward Brandon, his club pointing at him. "Pob!"

I continued forward but watched.

After giving a feeble nod, Brandon grabbed the handles of his wheelbarrow and lifted. But he just stood there. The guard smacked his club against the wheelbarrow's tray, which startled Brandon, who released his grip and stepped back.

The guard swung and struck Brandon in the arm. He dropped to his knees, then to his side. He let out a feeble moan as he clutched his bicep. The club rose again. It held there for a moment as Brandon began to cry. Then the guard shook his head and let the club fall to his side.

"Fohp," he said, and walked off.

"You can't do this!" Brandon yelled, still sobbing. "I have rights!"

The guard ignored him and kept walking. I hustled back to Brandon. He wiped tears from his face and looked up at me. "He's targeting me because I'm human."

"He's not targeting you," I said with a sigh. "He hit you because you weren't doing your job."

I helped Brandon to his feet. He winced, clutching his arm.

"What does fohp mean?" he asked.

"You don't want to know." I glanced at the rest of my crew, who were well in front of us, a good sixty yards. "You need to go home Brandon. There are other jobs you can do … you don't need to be a hauler."

His eyes moved from me to the wheelbarrow.

"I can walk you back if you want," I said.

Without looking at me, he shook his head. "I know the way."

It would be several weeks before I saw Brandon again, and when I did, he had three strikes.

CHAPTER 12

Shauna joined us for breakfast the next morning. It had been several days since I'd seen her outside. Rodrigo had taken a shift with Carla, who hadn't improved much and had only left her room once since she had been beaten. Rodrigo told me that Brandon had moved into house three and would start working with them tomorrow or the next day.

I finished eating and stood. As I began my trek to work, Shauna called to me.

"You're going to want to stay, Norman."

I turned and took a few steps back. "What do you mean? Why?"

She pointed past me, to a man in the distance.

"It's the messenger," she said.

As soon as the words left her mouth, I felt my stomach clench. I stared at the man as he moved toward us, wondering why the fuck he was walking so slowly. His skin was darker and his ratty beard was a few inches longer.

"Caulquier recien llegado?" he said.

"We have someone who only speaks English," Shauna said.

"Oh right, Dohring." He glanced at me, then turned back to Shauna. "Any newbies?"

I was about to ask about Jennifer, when Shauna responded to his question. "We had one, but he moved." Shauna pointed at the house across the street. "He's in number three now. Brandon Hebert?"

I bit down on my lip. I couldn't believe they were having this conversation.

"Yeah," the messenger said, looking down at his parchment. "I talked to him. Turns out he had an uncle in Central Bomba, but he died a few weeks ago." His eyes shifted to the other humans sitting around the table. "Anyone else new?"

I stepped in front of him, my hands on my hips. "We don't have any more goddamn novatos. Can you tell me about my daughter?"

"Yeah, I talked to her," the messenger said casually.

My throat was tight.

"It's her," he said. "I verified first name, last name, and address. She's definitely your daughter." He tapped a name on his parchment. "Jennifer Dohring."

I stood there with my mouth half open, unsure what to say. I guess I knew it was true, but hearing it now—the certainty of it—made my legs weak. They shook, as did my hands, which I squeezed into fists.

The messenger slid the parchment under his arm and wiped his forehead dry. "She considered coming here, to North Bomba, but I told her to stay put. It'd be too dangerous for such a young girl. I told her you would go to her."

I took a few shaky steps away from the messenger, giving myself space to think.

"But like we talked about last time, it'll cost you. I hope you've saved your money." His eyes fell to my right arm. "Good, still no strikes. That would make it impossible."

"But it's still a long, tough trek." Shauna said. "Do you think you're up for it?"

I nodded.

"You'll need money for supplies too," she said. "And for the tolls—the cost to get into the other regions."

"I do have some bad news though," the messenger said. "She's got two strikes."

I slid my coins into the pockets of my shorts. It wasn't much, but Shauna said it'd be enough for supplies—the bare minimum, but enough. I'd have to work a little longer to earn the money for the tolls.

Rodrigo offered to walk me to the supply store. As usual, he recommended that we travel in groups, but I was about to cross the whole fucking planet by myself, so it was about time I started doing things without a chaperone.

After work that day, I headed into the city. I had my hands stuffed into my pockets as I walked under a cloudy sky. It wasn't cold of course. This was security for my coins.

Shouts of 'fohp' started well before I reached the city. My mop vocabulary had improved, but I still couldn't understand most of the insults. And I received considerably more that when I walked with Rodrigo, Carla, and Brandon. The mops felt more emboldened when there were fewer humans around.

The supply store was in the poorest part of the city, probably because it was human-owned and all they could afford. The building was small, with rotting, uneven wood. TEDDY'S SUPPLIES was carved into a sign that hung out front.

The door creaked as I pushed it open.

A black man sat behind the counter, and I swear I heard him growl when he saw me. He had short hair and a trimmed beard, but both were uneven, as if he had cut them himself. He certainly had the tools for it. There was shit everywhere, hanging from the walls and ceiling, scattered on the shelves, in boxes and bins, and on the counter. There were shovels and trowels, hammers and nails, scissors, rope, clothes, blankets—I'd have to let Brandon know—shoes, socks, hats, backpacks, water containers, and knives—a big one lying next to his hand, which was missing two fingers. Most of the gear in the store looked handmade, but a few things had to have come from Earth, which meant that someone was wearing or carrying it when they went through the wormhole.

"You're Teddy?" I asked.

"I am." His voice was deep and raspy. "And you're new."

"New?"

"To Bomba," Teddy said.

I nodded. "How did you know that?"

"Your ID," he said, which meant he could read mop.

"Does that matter?" I asked. "That I'm new?"

"No, but we don't offer credit. A lot of the new guys have trouble understanding that, so I want to make sure you have the money to pay for whatever it is you want."

I shook my pockets and the coins rattled against each other.

"Very well." He cleared his throat, although it didn't help much with his gruff voice. "I have a security system too … just in case you get any ideas."

"I wouldn't—"

"I know, no one would," Teddy said. "Except the ones that do." His eyes dropped to the ground. "Sweep!"

I heard claws scratch against the floor, and within a few seconds, a German Shepherd trotted out from behind the counter. It stopped when it saw me and let out three loud barks. I guess it wasn't Teddy who'd growled at me after all. I took a slow step back as the dog moved closer.

"Heel!" he said.

The dog obeyed and moved back behind the counter, out of sight. But the growling continued.

"It's alright, girl," he said, glancing down. "He's just an honest, tax-paying customer."

I peered over the counter, trying to get another look at the dog. "She was with you when you went through?"

"Yeah, but I think she's the only one in Mafa Fah.

That's North Bomba."

"I know."

Teddy drank from his cup and then set it on the floor, where I could hear the dog's tongue slapping against the water. "We were hiking in Sloan Canyon when we went through."

"I'm surprised the mops let you keep her," I said.

He scratched his beard. "They don't like her, but I think they're scared of her. So they pretty much leave her alone." With his thumb, he pointed behind him. "I had to dig a latrine in the back so she has a place to go to the bathroom. The mops would probably kill her if they saw her piss or shit. We've had a few close calls." He picked up a piece of metal from the counter and began filing his dirty nails. "So what do you need?"

"A few water containers to start," I said. "And ones with lids if you got 'em."

Teddy stood, grabbed a bin of containers, and set it on the counter. "One coin will get you four of the homemade ones—you shouldn't have any trouble identifying those—and the plastic ones are a coin a piece."

I pulled out a few and looked them over, holding them up to the light coming through the open ceiling. Teddy had wedged a piece of plywood above the counter, to protect him from the rain and sun, but the rest of the store was exposed.

The homemade water containers were heavy and bulky. They had lids, but they were nothing more than plugs attached with string. There were about a dozen traditional water and sports bottles that I assumed humans had used for bartering purposes. Those were the ones I wanted, but at a coin a piece, it wouldn't leave me much money for anything else.

I looked up from the bin and noticed a hydration pack hanging on the wall behind him. It looked like a small backpack but was designed to hold water. Exactly what I needed.

"How much for that?" I said, pointing to it.

Teddy looked over his shoulder. "The CamelBak? Let's just say it's more than you have rattling around in your pockets. I was wearing it when I went through, so there's a sentimental markup as well."

I didn't bother asking the price. I knew I couldn't afford it. Letting out a sigh, I began to sift through the water bottles again.

"How many do you need?" Teddy asked.

"I don't know … three or four maybe."

Teddy sat back down. "Why so many?"

"I'm hiking to South Bomba," I said.

He looked at me for a moment. "You're crossing the desert?"

I nodded.

"Alone?"

"Yeah."

He leaned back in his chair. "I don't mind selling you supplies, friend, but I wouldn't recommend making that trip—not for someone so new."

I crossed my arms. "My daughter's in South Bomba.

With two strikes. So I'm definitely going."

Teddy gave me a slow nod. "Alright then, take four of the homemade containers because you're going to need money for other stuff." He began pulling containers out one by one, lining them up next to each other on the counter. "These are the best four I have. They'll add some weight, but they're the most economical."

"Okay ..."

He reached under the counter and pulled out a wooden box full of knives. "An essential if you're crossing the desert."

"To kill food," I said.

He rubbed the stub of one of his missing fingers. "Defense against the scavengers."

"Someone else mentioned them," I said. "Who are they?"

"Drifters usually, criminals ... they hate the government, hate paying taxes, and especially hate humans."

I slid the box across the counter and looked inside. The knives looked sturdy, with wooden handles, but were most certainly made on Bomba. "Are they sharp?"

"Sharp enough to cut a mop," Teddy said, and then picked one up. He ran it along the edge of his dark, dirty beard, and shavings fell to the counter.

"I guess I'll take that one."

He set the knife down, returned the box, and then set three plants in front of me. "Did you want to take any ointments?"

I assumed the ointments were in the leaves. I had to

keep reminding myself that substances on Bomba weren't packaged in plastic containers and available at your local department store.

"My skin has adjusted pretty well to the sun, so ..."

Teddy shook his head. "That's not what these are for."

Resting my forearms on the counter, I looked over the plants, studying the stems and leaves.

"These are for the creatures you'll encounter in the desert," he said. "There are lots of them out there, but I'll tell you about the three most common. And unlike the rest of the stuff in this shop, the advice will be free." Using the knife I had chosen, Teddy began trimming the plants as he talked. "First, there are the ants, which bite. They don't cause any long-term damage, but the itching will drive you mad—much worse than poison ivy. But what you should be most concerned about with the ants is dehydration. I don't know if it's from the constant scratching or maybe they release something inside you, but you'll need a lot of water if you get bit. The ointment in this one will help with the itching, and with any burns and cuts you might get."

He pushed the plant aside and began working on another. "Next are the tarantulas. They're bigger than standard Earth tarantulas, and they suck your blood ... like a tick. And they prefer humans over mops because our blood is thicker." Teddy shrugged. "At least, that's my theory." He shook one of the leaves. "Anyway, this stuff doesn't help much with the pain, but it should make the tarantula fall off." His eyes grew large. "And believe me, they're a pain in the ass to get off. For a few reasons really.

First, because of their size. They're as big as a rat. Second, when they feel threatened, they'll defecate on you, and let's just say their feces is a weapon."

With his knife, he pushed the plant away, then began trimming the third plant, which was taller and the leaves thicker. "Do you know what a hammerhead shark looks like?"

I nodded. "Yeah."

"Take the head of one of those, shrink it down, and screw it onto the body of a snake, and you have your worst predator in the desert." He stopped trimming and peeked up at me. "Well, except for the scavengers I guess. And these snakes aren't like hammerhead worms on Earth. I'm not sure if you know what those are, but these are bigger, more like traditional Earth snakes."

"So I'm assuming the snakes are venomous?" I asked.

"They are," he said. "And the problem is they're hard to spot because they blend in with the desert sand. So be careful where you step out there. I've seen it firsthand. The venom makes for a slow, brutal death." He broke off a leaf and peeled it open, revealing a cluster of blue berries. "You'll want to take one of these if you get bitten. They taste terrible, but they work."

"It's an antidote?"

The corner of Teddy's mouth turned up. "If only ... it's poison."

I stared at him, confused. "To kill the snake?"

He pointed the blade of the knife at me. "It's for you."

"A suicide capsule?"

"Yes. The effects of the venom are that bad. Believe me when I say it's worth it."

I reached into my pockets and moved the coins around with my fingers.

Teddy slid the other two plants over. "Four coins for each, or I'll give them all to you for ten."

My eyes moved between them as I thought about it.

"If you're looking for suggestions, I'd go with number three," Teddy said.

"The poison? That'd be my last choice. If I'm going to die anyway, who gives a shit."

"*You'll* give a shit," he said. "The pain is excruciating. You'll want those berries if it happens."

I shook my head. "I'm going to pass on the plants. I need that money for the tolls."

"That's fine," Teddy said with a shrug. "But remember, you could use the poison on someone else, too."

Reaching across the counter, I picked up the first plant and held it up to the light. "Couldn't I just go find these myself?"

"Sure," he said with a grin. "If you knew where to look."

Capitalism on Bomba.

Teddy rose from his chair and moved to the corner of the store, where a dozen backpacks hung on the wall. "And you'll need something to carry all this stuff in. I'd recommend this one. It's smaller, but well made and big enough to hold all your gear." He glanced back down at the knife. "It also has a slip for your knife. It's fine to keep it in there when you're traveling—it's flat out there, so you should be able to see who's coming—but I'd sleep with it at night."

My eyes wandered back to the box of knives, where I noticed one with a wide tip, like a putty knife.

The smell of paint filled my nose as I walked into my office. There was a paint can on the floor, with a brush and newspaper beside it. Camila stood facing the far wall, a putty knife in one hand and a container of spackle in the other.

"Camila?"

She flinched when she heard my voice.

"Mr. D—" she said, her mouth falling open. "I thought you were at a job?"

"We finished early," I said. "What are you doing?"

She took a step toward me, revealing an indentation in the wall. The putty knife began to shake in her hand.

"I uhhh …" she stuttered. "I fix uhhh …"

"Why are you fixing anything?" I asked. "What happened to the wall?"

Camila's eyes were downcast. "I'm sorry, Mr. Dohring," she said and began to tear up. "It was Leonardo."

I pulled the door back and noticed Leonardo standing in the corner. When he saw me, he began clapping his hands. But he wasn't applauding my arrival, and he was banging them with such force that I thought one of his fingers might snap off.

Then he started slapping his face. Camila stood with her mouth open as Leonardo moaned with each slap. After the slapping, he started biting his hand while simultaneously knocking his head against the wall. He would stop, cover his ears, and for a few seconds I thought it was over, but then it would all start again—clapping, slapping, moaning, biting, and then the head against the wall.

"I'm sorry, Mr. Dohring," she said, raising her voice over the moans. "My cousin drop him off here. She couldn't watch him. She—She—" Camila moved toward him. "It's okay, honey, it's okay."

Leonard babbled as she eased him to the ground, where she joined him, resting her back against the wall.

I shook my head and let out a long sigh. "I thought you took him to the facility on Tuesdays?" I asked. "The one over on Spring Valley."

"Uhhh … no, no, had to stop. Too much money."

I glanced around the room. "Is there more damage?"

"Yes, Mr. Dohring," she said, dropping her head. "By the missing person sign."

My eyes moved to Jennifer's picture and settled there for a moment. "You know the rule, Camila. Kids aren't allowed in the office." I inspected the wall near the missing person sign, then looked back at her. "I don't see anything."

She sniffled. "I already fixed that spot."

I leaned closer and squinted. "You did it yourself?"

"Yes, Mr. Dohring." She sighed. "I have a lot of practice."

Crossing my arms over my chest, I leaned against the wall. "I feel bad for you Camila, I really do, but you *cannot* bring your son to the office … or have him dropped off.

It's impossible for you to be effective while he's here." I glanced down at her hands, which were gripped tightly together. "I pay you well and expect a fair day's work. Whether that pay is enough to cover care for your son is not my problem."

I walked through the city streets with my hands clutching the straps of my new backpack. Mops routinely snatched loose items off humans, so I kept my distance and peeked over my shoulder every few seconds.

About halfway home, I saw my second bicycle—another invention the mops could thank humans for. I had heard the path through the desert was mostly hard, so making the trek on a bicycle would make the trip more efficient, but I couldn't afford one, and I didn't have the time or patience to build one myself. Not to mention, being a human and alone, I'd be lucky to make it to South Bomba without it being stolen.

I passed hordes of mops as I made my way out of the city. As usual, they pointed and berated me. Even the ones who didn't notice me were rowdy and boisterous; I had forgotten that today was North Bomba's Aba. The Ba who won would represent our region in the final Aba, which would be held in South Bomba.

The mops became louder, and as I kept walking, I realized why. A band of humans were being marched through the city. They looked like stick figures as they walked, so incredibly thin and malnourished, each with three K's etched into their arms.

Then I squinted and saw him. Two Strikes walked with his head down. A defeated, almost resigned look was spread across his sunken face.

The crowd threw rocks and pebbles as the humans were led toward the stadium, where another crowd of mops awaited. The humans would be served up as entertainment—beaten to death by the larger and stronger mops. As if having the same thought, and refusing to participate, Two Strikes suddenly stopped and dropped to his knees.

A cop waved for him to get up.

"No." Two Strikes shook his head. "No."

After pushing out a frustrated breath, the cop brushed passed the other humans, and then kicked Two Strikes in the ass.

"Pob," the cop said.

Straightening his back, Two Strikes folded his arms across his chest.

The cop pointed toward the stadium. "Pob!"

Two Strikes stared up at him, defiant. "Me vas a matar de todos modos," he said, then repeated it in English. "You kill me anyway!" Tears filled his eyes. "You no embarrass me! You no embarrass me!"

"Pob!!" the cop screamed, his long torso bent over.

More mops gathered around, hooting and hollering in their squeaky voices, encouraging the cop to beat him.

So he did.

The cop's club struck Two Strikes in the back of the head. His body went limp as he collapsed against the ground. The crowd cheered. I glared at them, my fists bunched at my sides. Then my eyes moved to Two Strikes who lay motionless, and my stomach tightened.

The cop left Two Strikes—left him to die—and shoved another human forward before screaming at all of them to keep moving. The humans were so emaciated, they hadn't the energy to react. They were robots now, with under one percent battery left—just enough juice to walk to the stadium and put up a feeble fight.

As the crowd followed them to the arena, I stood still, my eyes locked on Two Strikes. His eyes were shut, and his mouth hung open. Mops walked by him, casually turning their heads as if he had been a squirrel run over by a car.

Then I saw his right eye crack open. My pulse quickened and I shot forward, weaving through the mops. As Two Strikes let out a moan, a gang of mops stopped. They circled him, talking to each other, pointing down with their long, spongy fingers.

Two Strikes' hand inched forward across the ground. Then he pushed off with his foot and moved a little further. A mop set their heel against Two Strikes' forehead and pushed him back. The gang howled. Two Strikes groaned. With their feet, the mops began shoving him across the ground, back and forth, as if they were playing fucking Hacky Sack.

I moved to the side, slid off my backpack, and reached inside. I slid the knife out of its slip and held it against the side of my leg. With my other hand, I slung the backpack over my shoulder, then approached the crowd. The tip of the blade pricked the skin on my leg, and I winced.

The mops' kicks had become stronger, more violent, the latest striking Two Strikes across the jaw. He let out a faint whimper. Blood dripped from his mouth. The mops kicked and laughed, that stupid, squeaky laugh.

I wanted to stab them, stab them all and watch them die. The handle of the knife felt slippery in my hand as sweat filled my palm. But I could do it. They would never expect it. I could kill them all. Then my eyes settled on the three K's on Two Strikes' arm.

I would never make it to South Bomba with a strike.

Reason returned to my mind as I took a step back. Or perhaps it was cowardness, because instead of trying to help, instead of trying to save him, I watched Two Strikes get kicked and punched until he took his last breath.

CHAPTER 13

I didn't tell anyone from house six that I had seen Two Strikes. What would I have said? That I stood and watched as he was beaten to death? As a man, I should have risked a strike to help him. But as a father, I couldn't. My responsibility was to my daughter.

Still, I felt like a pussy.

I was glad to work the next day. Mentally, it helped me escape the awful thoughts that filled my mind. And shit, I needed the money. It would cost me to get into Central and South Bomba, and my taxes were coming due. But who the fuck cared about that? I guess I did. I had to. Because I'd end up with a strike if I didn't pay.

So I kept quiet, kept to myself, and worked. Day after day, I pushed that fucking wheelbarrow down death road, and day after day I earned my two coins. I got back into my routine—wake, eat, work, eat, sleep. Repeat. I paid my taxes, paid my rent, and saved money.

When the cop handed me the final two coins I would need for my trip, I let out a long breath.

"You're going tomorrow?" Rodrigo asked as we walked home.

I nodded. "In the morning."

"Start early," he said. "And remember to rest in the afternoons. Try to knock out most of your miles in the mornings and evenings when it's not as hot."

"Is it cold at night?" I asked. I hadn't thought about it until now, but deserts were usually cold at night, at least on Earth.

Rodrigo shrugged. "I wouldn't call it cold, but it'll definitely be cooler than your room," he said. "You'll welcome it at first, but it'll make the days seem hotter." His eyes moved to my forehead. "Did you pick up a hat while you were at the supply store?"

I shook my head. "I couldn't afford it."

"You're going to want one," he said. "Your skin may have adjusted out here, but it'll fry in the desert."

"I thought about that. But I should be able to rig something with my shirt and some sticks."

"So what supplies did you get?" he asked.

After I told him, Rodrigo nodded. "I would have bought a few more things, but those are fine," he said. "And I hope you're bringing extra money."

"A little," I said.

He slowed his pace and looked at me. "You might want to work a few more days. It's not just tolls you'll need money for."

"I know about the cost of the boat ride," I said.

"It's not that," he said. "What if the cost to get into each region has gone up? What if you run out of food and need to buy more in Central Bomba—are you hoping the humans will just give it to you?" He raised his shoulders. "And what if you need to bribe someone? I've had to do it from time to time. It's worth it if you can save yourself a strike."

I knew he was right; I had heard the same thing from the others. But I didn't care. I was ready to go. I needed to get my ass to South Bomba.

We saw Shauna moving toward us as we walked up the road to house six; she had stayed back with Carla again. As we got closer, we could see that her eyes were puffy and red. She didn't have to say why.

Shauna fell against Rodrigo and began to sob. When she finally pulled away, her glassy eyes moved between us. "I think it was a brain hemorrhage," she said. "I think there was bleeding." Her body began to shake. "The symptoms were there … I should have known. My God …"

Rodrigo cupped her face with his hands. They held each other for a long moment.

"It wouldn't have mattered, Shauna," Rodrigo said, and stepped back. "There's nothing you could have done."

"I'm so sorry," I said, then hugged her.

She wept against my bare chest, muttering her sister's name over and over.

Everyone was quiet at dinner that night, at least the ones

who ate. Most of house six passed on their meal and stayed in their rooms instead. Some of it was due to exhaustion—from digging Carla's grave and carrying her body to the cemetery. I helped with both. It was the first time I had carried a dead body.

Rodrigo stayed with Shauna, who had surprisingly made it to dinner. She had eaten very little since caring for Carla.

"I don't know what to do," she said, staring down at her food.

"About what?" Rodrigo asked.

She looked up slowly, her bloodshot eyes drifting to the darkening sky. "About this … this fucking place."

"You get up," Rodrigo said. "Each day you get up and you try to make it through."

She folded her arms and stared at him. "That's your advice? To get up?" She wiped her eyes. "Get up and go push my wheelbarrow? That's what I should do?"

"It's better than the alternative," he said.

"Is it?" she asked.

He gave her a hard look. "Yes. You have a lot to live for, Shauna. You know that."

Shauna shook her head.

"*You do*," Rodrigo said.

"I know what you mean, but it doesn't matter." Her eyes welled with tears. "This place is horrible. I hate it." She glared at two cops walking by. "And I hate *them*. Every one of them. They're horrible."

The cops, who had their clubs resting on their shoulders, glanced over as they moved passed us.

"Pob," Shauna said to them.

They stopped, said something to each other, then peered over at her.

Shauna pointed down the road. "Pob."

With their clubs now swinging at their sides, the cops strode toward her. Shauna stood.

"Sit down," Rodrigo said.

Her hands moved to her hips. Rodrigo rose from the table and stepped in front of her as the cops reached us. They pointed their clubs at her.

"Huma pob," a cop said. "Huma pob."

"Mop pob," Shauna said. She sat down and folded her arms. "This human isn't going anywhere."

The second cop motioned toward the sky, then to our house. "Pob. Pob."

"It's past our curfew," I said. "They want us to go inside."

"I know," Rodrigo said. He held up his hands. "Papa."

"*Mo*," Shauna said, her eyes still on them.

The cop's white eyes grew large. "Pob!"

Rodrigo gritted his teeth. "Shauna don't be stupid. Just go inside."

Shauna bit down on her lip, then let out a breath and stood. She faced them and was about to open her mouth but stopped herself.

"Papa," Rodrigo said, and then followed Shauna as she started toward the house. I did the same, as did the rest of our crew.

Then we heard "fohp," and Shauna stopped.

She turned, pushed passed Rodrigo, and sat back down. "No. I'm not done my dinner."

The cop's face filled with rage. He slammed his club against the table. It cracked the wood and the ceramic plates shook.

"Huma—pob!" the cop shouted.

Reaching under her armpits, Rodrigo tried to lift Shauna. She gripped the sides of the table as the cops continued to scream.

"Papa, papa," Rodrigo said to them.

A crowd of humans, and a few more mops, formed around us.

With his club, the cop jabbed Shauna, catching her on her bare breast. She winced.

Rodrigo screamed and shoved the cop back. "Get off her!"

It was the last thing Rodrigo ever said.

I gasped as the second cop raised his club. The sound of it against Rodrigo's skull was sickening. His body fell limply against the table. I pulled Shauna away as the cops continued to pound him. Then I held her and watched as their wooden clubs struck his head, his back, his legs. Every goddamn part of him. It was Two Strikes all over again. And as before, I stood there and stared. Rodrigo's body rolled from the table and onto the ground, where the clubs continued.

"Jesus ... go inside," I said to Shauna, who watched with her mouth hanging open.

But I was done watching, done standing there. I charged

them. I lowered my shoulder and rammed the cop that was straddling Rodrigo. He let out a squeaky yelp and crashed against the table.

Before I could get to my feet, the other cop's club crunched against my shoulder. Then his foot came down against my head and everything went dark.

I awoke to the smell of burning flesh. It took a few seconds to realize it was mine, and when I did, the pain was overwhelming. I howled as two spongy hands held me down. My body went rigid. My arm burned.

But at least I was alive.

Why they had killed Rodrigo and not me, I didn't know. What I did know is that Two Strikes was dead, Rodrigo was dead, and I had a strike, which meant that I would never make it into South Bomba.

As the mop's hands lifted off my chest, I squirmed on the table. I forced my eyes open and saw Ma peering down at me. My gaze drifted to the K singed into my skin. It was an ugly yellow, the edges dark and jagged.

My head began to pound. I ran my fingers over my forehead and felt a lump, and then remembered the kick to my face. I lay there, moaning, covered in dirt and sweat, wondering if I would ever see my daughter again.

Ma helped me off the table and walked me outside. My eyes were slits, stinging from the bright sun. It was the next day and based on the sun's position, probably mid-morning.

House six was quiet when I returned. Even with

Rodrigo's passing, my crew probably went to work. That was life on Bomba. Humans had to earn their money. Clutching my arm, I walked to my room and lay on my bed. A sprinkle of rain fell through the joists, which soothed my arm, but as the rain became steady, it began to sting.

The yellow coloring on the brand had turned pink. I raised my arm, craned my neck, and blew a soft breath against the K. I had just received the brand, but I already hated that fucking letter.

I didn't know how long I had slept for, but when I opened my eyes, Shauna was standing by my bed.

"I'm sorry, Norman," she said.

I sat up and immediately winced. My arm throbbed.

"Can you help me bury him?" she asked.

With most of the adults still at work, I helped Shauna and two ten-year-olds carry Rodrigo's body to the human graveyard. The kids offered to help dig, but Shauna asked them to work on the farm instead.

We dug Rodrigo's grave next to his father's. MATEO FLORES was carved into a wooden cross which sat at the edge of the graveyard. Shauna helped for about an hour, then began to wail. She sat under a tree, unable to stop crying, her hands clutching her stomach.

I glanced over at Carla's grave and wondered if Shauna had seen it. Or maybe it was Rodrigo's body, wrapped in cloth, lying just a few feet away. Or maybe it was all of it. I don't know what it was for me, but as my eyes moved from Carla's grave, to Rodrigo's body, to Shauna sobbing under the tree, I also began to cry.

Shauna eventually returned, though she didn't dig much. Instead, she cleared debris from the ground, refilled our waters, and worked on Rodrigo's cross.

A few hours later, Rodrigo's body lay in the grave. We said a prayer and then, painfully, began to throw dirt over his body.

Jennifer stood in front of Frederick's cross, which now leaned to the left. It had sat in the ground for nearly twenty years and the wood was soft and crumbly.

"Why didn't you use pressure-treated wood?" Jennifer asked, having remembered when she helped repair the front porch.

"I did," I said, standing next to her. "But even pressure-treated wood rots over time." I crouched in front of the cross and nudged it, so it stood upright. "I should have used a different type."

"What type?" she asked.

"There's wood that's designed for ground contact. I should have used that."

Jennifer leaned down and ran her finger along the edge. "So why didn't you? You always tell me to use the right equipment for the job."

I let out a small laugh and shrugged. "I don't know … I wasn't thinking straight that day."

"So what are you going to do with it?" she asked.

"Well," I said, staring at the cross. "Your mother and I think it has stood long enough, so …"

Jennifer crossed her arms. "So ... you're going to throw it out?"

"Well, I wasn't planning on throwing it in the trash," I said. "But yeah, I was going to pull it up. We thought it was better than letting it rot and fall down."

"Why don't you just build another one?" she asked.

For Amy and me, the cross had lasted as long as it needed to. I raised my shoulders. "I don't know ..."

She traced her finger around Frederick's name. "What if I did. What if I build it?"

When Jennifer was eight, we explained why I had made the cross in the first place. In the years that followed, whenever she would draw a picture of our family, Jennifer would include a fourth—an older boy, about a head taller, who she'd sketch in next to her. One of the drawings is still pinned in her room above her desk. The boy and girl are holding hands, waving to a figure in the distance.

As I left to pick up the supplies, Jennifer sat on the ground with the rotted cross resting on her lap.

Shauna and I sat on the front step of our house as the sun set. Humans and mops shuffled along the street in front of us. We were both exhausted from the day and stayed quiet for a long while.

"I realize what that means for you," Shauna finally said, her eyes settling on the fresh brand. "I'm sorry, Norman."

I was about to respond when she spoke again.

"Maybe we can get her to come here," she said.

She was referring to Jennifer.

"Would they let her leave?" I asked. "The messenger said she had two strikes."

"South Bomba will happily kick out any human, strikes or not. They just won't let you back in if you have one."

I glanced down the road. "Do you think a teenage girl could make it all this way?"

Shauna didn't answer, not directly. "What about meeting her halfway?" she asked.

"Halfway?"

"In Central Bomba," she said. "What about meeting her there?"

I gave a slow nod as I contemplated it. "That might work."

"And your part of the trip—through the desert—would be the hardest, which I know you'd prefer. She would just need to take the boat to Central Bomba."

"But how would we coordinate it? How would I communicate with her?"

Shauna took a swig of water. "We could write out a plan and send it with the messenger."

"But that means we'll have to wait for him again … and then wait for him to get to her … and probably for him to come all the way back here and confirm with us."

"Yeah, but it's probably your best chance," Shauna said.

"She'd be dead before all that happened." I rubbed the blisters on my hand. "If she isn't already."

We sat in silence for a few more minutes. The sun had dropped below the horizon, and humans were heading for their houses.

"We should go inside," I said, and stood.

Shauna remained sitting and ran a hand over her forearm. "There might be another way."

"To do what?"

"To get you to South Bomba," she said. "So that your daughter wouldn't have to travel, and you wouldn't have to wait for the messenger."

I sat back down. "How? I can't get into South Bomba with a strike."

"What if they couldn't see it," she said. "I heard there's a lady in Central Bomba who sells cosmetics. Apparently, her products are quite good." She shrugged. "I guess even on Bomba women want to look nice."

"Okay …"

"Anyway, I heard she has a side business, which is covering strikes."

I glanced down at the K on my arm, which still throbbed with pain.

"It's not permanent, but it could last long enough to get you into South Bomba," she said.

"Do you know her?" I asked, my voice low.

"No, I've never been to Central Bomba. Rodrigo told me. He met the woman when he went to bring his father back."

"How much does she charge?" I asked.

"I don't remember … fifteen coins maybe."

I wrapped my arms around my legs "Almost a week of work …"

"I could loan you the money," she said.

"I'm not taking your money," I said.

"It would be Rodrigo's money."

Even with the heat, I felt a chill run through my body.

"Why should *I* get it," I said. "That doesn't seem right."

"Rodrigo liked you. He would have wanted you to have it for this."

I blew out a long breath. "We both know that I might not make it to South Bomba. Which would mean I'd be wasting his money for nothing."

She nudged me with her elbow. "But you might. And you'd be doing me a favor too."

"What do you mean? How?"

"I need something from South Bomba."

"What?"

"It's a plant. It's abundant over there apparently. It's called a haba. Most humans should know where it is."

"Haba? What is it?"

Shauna looked down, hesitating. "It's kind of like pot."

I laughed. "You want to get high?"

She straightened her back and interlocked her fingers together. "It helps with pain."

"Are you in pain?"

"Not now …" Her hand moved to her bare breast, then to her stomach. "I'm pregnant."

I stared at her.

"Haba will help during the delivery," she said.

"I'm not going to South Bomba if you're pregnant," I said.

She grinned, which I was happy to see. "Are you an

obstetrician?"

"Of course not, but you're going to need help." I shifted on the step as I thought about our morning. "And you helped dig today. You should not be doing that shit."

"I know, I know," she said, nodding. "But I have a house full of people to help me. I'll be fine. And I'll eventually stop working."

"*Eventually*? Christ, Shauna. How far along are you?"

"Well, I haven't had my period for five mop weeks, so …" she cleared her throat. "I was planning on working two more weeks."

I shook my head. "You're not working two more weeks. And I'm not taking Rodrigo's money. You need it more than I do. Because the mops sure aren't going to give a shit that you're pregnant."

"You're right, they won't. But I am giving you the money. It's fifteen coins, Norman. It's not a big deal. And your daughter needs you more than I do."

My eyes dropped to her stomach as I thought about it. "So …"

"It's Rodrigo's."

I agreed to take the money. I thought the responsibility of paying her back—paying back Rodrigo's money and getting her the pot—would serve as additional motivation to return.

Shauna sat on my bed that evening as I organized my gear for the trip. I planned to leave in the morning. She filled my water containers and packed as much food as the house could spare. Then she drew a map for me, which showed the dirt road that stretched through the desert and the sea that separated Central and South Bomba.

"I'd stick to the main road in the desert, but when you see someone coming, I'd hide," she said. "If a mop finds you alone out there, they'll probably rob you. If you're lucky. And remember, there aren't any shit towns, so be careful where you go to the bathroom."

"How long will it take?" I asked.

"It's about a three-day walk," she said. "But that's just the desert. It's about a half day walk to get there and another half day from the desert to Central Bomba."

I loaded the water containers into my backpack.

"And make sure you ration your water, there's little to no rain out there," she said. "You can resupply in Central Bomba."

"Will the humans there charge me for food or water?" I asked.

"Probably not, but it'll depend on who you ask," she said. "Even humans will try to swindle a few coins from you if they think you're a sucker."

I glanced at the map. "Do I just follow the road all the way in?"

"Well, it's not really much of a road, but yeah," she said. "Look for the mountains—that'll be your landmark. You'll have to pass between them, through a valley, to get in." Her eyes moved to my brand. "I'd wear your shirt when you go through the checkpoint. Central Bomba doesn't really care about humans coming in with strikes—they just want your money—but if you get a mop in a bad mood, who knows." She shrugged. "You can always try to scale the mountains and try to bypass the checkpoint, which will save you money, but they'll beat the shit out of you if they catch you, and probably steal your coins, which means you won't be able to pay your way into South Bomba."

"Well, since that's the whole reason I'm going, I probably won't risk it," I said.

Shauna handed me the food, which I began loading.

"How are your sea legs?" she asked.

"Well, I was in the Navy," I said. "Why?"

"The boat ride from Central Bomba to South Bomba is pretty rough," she said. "The mops don't get seasick because, well, they don't have anything to throw up. But if you get sick on the boat, you can also forget about getting in."

I secured my knife, then closed the backpack.

Shauna held out a handful of coins. "Don't forget your extra money."

It was Rodrigo's.

"I'm paying it back," I said.

CHAPTER 14

I left before the sun came up. Since I hadn't taken this route before, I felt uneasy about walking in such little light, but I wanted to knock out as many miles as possible before it got too hot. Of course, it was all relative; it was already a fucking scorcher.

The landmarks Shauna had mentioned, helped. I passed the graveyard, passed the farm, and then walked along a stream for three or four miles before it dried up.

The sun peeked over the horizon, and I kept my head down as I moved along. My thoughts kept drifting to Jennifer, but I tried to push them aside and concentrate on my route. The grass, shrubs, and trees had thinned, which meant I was getting closer to the desert, but it also meant less coverage from the sun. But shit, walking with a backpack was still better than pushing a damn wheelbarrow.

Even with shoes and socks, the soles of my feet were

hot. An hour later I decided I had reached the desert. I mean it's not like there was a sign saying DESERT, but with the heat, lack of greenery, and brown landscape, I was pretty sure.

But it wasn't sandy, at least not where I was walking. The ground had become harder, and a few times I stopped and felt the terrain, which was hot to the touch. I was glad it was then, crouched down and mostly out of sight, that I saw my first mop.

He was on a bike, riding toward me, on his way from Central Bomba I assumed. Keeping my head low, I scurried off the road until I found a small crater. I dropped inside against my chest. My breaths were loud and labored. I waited a moment, then peeked over the rim.

His bike rolled to a stop about fifty yards from where I was hiding. He was talking, but it took me a minute to realize what he was saying.

"Huuuma?" he said.

I remained still.

"Mop aaww huma," he squeaked.

Mop saw human.

He stared in my direction, then hopped off his bike. Was he a scavenger? Lowering my head, I curled up inside the crater.

"Huummaaa."

His voice was closer. I let out a slow, soft breath.

"Huuuuuummaa."

I could hear his footsteps.

"Mop aaww huummaaa."

After easing off my backpack, I slipped my hand inside and felt for the handle of the knife.

"Huuuuuummaa."

My hand squeezed around the wooden handle. I slid it out and tucked it against my chest.

"Huuuuuummaa. Mop aaww huummaaa."

Based on the sound of his voice, and his footsteps against the hard ground, it seemed like he was right above me.

In one motion, I flipped onto my back and, with both hands gripping the handle of the knife, prepared to gut the fucker.

But his back was to me. He was walking away, still babbling.

"Huummaaa?"

The mop disappeared from my view, but a moment later, I heard the clang of a bicycle. I got to a knee and peered out from the crater.

He was pedaling again, heading north.

I trudged along the road taking extra care to look for travelers. And I walked with my knife in my hand so I wouldn't have to fumble around in my backpack if another mop rolled by.

It was about the middle of the day when I took my first break. I draped my shirt over my head and pulled out my water. My mouth was dry, but I only took a few sips, trying to conserve.

After a few minutes, I lifted my shirt and peered down

the road. It was clear. Then my eyes fell upon a bone. I stood and walked over to it. One bone became two, and then three, and eventually I could make out a full skeleton scattered along the terrain. Based on the smaller size, I assumed it was human and not mop. I wondered how this person had died. Were they killed by scavengers? Bitten by a snake? Heat exhaustion?

Then I saw ants file out from under a bone. I lifted my feet and peeked at the bottom of my shoe. An ant crossed the treads. I flicked it off with the knife. Three more ants crawled along the soles of my other shoe and I knocked those off as well.

Then I cut my break short and started back down the road.

I kept my shirt over my head as I walked. The shirt helped, but I wished I had spent a few extra coins and bought a hat. I had planned to make my own hat using my shirt and sticks, but never did. I contemplated wearing the shirt to save my skin, which felt like it was burning, but decided a cooler head was more important.

I took two more long breaks, then made up a few miles in the evening as the sun was setting. While there was still light, I found a place to camp—a spot far enough off the road to avoid being seen by anyone traveling at night. With it being cooler, I had contemplated walking through the night and sleeping during the day, but I was tired and didn't want to risk wandering off the road.

A steady breeze rippled my blanket as I laid it on the ground. I set my backpack on one end and sat on the other.

I ate a few pieces of fruit, then finished my second, of six, water containers. Assuming it was a three-day walk, I was on schedule with my water. I wished I had drunk a little less, but I was too damn thirsty.

I leaned back on the blanket and stared up at the stars. Without artificial light to muddy it up, it was a spectacular sight, peaceful and serene. My eyes drifted across the sky, taking in the vastness of it. I wondered if I could see Earth's sun, or at least the Milky Way. I wondered what Amy was doing. Was she on our back patio looking up at the same sky?

That's where we had been sitting when we received the call.

I waited on the patio as Amy answered the phone. We almost didn't pick it up. We sat there and let it ring a few times before Amy went inside. I told her not to bother. Jennifer didn't have a phone, so we knew it couldn't be her, and whoever it was could leave a message. There was no need to answer the phone every time it rang.

Only this time there was.

Earlier that day, Amy had asked me to drive Jennifer to work since she wouldn't be home in time. Amy would usually drive her, but I always made Jennifer walk. There was no reason not to. It was only a mile and a half. There weren't creeps hiding behind bushes or strangers lurking in the woods like Amy thought; most people were decent.

"Norm, did you take her?" Amy asked, standing in the doorway, the corded phone pressed against her flushed face.

"Jennifer? To work?" I asked, glancing over my shoulder. "She walked."

Amy's face went rigid, her mouth forming a hard line. "They said she didn't show up."

They were Pasquale's Pizzeria, where Jennifer had been working for about a year. I checked my Timex. It was almost seven. She should have arrived over two hours ago.

"Are they sure?" I knew it was a stupid question, but I really didn't know what to say.

"*Yes*," she said. Her voice was tense. "They're on the phone. She's not there."

As Amy called Jennifer's friends to ask if they had seen her, I walked Jennifer's route to work. When I didn't find her, I went through Pasquale's Pizzeria, still incredulous to the fact that she hadn't arrived. I was more deliberate on my return trip to our house, my pace slow, my eyes shifting. During the half-mile stretch that snaked through the woods, I screamed her name every few seconds. She never answered.

I made the round-trip four times that evening, twice with Amy, who walked it another five times the following day. At the end of each day, Amy would ask the same question.

"I still don't understand. Why didn't you drive her?"

Amy always drove her. She always walked her to school. She always watched her in the backyard.

Not me. I was always teaching her to be autonomous.

"Because I didn't think she needed to be driven!" I'd

say, and occasionally shout.

What I didn't say was, "I'm sorry." I don't know why. Maybe I was stubborn. Maybe I didn't think it was my fault. Or maybe I thought Jennifer would still return. But she never did, and the apology never came.

The FBI and local law enforcement had formed a task force to investigate all of the missing people. They entered Jennifer's name into their database. They asked for recent pictures. They asked for her height and weight. They asked for her eye color, her hair color, blood type, dental records, driver's license number, social security number, screen names, a description of what she was wearing, any notable items she might have been carrying. They talked to Jennifer's friends and teachers and coworkers. They took diligent notes and followed up with lots of phone calls and emails.

But it was all a formality. They knew they'd never find her. Shit, they hadn't found any of the people that had gone missing.

The task force also provided a missing person flyer that we could distribute. It was an electronic version that we'd have to print ourselves. They said they used the same template for everyone so that the layout and phone number remained the same. Isn't that great? I only needed to swap out the name, description, and picture. Task force efficiency.

Camila helped me print five hundred copies. It took four days to put them all up, the last one going on a telephone poll in Paradise, about six miles south of Vegas. We used a picture that Amy had taken on Jennifer's first day at Pasquale's Pizzeria. Jennifer had her hair pulled back and was wearing her red work shirt, with the Pasquale logo across the chest. It wasn't much of a design. The upper part of the P in Pasquale was in the shape of a pizza, and the bottom half of the letter, the vertical line, was the handle of a pizza peel.

We used that picture because Jennifer had been wearing that same shirt when she went missing. And with her hair pulled back, you could see her face, which at the time, wore a nervous grin; it was the first day of her first job.

My skin reddened as I walked the next morning. About every thirty minutes I'd move my shirt from my head to my shoulders, and then back again. I continued to ration my food and water and was now on pace to make it to Central Bomba with some to spare.

It was late morning when I heard an engine, although I didn't realize it at the time. I thought the heat was making me delirious. But when the engine grew louder, I stopped and squinted. A convertible was barreling down the road, dirt and dust flying up behind it.

Crouching down, I scurried off the road. After about a quarter mile, I dropped to my stomach and turned back.

The convertible rumbled by with two mops in the front seat, their long torsos sticking out awkwardly. I watched as the car sped by. It sounded like it needed a muffler, and as it began to sputter, I thought it might break down. But the engine kicked and the convertible kept going. Even from this distance, I could smell the fumes. It's not like there were emissions inspections on Bomba.

It was a relief not having to endure the constant douses of rain, but I sure could have used a soaking that afternoon. With the heat and lack of shade, it was a struggle not to drink every ounce of water I had.

The food helped with my thirst and also produced my first dump in the desert. I moved off the trail, checked both ways for travelers, then dropped my shorts. I felt like a dog, crouched out in the open, straining. The first few weeks on Bomba, my craps were yellow and runny, but my body had adjusted, and my shit returned to normal.

As I pulled up my shorts, I spotted an ant crawling on my shoe. I flicked it off, turned over my shoe and saw a dozen more. I tilted my other shoe and found another twenty scattered along its sole.

Then I stood flatfooted as a line of ants came out of the ground and across my shoes. After wiping sweat from my eyes, I noticed that I had taken my crap right on an ant hill. Fucking bullseye.

They moved from my shoes, up my legs. Perhaps they were heading for the source of the giant black mess that just bombed their house. The sensation of the ants crawling along my skin seemed to wake me though. I kicked off my shoes, took a few steps back, and, using my shirt, brushed the ants from my legs. Then I shook my shirt and a few more fell to the ground.

The ants swarmed over my shoes, under the laces, over

the tongue, and then inside, turning my white sneakers black. My eyes drifted from my shoes to my pale white feet, which were beginning to burn against the hot desert ground. I stood there, staring, wondering what I should do. It's not like I had bug spray. And it's not like I could wait for the ants to leave my shoes. Not with my limited supplies.

Teddy said the itching from ant bites would be severe. But what I was most worried about was the dehydration. I couldn't afford it. Not out here, no way.

Still, I contemplated digging them out of my shoes. I knew it would result in bites, but what was the alternative? Walking barefoot?

It was a quick decision, but that's what I did. I thought I'd have a better chance of reaching my daughter with hot feet than with dehydration. And hey, if the mops could walk without shoes, why couldn't I? Of course, the mops were also able to cool their feet by dispensing water. That wouldn't work for me. But as the soles of my feet burned with each step, I sure wished they were spongy.

As I crept along, I thought about tearing my shirt in two and wrapping the pieces around my feet, but it worked better as a single garment when using it over my head. Plus, I planned to wear the shirt when entering Central Bomba to avoid any issue with the strike on my arm.

My pace slowed from earlier in the day, and I had to take breaks every ten minutes to cool my feet. I was tempted to pour water over them but couldn't spare any. Thankfully, the ground began to cool as the sun set, and I was able to make up some time. But as with the previous evening, I decided to make camp while there was still daylight.

The thought of ants marching up my shorts motivated me to do a thorough search of the ground. I couldn't afford to lose anything else, especially my shorts. That's just what my daughter would want—her old man, tired and dehydrated, walking naked into South Bomba with a sunburned ass. But hell, if meant reaching her, I would have done it.

My right arm burned as I forced my eyes open the next morning. Teddy said the tarantulas on Bomba were as big as rats. Well, the one attached to my bicep's tendon—the part of your arm where they'd draw blood—had a shape and size closer to that of a snapping turtle, minus the shell, but with long, fury legs.

My mouth hung open as I stared at it. The veins in its throat pulsed as it sucked my blood. I didn't know when it had latched on, but my neck and back were stiff, my head throbbed, and a hot flash surged through me. There was ointment that I could rub around the bite. It would make the tarantula fall right off. But I never bought it. Kind of regretted that now.

The thought of touching the tarantula made me nauseous, but I didn't have a ton of options as I sat alone in the desert of an alien planet. So, I wrapped my fingers around two of its hairy legs and began to pull.

A trickle of blood oozed down my arm as it clamped

down with its teeth. I think it sensed what I was doing. That's when I remembered what Teddy had told me. He said these critters would defecate on you if they felt threatened. Not wanting to get crapped on by a Bomba tarantula, I released my grip.

As I watched its stomach swell with my blood, another wave of nausea swept over me. I felt faint. My muscles ached, and though it was cool—relatively speaking—a film of sweat covered my body. I struggled to keep my eyes open. If I couldn't get this fucking thing off me before I passed out, I doubted I would ever wake up. But I didn't see how I could do it. Setting aside the fact that it might crap on me, the tarantula was too big and the grip of its teeth too tight.

I thought I could pull off its head though, if that's all that was attached. Using my left arm—the free one—I reached into my backpack and pulled out the knife. I was half tempted to just stab myself in the heart and get this over with. Instead, I set the blade against the back of the tarantula's neck, drew a long breath, then began to cut, quick and deep.

The pain was immediate and intense. A stream of green pus seeped from underneath the tarantula and onto my skin, which started to bubble. I let out an agonizing scream as I sliced and sliced ... halfway, three-quarters ... almost there ...

I wasn't sure if it was the sight of the tarantula's severed head still attached to my arm, or the excruciating pain, but within a few seconds everything went black.

When I opened my eyes, I saw that my sunburned body was in the shade. Of course, that was impossible in this desolate place. The pain in my arm had subsided, but it was numb down to my fingers. I struggled into a sitting position.

Then my jaw dropped.

A man sat Indian-style in front of me. His back faced east and blocked most of the sunlight peering over the horizon. He had a long white beard, droopy eyes, and thick creases on his forehead. It was the man from the picture, the man I had seen on death road, the human wanted by the mops.

Fof.

He smiled at me, revealing a row of yellow, uneven teeth.

"The old has passed away," he said, then motioned to me with his right hand. "Behold, the new has come."

CHAPTER 15

The old man dropped his right arm, then lifted his left, which held the head of the tarantula.

"I was able to get it off," he said.

I glanced at my bicep, which was red and blistered, then back to the man.

He squinted as he raised the tarantula to eye level. He studied it, rotating the head with his fingers. His nails were long and as yellow as his teeth. "He's an interesting fellow. I like how these turned out."

Even though a tarantula head hung in front of me, my gaze kept returning to the old man.

"You're …" I stopped and cleared my throat, which was dry. "You're the guy from the posters. I saw you when I was … when I was working. You're the Fof."

The man grinned. "You speak mop."

"A little."

"A simple, but effective language," he said. "Best they

can do without tongues I suppose."

My eyes moved around the old man's wrinkly face, then down to his arms, which had no scars or brands.

"So you were the first human?" I asked. "To arrive on Bomba?"

He wiggled his toes. Again, he wasn't wearing shoes. "First maybe, but not to arrive."

"What do you mean?" I asked.

"I was the first human they saw, but I didn't go through the wormhole." He set the tarantula head next to him. "I've always been here."

I stared at him. "You've always been on Bomba?"

The old man gave a casual nod as he glanced around.

"So you were born here?" I asked.

"Born?" He gazed upward, reflecting. "I'm not sure I'd use that word, but … I've been here for as long as I can remember." He raised his shoulders. "Although most of that time has been spent on Santuario. Beautiful place, Santuario."

"But you said your son's on Earth?"

"He is," the old man said, and then his eyes began to water. "I built the wormhole for him."

"You *built* the wormhole?"

A proud smile spread across his face. "I did. Do you like it?"

"Uhhh …" I started, then shrugged. "Not really."

The old man frowned. "But yes, originally it was just me and Joshua on Santuario. Joshua's my son." The corners of his mouth curled back up. "It was wonderful. We swam in the ocean ... we fished ... we sang ... danced ..." He exhaled. "But as he got older, Joshua began asking for friends. He wanted others to join us. He thought we should share Santuario. That's when I started building the wormhole."

I squinted and rubbed my head. "So you built the wormhole to bring humans from Earth? To join you two on Santuario?"

"Yes, that's correct. But it wasn't easy—building the wormhole I mean. It didn't work at first." The old man picked up a handful of dirt and let it fall through his fingers. "I was able to connect two points, but the gravity inside was too strong. Anything I sent through got ripped to shreds, and Joshua wouldn't have been happy with me if his news friends died in my wormhole." He stroked his chin. "But I also couldn't figure out how to choose which points I wanted to connect—that was really frustrating." He casually lifted and dropped his shoulders. "But eventually I figured out those last two parts."

"How did you build it?" I asked.

"The wormhole? Well, there are lots of things to build with on Santuario." The old man smiled. "You'd like it there, Norman."

I peeked over my shoulder, suddenly anxious. "How do you know my name?"

"The wormhole told me," he said. "It knew your daughter was here—I think that one was an accident—and it sensed that she needed one of her parents."

"Wait—the *wormhole* told you?" I asked.

"Yeah," he said with another casual nod. "It ended up developing a mind of its own. Which is when it stopped listening to me and started deciding for itself whom to bring."

I raised an eyebrow. "A wormhole with free will?"

"Yes, although I didn't always agree with its choices. I thought some of the people it brought were unworthy. I didn't feel they belonged on Santuario. They didn't appreciate it … they were disrespectful … reckless … unruly." He bit down on his chapped lip. "So I banished them and made them live on Bomba with the mops. That's when other humans started showing up. I think the wormhole realized that those people—the ones I had banished—needed help or a companion or something … so it brought others, and then it realized *those* people needed someone too, so it brought more. It's gotten itself into a bit of a predicament."

"So it brought me here to help Jennifer?"

"Probably, but it's still having trouble pinpointing locations. I don't think it meant to put you so far away."

I didn't know if I believed him, if I believed anything he said, but when I went through the wormhole, the part I could recall anyway, it did feel like someone was there. I heard a pounding, like a heartbeat, and then moaning.

"Has it taken people the other way?" I asked. "Back to Earth?"

"Just once." He paused, and the water fell from his eyes. "It took Joshua."

"Why?"

He blew out a breath. "Well, Joshua told me that if I continued to cast people from Santuario—if I wasn't going to let everyone in—then he was going to leave and never come back. Because he didn't want to live in a place like that." The old man was quiet for a moment. "And I guess the wormhole heard him because it took him to a place far away from me ... a place with lots of humans." His voice was thick with emotion. "Everything I did was out of love for my son." He dried his eyes. "I was just trying to protect him."

"Maybe it'll bring him back," I said.

"I'm not sure he wants to come back." The old man dropped his head. "But people change ... I just need to be patient. There's a time for everything." The old man peeked up at me. "A time to be born. A time to die." He scooted forward and gently pressed his fingers against the tarantula's bite mark on my arm. With a soft circular motion, he began massaging the bruise. "A time to heal." Then, as if sensing something, he jerked his head up and peered across the open desert.

I turned in the direction of his gaze and saw the outline of three figures in the distance.

The old man released my arm and looked at me for a long moment, a deep searching gaze. "And a time to kill." He stood, his eyes on the figures approaching. "Don't be afraid, son. And remember, strength comes from within."

Then he disappeared into the desert.

What wasn't a mirage were the figures walking toward me. And they were close enough that I could tell they were mops.

Sliding my backpack over my shoulders, I moved onto the road and continued heading south. I walked casually as if I belonged there—just traveling to Central Bomba, that's all. No reason to run.

The three mops were moving perpendicular to me, coming from the outskirts of the desert. They crossed the road about fifty feet ahead of me, then stopped. I slowed, my heart racing in my chest. Then I let out a breath and picked up my pace. No need to slow down.

I waved as I approached, hoping the mops would step aside and let me pass by. They didn't. The three mops stood there, blocking the road, two of them with their arms folded across their chests.

So I gave a friendly nod and walked around them. That's when I felt a hand tighten around my bicep. I stopped, cocked my head and looked up at him. The mop had a long scar running diagonally across his face. He grinned. "Wheerree gooo huma?"

I wished I had taken the knife back out of my pack.

"Uhhh … South Bomba. Well, first Central Bomba. Ummm … Mafa Ba."

The two other mops closed around me. One was tall, and the other short and scrawny, at least for a male. He was still five or six inches taller than me though.

"Whhyy huma Mafa Ba?" asked the scar-faced mop.

I swallowed and looked down.

"Huma?" the tall mop said.

My eyes moved between them. Unlike the mops in

town, these mops had dry, flaky skin; there wasn't a lot of rain in the desert. And although all mops were lean, these were bony with sunken, hollow cheeks.

"I'm looking for someone," I answered.

Scar-face shook his head, confused.

"Uhhh …" I started, then touched my finger to my chest. "Me look for another huma. Another huma."

He nodded, apparently understanding. Then he released his grip, but as he did, shoved me back a few steps. "Huma mo Mafa Ba."

I glanced past him down the road, toward Central Bomba, toward Mafa Ba.

"Huma mo Mafa Ba," he said again. His lips were so dry they stuck together as he talked.

Standing there, with three mops towering over me, I considered my options. I could try to rush past them and outrun them to Central Bomba. But if these mops wanted to catch me, they could. Their long legs meant long strides, and those strides were quick and effortless.

I could beat the shit out of them. Only I couldn't. I wasn't big or strong enough to take down a single mop, let alone three. Part of me—the stubborn, masculine part I suppose—was tempted to risk one of those options. But my safety, and ultimately the safety of my daughter, was more important. So, I would go with option three, and turn around and head back.

Now, I wouldn't really go back. Instead, I'd walk about a mile, and then hide until these three assholes walked away. Then I'd continue on my way.

"Papa," I said to them.

I was worried about turning my back to them, but I did and began walking toward North Bomba. After about ten steps and not having received a fist to the back of my head, I blew out a breath.

Then I heard the shuffling of feet and suddenly scar-face was in front of me, blocking the road.

"Huma mo Mafa Fah," he said.

He doesn't want me to go to North Bomba. Of course, he also doesn't want me going to Central Bomba, so I really don't know what the fuck he wants me to do.

Peeking over my shoulder, I watched the tall and short mop scoot closer. But it was scar-face, the one blocking the road back to North Bomba, that poked me with his finger, tapping it hard against my chest.

"Mop mo baba huma."

He no like human.

Scar-face continued to berate me. He told me that the reason these three weren't working—the reason they spend most of their time in the desert—was because the humans had taken their jobs. The humans worked for less money. It wasn't fair. Then he told me how disgusting humans were with our eating and pissing and shitting.

For most of it, I nodded and said 'papa.' But as I stood there, my feet burning against the hot ground and the mops finger tapping against my chest, I grew irritated.

"Don't fucking touch me," I finally said, shoving his hand away. I pointed past him. "Huma go Mafa Fah."

Scar-face smirked. "Huma *mo* Mafa Fah."

I gritted my teeth. "You know what?" With my thumb, I pointed toward Central Bomba. "Huma go Mafa Ba."

The tall one poked me in the back. "Huma *mo* Mafa Ba."

Turning to face him, I said, "You either—don't touch me."

I'm not sure he understood what I was saying, but I think he could tell from my tone that I didn't like it. Still, the prick poked me again.

My eyes narrowed. I raised my hand and pointed at him. "I said don't touch me. If you do it again …"

He roared with laughter; they all did, as if I was a scrawny ten-year-old threatening a high school senior.

The tall one bent his long frame until I could feel his hot breath on my face. He inched his finger toward my chest, and when he finally made contact, said, "Boop."

He howled again, his body stretching backward. I thought about Rodrigo as the mop laughed, thought about Two Strikes and Carla. Rage swelled inside me. My eyes drifted to the mop's balls swaying between his legs. I wondered if it would have the same affect. With the soles of my feet burning and blistered, I thought it was a good time to lift one and find out.

In one swift motion, I swung up hard with my right. I could feel his penis and testicles against the bridge of my bare foot as it impacted. The mop's face, once laughing, filled with agony. He dropped to his knees, which lined up his head for a punch to the face.

I've hit a few guys in the face, but this one, without a doubt, felt the strangest. It was like punching a giant water balloon. But I must have got him good because he collapsed on the ground, his two hands pressed against his pudgy nose.

Then I felt a thump to the back of my head and went down face-first.

My only chance was to get my knife; otherwise I'd be beaten to death within five minutes. I rolled over, and in one motion, swung off my backpack. But as I reached inside, a foot caught me across the chin. Then there were more feet; it seemed like a hundred mops were kicking me at once.

When the blows stopped, I rolled gingerly onto my back. Groaning, I pushed myself across the ground, away from them, and then peered back over.

Scar-face was going through my backpack. My mouth dropped open when I saw him pull out my water containers. He handed them out, and I watched with wide eyes as they dumped the water, which I had been rationing so carefully, over their heads. They stretched their necks and let out a sigh, as if they hadn't absorbed water for days.

Scar-face tossed the container aside and then began chucking my food. From the expression on his face, I could tell that he hated even touching it. Then his eyes grew large as he stared into my bag. Slowly, he pulled out the knife and a grin spread over his face. The sun glinted off the blade as he held it in front of him.

"Pahhva," he said.

He reached back into the bag, pulled out my Navy shirt and tossed it to the short one, who slipped it over his head.

He looked ridiculous, like a man wearing a kid's shirt. And that little shit shouldn't have been wearing a Navy shirt if he wasn't in the Navy.

Scar-face opened the front pouch and peeked inside. He pulled out a handful of coins, and his grin grew wider. Then he closed the pouch and hurled my backpack at the tall one. The coins rattled as he caught it.

The tall one slid his empty water container inside, closed it, and strapped the bag to his back. "Pahhva."

My chest, which ached from the pounding, rose and fell as I watched them. I licked blood from the top of my lip and waited for them to leave. I thought I could still make it to Central Bomba without water, and I would just pick up my food when they left.

The short one—the one wearing my Navy shirt—said something to the others. Scar-face and the tall one laughed, nodded, and then strode toward me. They dropped to their knees and, while holding me down with one hand, used their other hand to slide off my shorts. Scar-face tossed them to the short one.

He slipped them on, then pointed at himself and laughed. "Me huma." Then he crouched down and grunted, pretending to take a shit. "Huuummmmaaaaa."

I cringed, half from his imitation and the other half from my bare ass searing against the ground. Then scar-face, still holding my knife, moved toward me. His grin turned menacing. When he reached me, he spread his legs and dropped down, straddling me. He pressed the blade of the knife under my chin, and I could feel a trickle of blood roll onto my chest.

Out of the corner of my eye, I noticed something slide across the ground. The hammerhead snake? I squinted and saw it weaving through the dirt, heading right for scar-face's leg.

Bite him. Bite that goddamn sponge.

But it didn't. Instead, just before reaching him, the thing turned and slithered away.

"No …" I muttered.

With both hands, scar-face raised the knife over his head. "Byyee huma."

I did end up buying the poison from Teddy and would have loved nothing more than to shove those blue berries right in the mop's spongy face. But they were hidden in my shorts, which another mop was now wearing.

But even though I was naked, I did have one weapon, and I had drunk enough to use it.

I arched my back and let go a stream of urine.

It took scar-face a few seconds to realize why he was getting wet, but when he did, disgust washed over his face. He yelped—like a little girl seeing a spider—and leaped off me. Now standing, scar-face wiggled and twisted, trying to shake my piss from his body.

Shifting my torso, I aimed my line of urine at his hand and began soaking it. He yelped again, dropped the knife, then fell to his knees and buried his dripping hand in the dirt.

I flipped over and scrambled toward the knife. The tall one charged. The handle of the knife was still wet, but I got a good grip, and as the mop reached me—his hand cocked back, ready to punch—I drove it into his chest.

It didn't slide in as easy as I thought considering the texture of their skin; maybe they have a tougher layer underneath or maybe I was still weak from the beating. With half the blade inside him, the mop wrapped his hand around my neck and squeezed.

I felt my grip on the knife loosen. I tried to suck in a breath but couldn't. He was too strong, too heavy. I was on my knees, and he was leaning over me, his force, his weight, too great. So I used it. I collapsed onto my back and let that tall mop, all two-hundred pounds of him—drop onto the blade.

He shrieked, and then his blood, pink and thin, spread over my chest. A few seconds later, I felt his body go limp.

With a grunt, I pushed him off. The other two mops stood there, wide-eyed, staring at the tall one. They took a step closer, then stopped when they saw me get to my feet and wave the knife. They glanced at each other, then took off in opposite directions. I let scar-face go and went after the short one, who was still wearing my clothes.

After a few steps, I realized I wouldn't catch him. So I'd have to risk a hole in my Navy shirt. I set my feet, turned my hips, and let the knife go. It hit him in the center of his back, which he arched in pain. The mop reached behind him, feeling for the knife.

Naked, my junk bouncing everywhere, I sprinted toward him.

Still twenty feet out, I saw the mop's six fingers wrap

around the handle. Awkwardly, bit by bit, he began to pull it out.

My feet burned as I raced across the ground. Five feet away, I saw the blade come out and the mop's body relax. Then it went rigid again as I jammed it back in. He fell to his knees, screaming.

Leaning my shoulder against him, I drove him to the ground. Then I pressed my knees against his lower back, slid the knife out with both hands, raised it above my head, and brought it down hard on the back of his neck.

The mop gasped, took a few shallow breaths, and then a moment later stopped breathing.

What food I could find was covered in ants and spiders. I checked each water container, holding them upside down above my mouth, but not a single drop fell from any of them.

Having expended so much energy fighting those fucking scavengers, I needed water, and now. I sat on the ground with my Navy shirt draped over my face. I knew I had to get moving, but without food or water, I didn't see how I could make it out of the desert. I licked sweat from the top of my lip and took long, deep breaths as I looked around.

My eyes fell upon the tall mop who lay dead on the ground. He was the reason—one of three—why I didn't have any water. Pulling the shirt off my head, I got to my feet and walked over to him. The ground around the mop was stained pink, but the desert had absorbed much of the blood. With my hands on my hips, I looked down at him. I screamed and gave him a hard kick to his side. A few drops of water seeped from his skin and onto the ground.

I froze, staring down at him, down at a giant sponge.

Squatting next to him, I looked over his body, wondering how I could extract his water.

Gravity. I needed to prop him up.

I rolled the mop onto his back. A thin layer of sand and dirt stuck to his chest and face. After pushing out a breath, I reached under his armpits and pulled him into a sitting position. I took a quick glance around to make sure scarface hadn't returned, then set a water container under the mop's hand. With a tight grip, I twisted one of his fingers as if I were wringing out a soaked rag.

A few drops fell into the container. Again, I twisted his finger, and again a trickle of water fell.

After I had wrung each of his six fingers, I held up the container. The water was mostly clear, about two or three ounces worth. I took a sip. It tasted warm, but not toxic or too salty or anything. I finished what was left, then sat there for about an hour. I didn't want to drink any more if it was going to make me sick.

But after that hour, I felt fine. Well, except for being dehydrated, bruised, sore, and badly sunburned.

Ounce by ounce, mop by mop, I twisted and wrung every part of their bodies, pushing and propping them to give me the best water flow. In the end, I was able to fill one of my containers about three-quarters of the way. It wasn't a lot, but hopefully enough to get me to Central Bomba.

After loading my remaining gear, I walked over to the tall mop, who now lay on his back. I crouched down and took a crap on his face.

CHAPTER 16

The mountains rose in front of me as I continued south. My spirits soared when I first saw them—two peaks in the distance, like two hands waving me over. I needed it too. With my water supply dwindling and my feet burning, I was a hot, delirious mess.

Patches of grass sprung up as I got closer. I moved passed bushes and brush, and eventually stumbled upon a fruit tree. The fruit reminded me of a prickly pear, although not as colorful. These were brown, but the skin was tough, and I had to use my knife to cut it open.

The inside looked and tasted like watermelon. I let out a giant sigh when I swallowed down my first bite. I ate about seven and packed two dozen more. The fruit gave me a surge of energy, but with darkness closing around me, I decided to camp instead of pushing through to the checkpoint. Luckily, that evening was uneventful.

I flinched when the mop brushed by me. He was on a bike, heading in the same direction—toward Central Bomba. I was relieved when he kept riding. Sure, he called me a 'fohp,' but in my condition I didn't really care. I was just glad he didn't rob me.

The checkpoint was in the valley. The mountains forced you to go between them. I considered scaling one of the mountains, but I was out of water and didn't think I had the energy to do it, even with the fruit I had found. What I did do though was put on my shirt. Rodrigo had said that Central Bomba, unlike South Bomba, would let humans enter even if they had strikes, but he also said it would depend on the guards. As I pulled the shirt over my sweat-covered body, I could smell mop. I tugged down on my sleeve so that it covered the strike, and kept walking.

Two mops stood at the checkpoint as I approached. Badges with blue insignias hung around their necks. A guardhouse stood just off the road and hanging outside was a sketch of Fof.

About twenty feet from the checkpoint, I heard a rumbling behind me. Peeking over my shoulder, I saw a car speeding down the road. It slowed as it reached the checkpoint. The mop inside looked like he was standing, but he was just that tall. When I noticed the tattoo on his arm, I realized it was the Ba—the gladiator I had seen in North Bomba, the same son of a bitch who had hit me with his car. He would be representing North Bomba in Aba, which was less than a week away. A mop week anyway.

The cops waved the Ba through without paying. I doubted they would do the same for me. They stood with their hands on their hips as I walked up. The last I heard, it was ten coins to enter.

One of the cops unfolded his arms and held up all twelve fingers.

"I thought it was …" I stopped and held up my own hands, flashing my ten fingers.

The mop shook his head. "Mo huma," he said, spreading his fingers wider, and flicking the ones on the end to emphasize.

I sighed and reached into the front pouch of my backpack. The coins clanged together as I counted twelve. I peeked up at them and saw they had edged closer. I was alone with two mop cops and almost three weeks' worth of wages.

Then I heard the puttering of engine. I watched as another car emerged from the desert. I waved dust from my face as it came to a stop at the checkpoint. Inside was Bob, the head of North Bomba, and sitting next to him was Ma. With the election approaching, Bob was planning to campaign in Central and South Bomba.

The guards waved them through, but when Bob noticed me, he stopped. He whispered something to Ma, who nodded.

With Ma translating, Bob said it was nice to see me again. He remembered meeting me at the bar. He told me they had taken my suggestions for making the mortar and cement, and early results were good. If they continued, he would recommend me for a construction manager job. Then, in his most sincere mop voice, Bob said he was proud to fight for me and the other humans of North Bomba.

I didn't believe him, but like a good taxpayer, I smiled and nodded.

Ma said something to him, and after contemplating it, Bob waved for me to get in the car. I dumped twelve coins into the cop's hand and hopped in the back.

Bob let me out a few miles outside of Central Bomba's main city, which they called Bah. He was fighting for humans but didn't want to be seen with one in his backseat.

It took me two hours to reach the city by foot, and then another hour to pass through it. During that final hour, I must have heard a hundred 'fohps,' much more than I would have in North Bomba. The mops here were also more physical. They wouldn't come up and punch me in the face, but they'd purposefully bump into me and then snicker as they walked away. The male mops were also more brazen with the females, rubbing and groping them right out in the open.

My priority upon leaving the city was water. Even with the fruit I had eaten, I was parched. My mouth was dry and my lips cracked. After laboring along for another hour, I finally spotted two human kids. Since it was late morning, the adult humans were probably working.

Naturally, the kids only spoke Spanish, but I had learned enough to ask for what I wanted.

"Agua?" I said to them.

"Tienes que ir al rio," one of the boys said, pointing past me.

I only saw trees. I held up my hands and shook my head. "Agua?"

Again, the boy pointed. His hands were filthy. "Rio."

They had to show me. After we passed under the trees and it came into view, I realized that 'rio' was 'river.'

"Gracias," I said to them, and then drank what felt like a rio's worth of agua. After filling my containers, I ate another piece of fruit and then found a man who spoke English. He explained how to get to the cosmetics store, which he said wasn't a store at all, but some woman's room. It was in the city, in a building that housed mostly mops.

The streets were nearly empty as I passed through the city. After another mile, I saw why. Hundreds of mops were packed around a stage, where three other mops stood with megaphones in their hands. One was Bob, and I learned the other two were the leaders of Central and South Bomba, Mafa Bah and Mafa Ahh.

A political debate.

I knew enough mop to understand parts of what they were saying, and a human next to me helped with the rest. I'll summarize, but leave out all the boring shit like jobs, education, and transportation. In fact, I'll just stick to their thoughts on humans.

The head of Central Bomba wanted to separate mops and humans. He would provide us with a small piece of land, which we wouldn't be able to leave. We'd also have to build a giant wall around the perimeter to keep ourselves, and our feces, inside. Considering how poorly mops treated us, this wasn't a terrible idea. At least they'd leave us the fuck alone.

The head of South Bomba wasn't just repulsed by humans, he hated us, and said so. What was his solution to the human crisis? He wanted to send us back. How did he plan on doing that? Well, he was a little short on specifics. Whatever the method, I'm sure he'd do so humanely.

Then my buddy Bob, from North Bomba, gave his usual spiel—humans need better pay, bathrooms in town, representatives in government, and a dozen other things, most of which got booed.

"Come in."

I waited for the stench to hit me as I pushed the door open. That was expected when entering a human-occupied room, even with the open ceilings. But I didn't get it. Instead, a floral, fruity aroma filled my nose.

The room was twice the size of mine. The walls were colored, and two padded chairs and a couch were arranged around a carpet. A circular table sat in the middle of the room, with jars and bottles filling every inch of it.

Sitting on the couch, wearing a clean tank top and shorts, was a petit Caucasian woman. She didn't look like your typical female on Bomba. Her hair was a stark blonde, almost white, and brushed straight back. And instead of the dirt, grime, and sunburn that coated most humans, this woman had clear, clean skin.

I felt dirty and out of place.

"Can I help you?" she asked, standing.

"I was looking for … cosmetics … like makeup."

She flashed a smile, showing her straight, white teeth. "For your girlfriend?"

"No, it's uhhh … for me." I shifted my feet "For the brand."

The woman stared at me for a few seconds, then brushed by me and walked to the door. She peeked outside.

"It's against the law to conceal a brand," she said, and eased the door closed.

"I know."

Her eyes, which were coated with blue eye shadow, moved to my right arm. "You only have one strike," she said. "I could do it for you, sure, but what's the point?"

I pulled off my backpack and set it on the ground. "I need to get into South Bomba."

"Why?" she asked.

"My daughter's there."

The woman crossed her arms and gave a slow nod. "Covering a brand … it takes a lot of cosmetics to do the job."

I nodded. "I know. Fifteen coins? I have it."

She raised her shoulders. "Mops robbed me last week, so my prices have gone up. It's seventeen now."

After subtracting what I'd need for the boat ride, the entrance into South Bomba, as well as the human markup for both, I wouldn't be left with much. A few coins maybe. But what choice did I have? I nodded and pushed out a breath.

She walked to the table. "I'm going to need half of it now—say nine coins—but I'll need to *see* all seventeen."

After showing her the money, I brushed dirt from my shorts and sat on the couch. My ass welcomed the cushy surface.

Holding a cloth and small bowl, the woman slid next to me, facing my right arm.

"First we need to get this crud off," she said, scooting closer. "I'm Doll by the way."

I peeked down at my arm as she ran a wet cloth over it. "Your name is Doll?"

She nodded.

The woman kind of looked like a doll.

"Is that your given name?" I asked.

"What do you think?" she said.

Doll dabbed the cloth in the bowl and then went up and down again, pressing firmly against my arm. When she was finished, her white cloth had turned brown.

"All that's from my arm?" I asked.

Doll nodded as she studied the brand. "Yeah, but you're not as bad as some of the others I've seen. You must be new."

I shrugged. "I've been here a few months."

"Well you're definitely new if you're still using the word 'months,'" she said. "What's your name?"

"Norman."

"Alright, Norman," she said, standing. "Next we need to put on a primer."

Doll stepped back to the table and grabbed a brush and container.

"It sounds like you're preparing to paint wood," I said.

"Same type of approach," Doll said, returning to the couch. She dipped the brush in a clear liquid, then ran it along my skin with long, smooth strokes. I squinched my nose. The shit actually smelled like paint primer. Doll set one hand against my chest, leaned in, and blew against my arm. The clean patch of skin looked awkward compared to the rest of my body.

"We'll let that dry for a few minutes," she said.

Relaxing my arm, I sunk back against the couch and glanced around. "How can you afford this place?"

"Business is surprisingly good," she said. "Especially with the teenage girls. The older gals here don't really care about their looks, but the teenagers, hell, they'll steal their parents' coins for a little cover up, or maybe some highlights." Doll stood and returned to the table. "I've even had a few mop customers."

"What do they ask for?"

"Streaks of color mostly … it's just hard to get it to stick to their skin." She plopped down next to me with a mirror and a few other supplies. "But the mops tend to leave water marks on my sofa."

As I straightened on the couch, Doll began mixing substances with a small wooden spoon. After a few minutes, she used her finger to wipe it vertically across my branded K. She squinted and tilted her head. "I think it's a little dark."

"How do you make this stuff?" I asked as she began mixing again.

"Combination of plant leaves, stems, a little animal fat, and some coloring, which also comes from their plants." She dabbed her finger and ran another streak across the K. "That's it."

The streak matched the coloring of the rest of my arm, as if the middle of the K had been erased.

"Remember," she said, scooping more paste with her finger. "This isn't a tattoo. It'll come off if it gets too wet." Using two fingers, Doll pressed against my arm in a circular motion. "A little water's fine. I know you'll be sweating. But don't expect it to last more than a few weeks." She leaned back and stared at it. "And that's mop weeks, Norman." She picked up a brush, dipped it into a separate bowl of brown powder and began running it lightly over the clean patch of skin that surrounded the brand. "Now I need to blend it with the rest of your arm." Her eyes were narrowed and focused. "You'll want to avoid rubbing it or sleeping on your right side."

"Understood," I said.

Doll picked up her mirror and turned it toward me. My mouth fell open when I saw the reflection. Not because of my arm, but because of my face. It was the first time I had seen my reflection since arriving on Bomba. My high, tight haircut was gone. It was a scraggily mess, as was the beard covering my suntanned face.

"Impressive, huh?" Doll said.

"Uhhh … sorry, I was looking at my …"

Doll smiled and stroked my chin. "I know." She adjusted the mirror so I could see my arm.

And just like that my brand was gone. At least temporarily.

"Thank you," I said. "It looks good."

As I began to stand, she pushed me back down. "Hold on cowboy, I still need to put on the sealant."

"I'm surprised the mops let you run a business out of your house," I said as she walked to the table.

"What business?" Doll said with a smirk. "I couldn't afford this place or all of this furniture if I had to pay rent for a store too." She returned to the couch and slid next to me. I could feel her shaved legs resting against my thighs. "They suspect I'm up to something but can't figure it out since my customers never leave with any goods. None they notice anyway. I'll just have to be careful if I expand my mop business."

When she was done applying the sealant, she moved her face within an inch of my arm and blew a long, soft breath. "Like I said, a little water is fine, but keep it dry for at least the first day."

"Yes, ma'am."

Doll leaned to her left, and her tank top strap slid off. "I'd be happy to earn my tip now."

"Sorry, I'm a little short on money. I need the rest to get into South Bomba."

An exaggerated frown spread across her face. "Well, I guess I'll let you work for it then." She tapped my nose. "Just this once."

"Thanks, but I'm good," I said.

Doll's finger dropped to my chest and lingered there a few seconds.

"I'm married," I said, standing.

"You're on a different planet, Norman. I bet your wife would give you a pass."

I shook my head. "I'm not so sure about that. But it wouldn't matter if she did."

Doll blew out a disgusted breath. "You know, the only reason I even offered is because you're new," she said. "You're cleaner than most of the other filthy fucks around here."

"I'm flattered."

Shaking her head, Doll stood. "Give me my money."

CHAPTER 17

The mop's hand stayed extended. The eight coins I dropped into his palm wasn't enough. He wanted ten for me to board the boat, even though the sign said eight.

The boat ride, which would take three hours, was the only way to reach South Bomba, Mafa Ahh. The sea was too rough to swim. Even if I were well-rested, well-fed, and in good shape, I doubted I could have made it across.

It was the moons; three of them made for stronger currents and higher tides. Except for the voyage between Central and South Bomba, the mops hadn't ventured very far on the water. Boat construction was part of the problem. The mops were still using wood, and it would only last so long under the force of these waves.

But the mops also couldn't swim. I suppose they could have learned, but it wouldn't have done them much good. The more water they take in, the fewer the air pockets, and the heavier they become. Eventually, they sink.

So even if Santuario did exist, the mops would never reach it.

"Ubu," the mop said, his arm still extended.

I shook my head and dumped two more coins into his hand.

He waved for me to pass. "Pob."

With two hands gripping the straps of my backpack, I stepped onto the wooden pier. Water washed over my feet as I walked toward the sailboat, which rocked up and down at the far end. The boat, which was probably designed by humans, was fifty feet long with a curved hull and a mast, which held the mainsail and jib. There wasn't a cabin though because the mops didn't care about getting wet. Instead, the deck was lined with seats, about twenty of them, and several crates of supplies—goods going from Central to South Bomba.

Looks of disgust filled the mops' faces as I hopped on board. The boat swayed. With one hand against the boom, I stepped across the deck and plopped down in the last row. As soon as my ass hit the seat, the mop next me—an older woman with wrinkly, saggy skin—scooted over, leaving a seat between us.

I was the only human on board.

Mops continued to stare. They turned and pointed and shook their heads, even the kids, who yelled 'huma' and 'fohp.'

I let out a sigh when we finally pushed off and raised our sails. My hands clutched the edge of my seat as the boat sliced through the waves. The mops hung on too, their faces strained. For them, going overboard would be death.

Suddenly, a shiver spread through me as water ran down my face and onto my chest. I looked over and saw the old woman with her right hand held above my head. Her fist was clenched into a tight ball; she had just flushed it of water.

"What the fuck …" I said to her.

Her smirk turned into a squeaky laugh as she pulled her arm back. "Fohp," she said.

The passengers and crew held on as the wind filled the sails. The bow rose, then shot back down as the boat went up and over a wave. I served in the Navy for eight years, but rarely had I seen seas this rough.

When I had adjusted to the rocking, I glanced around. Hanging in the stern were NO PISSING and NO SHITTING signs. That was fine, I could hold both for the boat ride. Based on what I had been told about North Bomba, I was just happy they let me board.

I slammed my eyes shut as water pelted my face. After wiping my eyes, I peeked over at the old lady again. She was looking the other way, and her hands were in her lap. Then I heard giggling, and when my eyes settled on the source—a kid two seats in front of me—I frowned. His hands were joined together, pointed at me. Like the asshole who branded me when I arrived, the kid had shot me using his hands as a water gun.

He dropped his arms at his sides and shook them, I guess to reload. He aimed and fired again, soaking my neck. Water ran down my chest and onto my arm.

My arm.

With wide eyes, I stared down at my bicep. A bit of color had run off, but the concealer was mostly intact. At least for now. The little shit was ready to fire again. I shifted in my seat so that my right side was shielded. More water doused me, but my right arm stayed dry.

The kid sat there, staring at me with a stupid grin on his face. "Huma," he said, his voice high and squeaky.

If it wasn't for my arm, I would have leaned forward and slapped his little ass. Although he wasn't exactly little, at least not compared to me. He was almost my height.

So instead I gave him the finger. The pores on his forehead wrinkled into confusion. He said something to his mother, who glanced back at me. I kept my finger upright. After whispering something to her son, she turned her nose up and looked away.

The kid continued to stare at my finger. Then he turned the back of his hand toward me and flipped me the bird right back. Of course, it wasn't his middle finger because he had six, so I wasn't exactly offended by his third-from-the-left finger being up.

The boat lurched. There was a scream, and several mops sprung from their seats. Using the back of my chair for support, I stood and scanned the deck as the boat rocked. A crowd of mops had gathered on the starboard side. A crewmember, a mop, had gone overboard.

He flapped his arms in the water, struggling to stay afloat. Waves crashed over him. His head went under, but his hand caught hold of a rope that had been thrown. The crew pulled him up and dropped his fat, bloated body at the bow. He lay there, a saturated sponge, unable to move. A mop knelt beside him and thrust his hands against his chest like he was giving him CPR. Water seeped from the mop's pores and across the ship's deck.

It was an hour before the mop could sit up. His head and body were still swollen with water, but he could move, and I'm guessing, would survive, though I didn't know what affect the salt water would have on him.

The whole thing was a welcomed distraction. I had grown tired of the verbal insults and squirts of water. I just wanted to get to my daughter.

I hurried off the boat and was the third passenger to reach the checkpoint. I held my backpack against my chest as I waited in line. With barely enough coins for the toll, I couldn't afford for even one to be swiped.

I could see the city just past the checkpoint and wondered how long it would take to find Jennifer. That's assuming I made it through.

The mop ahead of me handed over his coins, then passed the guards. I was about to step forward when the old lady from the boat cut in front of me. Her pore-covered skin was a shade darker than the other mops. A hundred years in the sun I guess.

She shook her head. "Huma mo hop."

Human no first.

I wanted to tell the bitch to wait her turn, but I didn't know how to say it in mop, and even if I did, I'm sure I would have gotten clubbed for it.

She took her time, counting each coin as she handed them to the guards. "Hop … ubu … owp …"

Just as she finished counting, another mop cut in front of me.

"Come on …" I said with a shake of my head.

The mop turned and glared down at me. "Fohp."

Within five minutes, I had been pushed to the back of the line. And now I had to piss. I glanced over my shoulder, then squeezed out a little urine, soiling part of my shorts.

The mop in front of me, a tall, lanky male, turned and sniffed. I could feel my face flush. The mop's eyes drifted to my shorts. With my palm, I wiped sweat from my forehead and then smeared it against the wet spot. I let out an exaggerated breath. The mop stared at me, shook his head, then called to the guards.

My heart began to pump as a guard strode along the line of passengers. When he reached me, the lanky mop said something to him. The guard glanced at my shorts, craned his neck forward, and then inhaled through his nose.

He pointed at my crotch. "Mo baba."

"No, no," I said, shaking my head. "*Mo*. Someone squirted me." I pressed my hands together as the kid had done on the boat. "*Mop*."

The lanky one demonstrated, shooting me with a stream of water, further soiling my shorts. "Papa?"

Yeah, kind of like that asshole.

The guard snickered, then squirted me too, showering

my chest and arm. I gasped as more coverup washed away.

"Papa, papa," I said, turning away.

As the guard returned to the checkpoint, I used my finger to try to blend the coloring. But I could see the top of the K.

"No ..."

I spat on my fingers, ran them along the ground, and then worked the mud around the brand. It was a shoddy job, but I couldn't wait another minute. I was at my daughter's doorstep.

When the last mop had paid and walked through, I blew out a long breath. Then I stepped forward.

Looks of contempt filled the guards faces as they looked me over. Their eyes moved along my dirty, sunburned body. One of the guards circled me, eventually stopping on my right side, his eyes settling on my arm.

I squeezed my trembling hands into fists.

The guard ran his hand over my bicep, then tilted his head and squinted. He waved the other guard over, and they stood there with their arms folded, studying my arm.

Sweat pooled at the corners of my eyes. I peeked down and could see the top of the brand again.

But the guards asked for my money.

I sighed and my shoulders relaxed. Until I realized how much they were charging. Twenty coins. Twice as much as Central Bomba's toll. And seven more than what I had. *Seven.*

"This is all I have," I said, my shaking hands dropping the coins onto the guard's palm.

He counted them, then held up seven fingers.

I pulled out the insides of my short's pockets. "That's all I have. Mo. Mo. No more."

The guard shook his head. "Huma mo Mafa Ahh."

My eyes begin to water. I pointed passed the checkpoint, then pressed my hands together, pleading with him. "Please ... I have to get in … please …"

"Mo," the guard said.

I forced my backpack into his arms and showed him the water containers, the knife, everything I had. "Here," I said, breathing heavily. "All this stuff—it has to be worth at least ten coins."

He looked over my gear, then held up a single finger. One more coin. The fucking asshole wanted one more coin.

The guard's finger stood there, almost like a middle finger telling me to fuck off and never come back. But I had nothing else to give. Nothing.

"Please let me in," I said, turning my empty palms toward him. "That's all I have."

The guard shook his head. "Mo huma."

With my arms still extended, I noticed my watch. My Timex. It had stopped. I stared at it for a long moment, then took it off and wound it.

"Here," I said. My voice was thick with anguish. "Take this."

The guard held the watch, his white eyes following the seconds hand as it turned. Then he stepped to the side and waved me into Mafa Ahh.

I winced as a rock glanced off my temple. It was the third object that had been throw at me since I passed the checkpoint, a stick and a piece of fruit the others.

The males in Mafa Ahh treated the females almost as bad as they treated humans. They didn't throw anything at them, but they grabbed and groped them whenever they felt like it. And the sex, which I doubted was consensual, was blatant—in alleyways, in stores, upside trees.

The soles of my feet throbbed with pain as I hustled through the city. The sun was setting, but as usual I was soaked in sweat. I needed a drink, I needed to eat, but I kept running. I was so close I couldn't stand it. I had already seen three cars on Mafa Ahh, but still no humans.

When I finally saw my first, I grabbed the poor Hispanic woman by the shoulders and asked if she knew my daughter.

"Jennifer," I said, panting.

Her eyes were wide.

"Jen Dohring," I said.

The woman shook her head. "No inglesa."

"Christ," I said, and kept moving.

I weaved through crowds of mops, who shoved and pushed me as I searched for humans. More shit was thrown at me and more insults hurled my way.

Humans. I need to find humans.

I found three. All of them spoke English, but none knew Jennifer.

"Try down that road," a man told me, pointing to my

right. "Try house seventeen. I don't know her name, but a girl there kind of matches that description."

My heart pounded as I lumbered toward the house. Two Caucasian women stood out front as I rushed up the steps.

My chest rose and fell as I tried to speak. "Jen—I'm looking for Jennifer Dohring. Does she live here? Jen Dohring."

They looked at me, their arms folded across their chests.

"Who are you?" the taller one asked. She had long, grey hair which didn't match her youthful face.

I dropped to a knee to avoid falling. "I'm her father … I'm …"

"What's your name?" she asked.

"Norman Dohring," I said, pushing out a breath.

The women exchanged glances, and then the tall one said, "Wait here, okay?"

"Wait?" I said. "Is she here? Does she live here?"

"I'll go look. Just hang on a second."

I wiped sweat from my face and nodded.

When the door creaked opened a few minutes later, I got to my feet. My pulse raced.

Next to the tall woman with grey hair, stood a teenager. She was tall too, but with bright red hair and fair skin. Her eyes took me in.

"Can I help you?" she asked, her hands at her side.

"I'm looking for Jen Dohring."

"I'm Jen Dohring."

"What?" I studied her face. "You're Jen Dohring?"

The girl gave a quick, confused nod.

I blinked hard. "And you're from Henderson?"

She scooted behind the other woman, peering at me from over her shoulder. "Yeah."

"Wait ... no ... how do you spell your last name?"

She spelled it just like mine.

"Can't be ..." I said.

My knees were weak. I set my hand against the house to steady myself. Then I slid down onto my ass and put my head in my hands.

"No ... no ..." I began to sob. "No ..."

My daughter's not in Mafa Ahh. She's probably not even on Bomba. But I am. I'm stuck here with no food, no money, sore, dirty, and tired.

"Dad?"

I dried my eyes.

The voice became louder. "Dad?"

Craning my neck, I looked up. The first thing I noticed, before reaching the person's face, was the red shirt. Then the logo—the top part of the P in the shape of a pizza. PASQUALE'S PIZZERIA. The shirt was stained and the sleeves had been cut off.

My eyes drifted up, and I saw the slender frame, the straight auburn hair—now short and uneven—and those buggy eyes.

"Jennifer," I said, my mouth hanging open.

She had lost weight, and there were smears of dirt across her arms and face. Her wide eyes filled with tears as she stared at me. "Oh my God."

I staggered to my feet. "*Jennifer.*"

She began to cry.

"Sorry about the other girl," the older woman said. "There's a lot of creeps on Bomba who say they're someone they're not. We just wanted to be sure."

I stumbled toward my daughter, who reached to hug me. But it was a spongy arm I felt.

What?

Then I heard those squeaky voices. When I stepped back, two cops stood between Jennifer and me. Badges with blue insignias hung from their necks.

They looked me up and down, then turned to another mop, who waited at the bottom of the steps. He wasn't wearing a badge. My eyes bulged wide when I saw the long scar running across his face. He had flaky skin with sunken, hollow cheeks.

Scar-face.

It was the scavenger from the desert, the one who had gotten away.

His eyes narrowed. He moved toward us, then raised his long arm and pointed. "Huma."

The cops closed in around me.

"No!" I yelled, pushing them away. "Jennifer!"

I roared, struggling to get through them. "Jennifer!" I flailed my arms, punching and kicking. "Jennifer!" Her red shirt flashed between them as I tried to break free. "Jennifer! Jennifer!"

But out came the clubs, and down I went.

The mops yanked me off the porch, and I heard Jennifer scream as my head bounced against the steps. Then scar-face kicked me when I reached the bottom.

My eyes locked with Jennifer as the cops dragged me across the ground. She stood hunched over as tears rolled down her sunburned face.

CHAPTER 18

The cops branded me twice—once for each of my victims. I had three K's now, the latter two pink and swollen.

I sat on the dirt floor of the jail cell with my head down. Bitterness ran through every inch of my bruised and beaten body. I sobbed and pounded my fist weakly against the ground. I had her.

I had her.

But I didn't. She was alone again. And now I was struggling to remember what Jennifer even looked like. Her short hair, her face flush from the sun, her work shirt dirty and without sleeves. Longing filled my chest as I thought about her, as I thought about Amy. Lord, I missed my family.

The jail stank like piss, shit, and sweat. Because that's all there was—twelve humans crammed into a ten by ten jail cell with one trip a day to the bathroom; if we were lucky.

Not that we needed to go that often. Cops tossed in

fruit every couple of days. I'm sure they hoped we'd fight over it like hungry wolves, but we didn't. Because fuck them. Instead, we split it up evenly, and occasionally gave more to those who were worse off, and sometimes less. We had to be sensible. Why give food to someone who would be dead by morning?

"Your timing isn't exactly great," Oscar said. He was one of the inmates and hadn't stopped talking since I arrived.

"Why?" I asked.

Oscar was Caucasian but was so filthy that he looked black. "Aba is in two days," he said.

I didn't respond.

"They'll take us to the arena." He nodded, knowingly. "And use us as pawns in their grand little game."

I rested the back of my head against the stone wall and sighed.

"We're all going to be slaughtered," Oscar continued. "Beaten by a mop—by a Ba."

"I know how Aba works," I said.

"We all know, Oscar," another inmate said. "We'll all be dead in two days. We get it."

A grin spread over Oscar's face. His teeth were as dirty as his hands. "But I bet you didn't know this," he said.

I straightened my back and peered over at him.

"If you win Aba—if a human wins Aba—they'll release you."

The other inmates leaned forward. Even the ones that had been curled up on the ground, sat up.

"They'll let you go free. They'll let you and your three K's walk right on home," Oscar said.

"Bullshit," an inmate said.

Oscar gave a dramatic shake of his head. "It's true, it's true. It's in the rules, look it up. And do you know what they'd serve you for your victory dinner?"

We all stared at him.

"Pom," Oscar said. "They added these rules so humans would put up a good fight."

"Does it even matter?" an inmate asked. "It's a joke to them. The Bas are bigger. They're stronger. They have clubs. There's no way a human could win."

"We'll see about that." Oscar got to his feet. He was barely a hundred pounds. "Do you know who you're looking at?" he asked. "The next winner of Aba. Right here, standing right in front of you. I'm going to make history. The first human to win Aba."

The pounding of footsteps echoed down the hall. Oscar set his hands against the rusty bars and peered through. "Someone's coming. A whole bunch of mops."

A dozen mops stopped in front of our cell. All but one were cops. And that one, the tallest of the bunch, I recognized. His name was Hapa. He was the leader of South Bomba. I remembered his campaign slogan from the debate. *A World Without Humans.*

The mops' eyes drifted from inmate to inmate. Reaching his hand through the bars, a cop pointed at me. Then he unlocked the cell, stepped inside, yanked me up from under my arms, and forced me to the entranceway until I was standing in front of Hapa.

I raised my shoulders. "What …"

Ma emerged from behind the cops. The corners of her mouth dropped into a sympathetic frown. She told me that one of the mops I had killed in the desert—the tall son of a bitch—was Hapa's son.

"Oh. Well, tell him that his son was an asshole." I peered up at Hapa. "I bet you're a terrible father."

It was quiet for a moment. I peeked over at Ma, who had a perplexed look on her face.

"Tell him I don't care," I began. "And tell him I took a shit on his son's head."

Ma hesitated, swallowed, and then said something. Hapa's eyes filled with rage, and his six fingers closed around my neck. With his free hand, he reached back and slugged me in the face.

I tasted blood and spat, and because I did—because of how gross my saliva was—he punched me again.

"Whhhyyyy?" Ma said.

Hapa released his grip and folded his arms across his chest.

"Whhhyyyy?" she said again.

With the back of my hand, I wiped blood from my mouth. "He wants to know why? Why I killed his son?"

Ma nodded.

I cleared my throat. "It was my only choice," I said. "His son was going to kill me—him and his mop buddies." I swallowed. "It was either him or me."

After she translated, Hapa nodded his head. He tapped

his finger against his tiny mouth, contemplating something. His white eyes stayed locked with mine as he said something to Ma.

Looking down, she passed on his message. It was choppy and I had to have her repeat it, but eventually I got it. Hapa was going to bring Jennifer to Aba so she could watch me die. Payback for killing his son.

Before I blacked out from the beating, I got one punch in—right against Hapa's little, spongy nose.

Oscar extended his hand, which held two pieces from a granana. "I saved you some fruit."

I lay on my side, staring at it. The ground stank. I bet a lot of humans had pissed there.

Groaning, I sat up and ate both pieces. "Thanks."

"We've got to get some food in us if we're going to win Aba," Oscar said. "You want that victory pom, right?"

I licked my lips, savoring the taste of the granana. "I don't think I'm going to be eating any pom."

Oscar smiled. "That's because I am," he said. "But if you survive, I'll share it with you."

"What day is it?" I asked.

His smile widened. "It's game day. They're going to come get us in a few hours. To take us to the arena."

The door to our cell swung open. I thought it was time for our daily bathroom break, but the cop standing there had his head turned, waiting for someone.

"Looks like a human," Oscar said, peering down the hall. "I think we're getting another roommate."

The first thing I noticed when the human reached our cell, was his skinny jeans, which now sagged from his thin frame. As my eyes drifted up, I saw Brandon's three strikes, two black eyes, and one long gash across his forehead.

The cop shoved him inside. I tried to catch Brandon, but having sat motionless for days, I barely raised a hand before he hit the ground.

"Sorry," I said. "Are you okay?"

When his glassy eyes met mine, Brandon cracked a small smile. His fair skin had darkened.

"Hey." He winced as he sat up. The gash on his forehead began to bleed.

I glanced at his three K's. The third was pink and puffy. "What happened? What did you do?"

"I stood up for human rights," he said, out of breath. He wiped blood from his forehead. "It's a boy's club here. This whole planet is one giant boy's club. Have you seen how they treat the women?"

"I've seen it, Brandon."

He wrapped his arms around his knees and leaned toward me. "We need to start a revolution."

The inmates laughed. Except for Oscar, who told Brandon that he would join him in his revolution, right after he wins Aba.

I hung my head when I heard the guards' footsteps. They were coming for us, coming to take us to Aba.

It was a strange feeling knowing that I'd be dead in a few hours, even stranger that it was going to happen on my birthday—fifty-three as of today. At least I thought it was. I lost track of the days after Rodrigo died.

I had been looking forward to growing old. I really had. After retiring, I planned to spend my mornings reading the paper in my recliner. I'd have lunch at Black Bear Diner in the afternoons, shooting the shit with all the other old fucks. In the evenings, I'd watch the news and then cook dinner for Amy and me. That would be followed by a walk around our community, where I'd show off my beautiful wife and yell at the teenage drivers to slow down.

But I wouldn't be doing any of that now.

A stench filled my nostrils as we stood. It was from all of us—all our filth standing at once. As we formed a line to leave the cell, I noticed an inmate hadn't gotten up. I nudged him with my foot. He didn't move, and after nudging him again, I realized he was dead.

He was wearing brown, leather work boots, similar to the ones I wore out on jobs. I love wearing boots. I love lacing them up and stomping around as I put in a hard day's work. As the other inmates began to file out, I crouched down and wiggled off the guy's boots. Then I slid my feet inside and followed Brandon out of the cell.

A sliver of hope rose inside me. With leather work boots, I might just have a chance at Aba.

Shielding my eyes from the sun, I could see the arena in the distance. It looked larger than the North Bomba arena, even bigger than the one that was under construction. The mops spared no expense when murdering humans as entertainment.

Mops lined the street as we were marched through town. They heckled us, and threw stones and rocks. I kept my head down, my eyes focused on Brandon's shoes as we walked. My legs quivered with each step. The last time I had been outside was twenty hours ago during our trip to the bathroom.

I squeezed my eyes shut as an object glanced off my temple. But it didn't hurt; whatever hit me was soft. After I wiped my face and licked my fingers, I could taste it. *Fruit.*

It wasn't the first time mops had thrown food at me. They knew we needed it to survive. To them, it was a game—feed the savages.

"Eat it, Brandon," I said.

He peeked over his shoulder. "What?"

"If they throw fruit at you, pick it up and eat it," I said. "It'll give you energy."

He did. And so did I, picking six pieces off the ground. I caught another two with my bare hands.

A gate swung open as we approached the arena. They led us through the opening and down a long, dark tunnel under the stands. I could hear the crowd above us, yelling and pounding their feet. My heart thumped. The sun peeked over the stone wall as we emerged from the tunnel and into the arena.

After the door had been closed behind me, I turned in place. There were four levels, each jammed with mops. Females stood in the first row, dancing and twisting as fans fondled them. Mop cheerleaders. The ground level was divided into three sections, one for each of Bomba's regions, with cheerleaders serving as the borders. The cheerleaders had batons, which they twirled above their heads and between their hands. In the center of the arena stood a water tower, supported by four wooden stilts. Bursts of water shot from the tower and into the crowd, and the mops hooted and hollered with each dousing.

Once all the humans had entered the arena, about a dozen to each section, a mop strode to the water tower. He spoke to the crowd through a megaphone, similar to the ones the politicians had used. I was able to pick up about every third word, but the gist was this: the winning Ba would get to bang a cheerleader, a lot of humas were going to die, and the whole thing was going to be pahhva—awesome.

After running his hand over the breasts of a cheerleader, the announcer introduced the first Ba. On cue, a door opened and out roared a convertible with the Ba behind the wheel. My mouth dropped open when I heard an American pop song blasting from the car's speakers. I assumed it was from a smartphone that hadn't fried in the wormhole. Unfortunately, it was the same shitty music that Camila played at her desk. Naturally the mops loved it, dancing their spongy asses off to the awful beat.

"I love this song," said Brandon.

Of course he did.

The car, which must have had a manual transmission, jerked as the Ba drove it. The stupid mop couldn't drive stick. I could hear the gears grind as he sped—or at least tried to—around the arena. When he finished his circle, he jumped onto the hood. A spray of water shot from the tower, soaking him. He thrusted his arms into the air and yelled, "Pahhva." Then the Ba leaped off and began molesting the cheerleaders, who playfully pushed him away with their batons.

That Ba was followed by the mops representing Mafa Bah and Mafa Fah. They were even worse drivers, the final Ba stalling his car halfway through his lap. They also had the same terrible taste in music and performed the same deplorable act against the cheerleaders. But all three were gigantic, standing nearly eight-feet-tall.

Two of the cars were driven out of the arena, but the third—the one that had stalled—was abandoned since no one could figure out how to start it. Dumbasses.

As the announcer walked off the field, grabbing cheerleaders' asses as he did so, I glanced into the crowd and saw Hapa—the leader of Mafa Ahh. He had a smug look on his face as he pointed and laughed at the frail humans. The only consolation was his swollen lip.

Then a chill ran through me when I noticed the dirty, sleeveless Pasquale's Pizzeria shirt. To Hapa's left, sitting by herself, was Jennifer. She had been given one of the best seats in the arena. A perfect view to watch her father die.

She stood and ours eyes met. We stared at each other for a long moment. She wiped a tear rolling down her cheek, then squeezed her hands into fists, held them in a fighting position, and mouthed 'Come on.'

It made me think of Two Strikes. Not because he

fought, but because he didn't. I understood why Two Strikes had given himself up—even respected him for it—but I wasn't planning on doing the same. Not with my daughter watching. I'd rather her see me fight and die, then not fight at all. So yeah, honey, I'll raise my fists and keep punching until they knock the last breath out of me.

The announcer spoke into the megaphone, and the crowd fell silent. A few seconds later, music echoed through the arena. But it wasn't another American pop song. A row of mops played instruments that looked like drums and trumpets. The audience sang along, their arms swaying back and forth. The mop fight song perhaps, or maybe their anthem. But the crowd's voices, much like their choices in songs, were terrible—high and squeaky.

Brandon, who stood next to me, began to drop to a knee.

I grabbed his arm and yanked him up. "If you take a knee, I'm going to punch you in the face."

He remained standing until the anthem finished.

So what's the goal of Aba? Well, it's quite simple really. To kill everything. If you kill the other gladiators, and any pesky humans that happen to get in your way, you win. Each Ba must slaughter a dozen or so humans, along with a giant pom, before moving on to face each other.

Three successive blasts of water shot from the tower, soaking the crowd. They were frantic with anticipation. I glanced down and noticed a puddle on the ground in front of me. I dropped to my knees and slurped up a few ounces.

A horn sounded, and each Ba raised his club, gripping it

like a baseball bat. My chest tightened. I ran my damp hands against my shorts and blew out a long breath.

Oscar turned to me and the other humans behind him. "You're looking at the next winner of Aba!" he shouted, pounding his chest. "Let's go!"

As he turned back around, the Ba's club struck him in the forehead, killing him instantly.

I guess Aba had started.

Everyone scattered. I peeked over my shoulder as I ran and saw the Ba take down two more humans. Then I crashed into Brandon who had stopped in front of me. I wiped sweat from my eyes and saw a pom charging. That must have been protocol—the Ba would whack a couple humans, causing the others to run in the opposite direction, and then they'd release the pom. It trampled three humans before I had even blinked, which I did, hard. I shoved Brandon to my left, waited a half-second, then jumped to my right. The ground shook as the pom barreled by us.

From my knees, I saw the Ba club the guy behind me, and then the one behind him. Less than two minutes had gone by, and eight humans were dead.

The Ba's foot came down on the neck of an old man from our cell, and the count rose to nine. And based on the 'oohs' and 'ahhs' from the crowd, I assumed the same thing was happening in the other sections. Then the Ba's eyes locked on me, and he charged. With my chest heaving, I scrambled away, toward the cheerleaders. Two of them raised their batons as I got near, causing me to gasp and skid to a stop. I guess these gals did more than cheer; they were also security—to keep the humans in their designated sections. After all, it wouldn't be fair for a Ba to only kill eleven humans when he had been promised twelve.

I crouched down and swung my head around, then watched as the Ba whacked another human. Ten dead. Just Brandon and I remained. With my hands trembling, still crouched in front of the cheerleaders, I snuck a look at my daughter. Again, she squeezed her hands into fists.

I hadn't fought. Like all of the other humans, I had run. I was just trying to survive.

But as I stared at her two clenched fists, I realized I would have to fight eventually. And maybe if I started right-the-fuck-now, I could take the prick by surprise.

With gritted teeth, I shot toward him. Before he had a chance to raise his club, my right shoulder slammed against his chest. He was bigger, so I took the brunt of the collision, but we both went down. I watched him get to his feet and search for his club. But Brandon had it and was running away in a full sprint.

As the Ba started after Brandon, I landed a right cross against his cheek. Then a left hook to his ribs. And then another right, this one knocking him square in the jaw. The impact against the Ba felt different than the guy I hit in the desert. Maybe because he was more hydrated. He was definitely more angry, and let his own punch fly, nailing me on the bridge of my nose.

Being hit in the face by a mop is both better and worse than being hit by a human. It's better because their hands have more cushion due to their spongy skin—almost like boxing gloves. But it's worse because the mops are so much stronger. The force was noticeable, and his third shot sent me to the ground.

His punches came hard and fast. My vision grew blurry. Then I could feel his long fingers wrap around my neck. I gasped for breath as he squeezed. My body tingled. My hands had lost most of their feeling, but one had enough to slide into my shorts. I wiggled opened the inside pocket and slid out a handful of berries. Then I smashed them over the Ba's head and the blue juice soaked into his skin.

There are pros and cons to being so absorbent. One pro is that you don't have to worry about drinking water. You just absorb it. But a con is that you absorb all liquids. Even poisons. When the Ba felt the berries' juice seep into his head, he grabbed my hand and held it in front of his face. His eyes narrowed as he studied the blue stain on my palm. Then he laughed. How could I have possibly hurt him with that?

A few seconds later, he began to cough, which quickly turned into short, labored breathing. A pained look filled his face and, still on top of me, he began to wobble. His white eyes rolled back in his head, then he collapsed onto my chest. Dead.

Still on the ground, I saw two human feet walk up.

"Here you go," Brandon said, handing me the club.

"You know," I said, trying to catch my breath, "I could have used that a few minutes ago."

Brandon helped roll the mop off me. I got to a knee, wiped blood from my nose, and let my breathing settle. But before it could, my eyes flickered wide. The cheerleaders had parted and sprinting toward us was a Ba, his club raised, ready to swing. I guess he had already slaughtered all the humans in his section. I was sure his mother would be proud.

I grabbed Brandon by his jeans and yanked him down, just as the club went screaming over his head. The Ba stumbled but stayed on his feet. I got to mine and yelled to Brandon. "Get out of here!"

The Ba took two long steps and swung hard. I got the club up quick enough to save my face, but the impact sent my club hurling through the air. Before it had even landed, the Ba was halfway to it. Even if I had reached it first, it wouldn't have mattered. I couldn't beat a Ba in a sword fight. They were too strong.

I needed something bigger.

After scanning the arena, my eyes settled on the stalled car near the water tower.

Yeah, that'll work.

My boots pounded against the ground as I sprinted toward it. I hoped that the idiot had just flooded it and enough time had passed. After leaping into the driver's seat, my eyes jumped from instrument to instrument—steering wheel, shifter, gas, break. Must have been designed by humans.

I turned the ignition, and the son of a bitch roared to life. I revved the engine and screamed, "Yeah!"

The Ba slowed, peering into the car as he circled me.

My eyes traced the wires from the speakers to a

smartphone lying on the passenger seat. I scrolled through the list of songs, finding one horrible tune after another. Then I stopped.

The Clash. *Should I Stay or Should I Go.*

"Hell yeah," I muttered.

I tapped the song, and the speakers blared to life. Based on the scrunched-up faces in the crowd, I doubted the mops liked it.

So I went ahead and turned it up.

I peeked over my shoulder and saw the Ba sneaking up behind me. I pressed the clutch down, stuck it in first, and waited. The Ba was twenty feet away, then ten. Five. I turned the volume up as far as it would go, then released the clutch and floored it, spraying dirt over his pristine white skin.

With my head bobbing to the music, I tore around the arena. The cheerleaders retreated to the stands. I tapped my hands against the wheel as the song blared. The announcer, who was describing the whole thing through his megaphone, began backpedaling as I sped toward him. I dropped it into fourth and caught him in his ass.

"Pervert," I said as he tumbled to the ground.

Then I turned hard, dropped it back into third, then second, and took off toward the Ba. He took a few steps back as I lined him up. I shifted into third, then fourth, and slammed the accelerator against the floor. I wanted to run the sponge over.

The Ba stopped backpedaling, and lurched left and right. He was going to wait and jump out of the way. I would just need to guess right. And I did, though I didn't hit him cleanly. He bounced off my fender, which sent him, and his club, to the ground. Then I slammed on the brakes to avoid crashing into the crowd.

As I reversed, Brandon wandered out. I think he wanted to help. But from behind him, I saw the pom charge.

"Shit."

Still in reverse, I gunned it, zipping past Brandon and slamming into the pom. My head jerked as the pom crunched against the back of the car. It squealed and went down in a heap.

Then I shoved it into first and hit the gas.

"Get out of here!" I yelled as I tore past him.

The Ba picked up the club, slammed it against the ground, then waved for me to come back. The crowd roared. I started slow, keeping it in first as I rolled along. I needed to corner him. Otherwise his spongy ass would just keep bouncing off the car.

Again, he waved for me to come. I kept rolling, nice and easy as he shifted on his feet. I began a slow weave as I approached, moving him left, then right. With his back ten feet from the wall, I think the Ba realized what I was doing and scrambled to his left. I jammed it into second, released the clutch, and flattened the accelerator. The car hit his side, sending him into the wall. He staggered in place.

Then I hit him again and he dropped to his knees. He shrieked, his mouth stretched open. I reversed a few feet, then again, bam, into his chest. The Ba hunched over, and his head lined up with the front end of the car. I drifted back, blew out a breath, then jammed it into first and dropped my heavy boot against the pedal.

The Ba's head exploded, water and brain splattering against the windshield.

The crowd let out a collective sigh.

The front wheels scraped against the frame as I backed up. I doubted the car would last much longer. I shifted into first and as the car rumbled forward, I saw the final Ba jogging over. He was the Ba representing North Bomba, the same bastard who had hit me with his car. We were the only two who remained.

I drifted by the water tower, then stopped. The car rattled and shook. The Ba slowed, moving the club from his right hand to his left. I revved the engine as *Should I Stay or Should I Go* wound down.

As the Ba drew closer, I slipped the gear stick into reverse and began to ease the car backward. The crowd roared and pounded their feet.

Unlike the previous Ba, this one didn't dance around. He walked steadily toward me, his gaze locked with mine.

"Keep coming," I whispered.

From the look in his eyes, I could tell he wanted me to charge him. And I don't think he planned to jump out of the way. This Ba was going leap into the car and club me to death right there in the front seat.

I continued in reverse, drifting toward the tower.

"Come on."

The car squeaked as it rolled along. I turned the wheel slightly, lining up the back end with my target.

Then, just as the song ended, I let out the clutch and floored it. The back of the car crashed through the water tower's left-front stilt. As the Ba looked up, down came the tank, obliterating him in one gigantic explosion of water and debris. The crowd gasped as a loud BOOM echoed through the air.

Water surged across the ground, crashing against the stands and soaking the crowd. I crawled out of the seat and stepped onto the hood.

I raised my clenched fists and yelled, "Pahhva!"

CHAPTER 19

The crowd glanced around awkwardly, their tiny mouths hanging open. Now that the song had finished and Aba was over, the arena was eerily quiet.

Well, except for the screaming human girl.

I hopped off the hood of the car and slugged through ankle-high water, passing dead humans and mops. I climbed into the stands as rain began to fall.

"Jennifer!"

Mops tried to high-five me as I pushed through them, jumping from row to row, seat to seat. Jennifer hurried down to meet me. When we finally reached the same row, we stopped and faced each other. A smile sat proudly on her face, and her eyes glistened.

Then we hugged, shaking and sobbing as every white eye in the arena watched. It felt like the first time Jennifer and I had ever embraced. Our dirty, sweaty bodies stuck together. She smelled terrible. I held her tightly and stroked her hair as tears ran down my cheeks.

"Dad," she said, leaning back and pointing behind me. "That kid's still in the corner."

Oh, yeah. Brandon.

We waved him over. Brandon climbed into the stands and began jogging toward us along the bottom walkway of the arena.

The announcer, who I'd hit with the car, limped onto a stone block and motioned me over. I took Jennifer's hand, and the crowd parted as we walked down. I had heard the celebration for the winner was elaborate, but since the winner was human, I suspected they'd need a plan B.

When I arrived and stepped onto the block, the announcer sighed and raised the megaphone to his mouth. "Ahhpp Aba ... mo Mafa Ahh, mo Mafa Bah, mo Mafa Fah." He rolled his eyes and gestured to me. "Ahhpp Aba ... *huma*."

The crowd was silent.

"You know, he has an actual name," Jennifer said. "And it's not huma." She pointed at me. "Norman. His name is *Norman*." Then she smiled. "He's my father."

The announcer shook his head and gestured to me again, this one exaggerated. "Ahhpp Aba ... *Orma*."

Without a tongue, he couldn't pronounce the N's in my name. Good thing he didn't have to say Dohring.

Jennifer clapped, as did Brandon who had walked up, out of breath. The rest of the crowd stayed quiet.

Ma made her way down and asked if I wanted to say anything.

"Sure," I said, glancing around the arena. "I'm sorry I destroyed your water tower ... and flooded your little stadium here." I cleared my throat. "But aside from that, and all the dead people, it was great. Go North Bomba. Go Mafa Fah."

The announcer handed Ma the megaphone and she passed on my message. The mops exchanged looks but remained silent. Then a cop dropped a sack of coins at my feet. Ma said the winnings were a little less because I was human.

I raised my shoulders. "So is that it?" I asked. "We can just go home? There's not like a trophy presentation or anything?"

The announcer glanced at Hapa, who began to shout at me.

Jennifer tugged on my arm.

"We should probably go, Dad."

Before we did, Brandon turned to one of the cheerleaders. "Remember," he said to her. "You are not an object. You are a strong, independent woman who deserves respect."

I watched the corners of Jen's mouth stretch into a smile. The cheerleader tilted her head and stared at Brandon. Then Jennifer grabbed Brandon's hand, and we all walked down the tunnel.

The rain had passed as we emerged from the arena and into the city. We shielded our eyes from the sun, and then the three of us walked hand in hand down the main corridor. Mops stared and pointed as we passed them. But it wasn't like before. Word of my victory had reached the streets, and mops wanted to get a look at the first human to ever win Aba.

Although the adult mops stayed back, many of the kids approached, slapping my hand and rubbing my head.

"Huma ahhpp Aba! Huma ahhpp Aba!"

Human won Aba. Human won Aba.

Jennifer, Brandon, and I sat outside her residence eating our victory dinner. We had to cook and cut the pom ourselves, which had been dropped on her front step. They had just tossed it and left. We walked outside for water and there it was, lying dead on the ground.

Congratulations huma!

But I savored each bite, which I worked around my mouth before swallowing down. It tasted like beef tenderloin but was lighter in color. And that was all we ate, just the pom. There were no sides—no green beans or potatoes or salad. Just the meat, which we ate by hand. Even Brandon partook, despite having given up red meat earlier that year. He had initially refused the pom when we began eating, citing his newfound vegetarianism. I almost choked him on the spot. But thankfully, for the both of us, he wavered.

I stared at Jennifer as we finished our meal. I watched her mannerisms and facial expressions, and memories of the past seventeen years came flooding back. And these were good memories, not those of a missing child. I even enjoyed listening to Jennifer and Brandon talk because I got to hear her sweet voice, which sounded more like a woman's now.

My eyes drifted to her arms, which were thin, but I could make out ridges of muscle on her triceps and shoulders. The two K's on her right arm, and the ID on her left, had healed well. Better than mine. But it was her two strikes, and the thought of her screaming as they pressed the scorching iron against her skin, that still made me sick.

Jennifer said her first two weeks on Bomba were the toughest, and when she had received her two strikes. She hadn't been able to adjust to the heat, the length of days, or the manual labor, which consisted of hauling lumber for a building contractor. She eventually moved from hauling the wood to building with it. Having helped me finish the basement at our house in Henderson, she knew how to frame and finish rooms. She still struggled through the long days, but physically, the job was less demanding. And she worked smart. When she'd frame a wall, she'd position it so that the wall blocked the sun as she worked. She also invested in a large water container. Since Jennifer didn't have to lug her water throughout the day as I did, she was able to bring more and stay hydrated.

After Brandon had laid his head on the table and fallen asleep, I folded my hands together and cleared my throat.

"Jen, I uhhh …" I swallowed. "I want to let you know that I'm sorry."

She licked pom juice from her fingers. "For what?"

"For not driving you to work."

Her eyes were downcast, and she was quiet for a minute.

Then she said, "It was a nice day. There was no reason I couldn't walk." She peeked up at me. "Right?"

"That's what I said, Jen. That's what I said that day."

"I know," she said.

I gave a long, slow nod as despair filled my chest.

"But you're here now," she said.

Maybe so, but I was still the reason she was on Bomba. And still the reason she was without her mother.

I bit down on my lip. "Your mother misses you."

Her eyes fell again, then began to water. "How is Mom?"

"She loves you, Jen. Very much."

Jennifer waited for me to continue, but I stopped there. "So … how is she?"

Shifting in my seat, I rubbed my hands against my legs. "Well, she spent a long time—we both did—looking for you." Again, I cleared my throat. "And when we finally stopped, she became … lethargic. Depressed I guess."

Brandon mumbled something but appeared to stay asleep.

"Is the house quiet without me?" Jennifer asked.

With Amy and I having effectively stopped talking—any conversation with substance, anyway—the house wasn't just quiet, it was depressing.

I nodded.

Because we were human, Brandon and I weren't allowed to stay in Jennifer's room. Luckily their residence had openings, so I used part of my winnings to rent us rooms.

Usually the winner of Ba gets a thousand coins but because I was human, I received three-hundred. It would be enough to get us back to North Bomba, get us settled, and pay back Rodrigo's money. There might even be a few coins left over to finally buy myself a hat, or perhaps a drink at the bar.

Although I did pay for a separate room, I didn't sleep there. When night came, I snuck over and slept on Jennifer's floor. She wouldn't be leaving my sight anytime soon.

As I lay there, staring up at the starry night with my sore back resting against the wooden floor, I heard Jennifer's faint voice as I faded into sleep.

"Happy Birthday, Dad."

She had kept track of the days, too.

I could feel the sun against my face as I forced my eyes open the next morning. I considered sitting up, but with my back still aching—with everything still aching—I stayed curled up against the damp floor. It had rained overnight. Having been so tired, I must have slept through it.

"Are you awake?" I asked.

She didn't answer.

I struggled to my feet and saw that her bed was empty. I crept to the door and was about to open it when it cracked me in the head.

"Oh gosh. Sorry, Dad."

Jennifer stood in the doorway, holding something in her hand.

"Are you okay?" she asked.

"Yeah, yeah," I said, rubbing my forehead. "I'm fine."

She came in, closed the door behind her, and held up a carved piece of wood.

"I made you a present," she said.

"Jen, you didn't—"

"It's not for your birthday," she said.

I squinted, studying it. It was a wooden figurine—a man with two arms stretched in the air.

"What is it?" I asked.

"It's a trophy," she said with a smile. "For winning Aba."

We grabbed Brandon and walked down for breakfast, where I proudly showed off my trophy. Brandon said the figurine looked too thin to be me and then asked why he hadn't received a participation trophy for Aba.

As we ate, I explained our plan for getting back to North Bomba. We'd have to take the boat to Central Bomba. There, I'd buy bicycles for our trip through the desert. We would also need food, water, and supplies. Thankfully, my winnings would cover it all. But it wouldn't help much with scavengers, except maybe for a bribe.

As Jennifer explained where we could resupply, I heard a car approach. Bob, the leader of North Bomba, was driving and Ma was in the passenger seat. They stopped and said something to a human, who pointed toward us. After they drove over, we stood to greet them.

Bob extended his hand, and his small mouth stretched into a smile. He congratulated me for winning Aba. At least

I thought he did. Bob used words like ahhpp, pahhva, and Aba. The rest of what he said had to be translated.

I shook my head as I listened. Bob wanted me to campaign with him. He thought having the winner of Aba at his side could swing a few votes, at least liberal votes.

My eyes stayed on Bob as Ma finished.

"Tell him I'll pass," I said without hesitation.

Ma scratched her head.

"Tell him no," I said. "*Mo*."

After she relayed my message, Bob's phony smile shrunk into a hard line. Then he spoke again, his voice raised.

Jennifer explained that he was insulted. Bob was fighting for the rights of humans, and I was refusing to help.

"He's full of shit," I said. "He just wants to get elected. The only thing he's fighting for is more votes."

"He's also offering protection, Dad," she said.

"Protection from whom?"

Jennifer's eyes shifted from Bob, to Ma, to me. "From the police. And the politicians."

I shook my head. "Tell him I don't need it. Remind him that I won Aba. I'm free."

It was Ma who passed on my reply, and it was Ma who passed on Bob's counter, with her finger pointed at Jennifer.

"It's for me, Dad." Jennifer's eyes dropped to the two K's on her arm. "For my protection."

My throat tightened. I squeezed my hands into balls.

"No way, Jen, I'm not doing it. This guy's a hypocrite. He's just using us."

She nudged me. "Is he using us to get what he wants … or are we using him to get what we want?"

I glanced again at her brands. I didn't want to be a pawn in his political game, but if Jennifer made just one mistake, she'd be done. It might not even take that. If I didn't help Bob, they'd find something on her for sure. We might not even make it out of South Bomba before they singed her arm with that final K—the death brand.

Amy would have done it. She'd have accepted Bob's offer, wouldn't have thought twice about it. She would have done whatever was necessary to protect her daughter. I could hear her voice in my head. "How can you even consider not doing it?"

I shifted my feet, took Jennifer's hand, then blew out a breath. I fixed my gaze on Bob and nodded. "Papa."

His smile returned and he puffed out his chest. Bob went on to explain that we'd be attending rallies with him over the next week. He'd bring me on stage, and I'd wave to the crowd and tell them how awesome he is. "Bob pahhva!" I'd shout.

And that's exactly what I did. I spent the week attending two rallies a day. Bob called me up on stage and told the crowd that the winner of Aba had endorsed him for president. He told them that I was fluent in mop, that I had purchased my own house, and that I had a successful business with both human and mop employees. None of this was true of course, but he's a politician so the truth didn't really matter.

Jennifer and Brandon joined me at each rally. Despite

Bob's promise to protect my daughter, I kept Jen close. Even during the rallies, my eyes searched for her in the crowd, and when I found her, I'd check back to the same spot every couple of minutes.

I gave Brandon precise instructions. He was to stand by Jennifer's side while I was on stage. He would hold her hand—it was Brandon, so I wasn't worried about it—and not let anyone touch or talk to her. *No one.* If anyone did, or he felt they were in danger, he was to call out to me. I was worried about Brandon projecting his soft voice, so I asked Jen to call out as well.

So, rally after rally, I went on stage and yelled, "Bob pahhva!" to a mix of cheers and boos.

Though I despised the rallies, I enjoyed the time we spent traveling between them. I'd sit in the back of Bob's car with my arm slung across Jennifer's back and my fingers wedged between her and Brandon. We'd make fun of Bob's driving and wave to mops who were walking to work. I enjoyed seeing their bewildered expressions when they saw us—three disgusting humans taking a joyride with the next president of Bomba. Potentially. I even insisted that Bob give humans a ride to work occasionally. He wouldn't let them inside the car, so they'd sit on the trunk with their legs hanging over as Bob drove them to their jobs.

In the evenings, I'd lay on the floor of our room and listen to Jennifer and Brandon talk politics. They'd sit on the bed facing each other. Brandon would bring up social issues, and Jennifer would argue her more conservative side, which she no doubt got from me. I'd wake up in the middle of the night—after a dousing of rain—and still hear them debating. Brandon would emphasis words like "diversity" and "inclusion." And Jennifer's response would usually be, "And how do you plan to pay for it?"

The election ceremony would be held in Central Bomba, Mafa Bah, where they would announce the winner. We would need to travel by boat across the sea.

Before heading to the pier, I tracked down a haba plant for Shauna. She wanted it for her delivery, to help with the pain. I stuffed the pot into my sack of coins and instantly felt like a gangster. When I mentioned this to Jennifer, she said the hipper version was pronounced "gangsta." But when I said it, she laughed.

Since we were leaving South Bomba, and not entering it, we didn't have to pass through the checkpoint. But I stopped there anyway. As Jennifer and Brandon walked to the boat, I approached the guards. I glanced at their hands and was relieved to see my Timex wrapped around one of their wrists.

"I gave that to you," I said to the guard, and repeated it in mop. Then I offered to buy it. Although it was only worth one coin to him at the time, the dick charged me twenty to get it back.

I didn't hesitate.

Brandon threw up on the boat ride to Mafa Ba. The only reason he wasn't beaten was because of Bob. He protected us. I had helped him, so he helped me. A political favor. A quid pro quo.

Of course, we still had to clean it up. And since Brandon was too sick, that responsibility fell to Jennifer and me. We scooped up his vomit with our bare hands and tossed it overboard. I guess I deserved it for encouraging him to eat the pom.

"Sorry," said Brandon, who lay curled in a ball on the deck of the ship.

"Jennifer knelt beside him and wiped her hands against her shorts. "It's okay. Is there anything we can do for you?"

"He likes ginger ale," I said. "It makes his tummy feel better."

"Dad—" Jennifer said.

"I'm fine … thank you." Brandon's voice was weak and his face pale. "I should have kept my eyes on the horizon. Like my Dad taught me."

"Was your father a sailor?" Jennifer asked.

He nodded. "He was in the Navy."

I crossed my arms and stared down at him. "Your father was in the Navy?"

"Yeah," Brandon said.

"I don't believe it."

Brandon peeked up at me. "Why … what do you mean?"

"There's no way that you're the son of a Navy man."

"No, I am," he said, wiping his mouth. "Were you …"

"In the Navy, yes," I said.

"So that's why you curse so much," Brandon said.

After reaching Mafa Ba, we drove into the city, passing hordes of mops as they headed for the event. As before, they threw up their arms when they saw us in the backseat.

I asked Jennifer and Brandon to wait by the car when we arrived. Mops stared at me as I followed Bob through the crowd and up onto the stage.

Each politician spoke before they announced the winner. I shook my head as I listened. What a bunch of malarkey. And I didn't give a shit who won. I just wanted to get us back to North Bomba, back to my family at house six, the ones who were left anyway.

Bob was the last to speak. He said a few words, then waved me over. "Bob pahhva!" I shouted, striding toward him. I was such a punk. I was tired of being his puppet, tired of telling everyone how great he was. But I did it anyway. "Bob pahhva!"

Glancing over the crowd, I searched for Jennifer. I spotted her and Brandon with their backs against the car, and as instructed, Brandon had his hand in hers. They were talking, the corners of their mouths stretching into a smile every couple of seconds.

After Bob finished speaking, another mop with loose, wrinkly skin walked onto the stage. He had a megaphone in one hand and a folded piece of parchment in the other.

It was time to announce the winner—the next president of Bomba.

Motioning to each politician, the man gave their names and the region they represented.

"Bob—Mafa Fah. Bob—Mafa Bah. Hapa—Mafa Ahh."

Then he paused. The crowd was silent. A nervous energy filled the air as he unfolded the parchment.

"Ahhpp Bomba …" the man said. He brought the parchment to his eyes and read. "Hapa—Mafa Ahh!"

A mix of moans and cheers tore through the crowd. I could feel the stage shake as Hapa pumped his clenched fists.

"Mafa Ahh!" Hapa yelled. "Mafa Ahh!"

Didn't the idiot realize he was in Mafa Bah?

The two Bobs hung their heads. The older mop slung his arm around Hapa and asked if he wanted to say anything. He did, and when he finished, the crowd cheered. Then the older mop asked Hapa what he planned to do on his first day as president of Bomba, which apparently started right then. Why bother with a transition when you can start killing humans immediately?

Hapa took the megaphone and walked to the edge of the stage. Slowly, he turned his head, his eyes moving between the two Bobs before finally settling on me. Hapa began speaking again, motioning to me every few seconds.

Ma scooted closer and translated. I stood with my mouth half open as she whispered in my ear.

Hapa's first act as president would be to change the rules of Aba. Humans were now prohibited from winning. If they happened to survive, as I had, they'd simply be tossed back in jail, where they'd languish until the next match. If they made it that long.

And the best part of this important legislation? It would be retroactive. There would be no vote either. No consensus was needed. The president of Bomba had made a law and that was that.

"So what does it mean?" I asked Ma. "Am I still free?"

"Mo," she said with hunched shoulders.

Panic filled my chest. I couldn't believe this was happening. I was a regular human again. A human with three strikes. A convict.

Hapa's face contorted into a grin. He raised his arm and pointed at me. "Boh huma."

Get human.

A convict about to be sent back to jail.

With that thought, I took three steps and leaped off the stage. I crashed against two mops, then charged through the crowd.

"Start the car, Brandon! Start the car!"

I kept my head low as I ran, out of sight of cops, who lined the perimeter.

"Start the car!"

When I emerged from the back of the crowd, I spotted the convertible and sprinted toward it. Cops closed in behind me, their clubs clutched in their hands. As Brandon and Jennifer jumped into the front seat, I hurled myself into the back.

"Go! Go! Go!"

The engine fired.

"Go!"

But we didn't move, and a long moment ticked by. "What are you doing?" I jerked my head up and yelled to Brandon. "Go!"

His hands shook on the steering wheel. "I don't know how to drive stick."

Jennifer stepped over him and plopped down in the driver's seat. Then she jammed it into first, let out the clutch, and floored it. The tires spun against the dirt, showering the crowd behind us.

Then the car thrust forward. She dropped it into second, then third.

"Dad, where are we going?" she yelled as we barreled down the road.

"The desert! Head for the desert!"

With his head pressed against the seat, Brandon stared at Jennifer as she jammed it into fourth. He clutched the car door as wind funneled through the convertible.

Jennifer weaved through the street, screaming at mops to move. As she took the turn onto the main corridor—the one that would take us to the desert, and hopefully Mafa Fah—a mop stepped in front of the car. Jennifer jerked the wheel hard right. She missed the mop, but the car veered off the road, down an embankment, and crashed against a tree. Our heads whipped forward.

"Out! Out! Out!" I said, grabbing my sack.

Smoke rose from the engine. I climbed the embankment and peered into the street. Two cops ran past us, and I ducked back down.

"What are we going to do?" Brandon asked.

My eyes fixed on a building across from us. "I have an idea."

After she opened the door, Doll crossed her arms and stared at me.

"What the hell are you doing here?" she asked, then glanced at my strikes. "I told you not to get it wet. You're not getting a refund."

"I'm not here about that," I said, out of breath.

Doll's eyes moved past me to Jennifer and Brandon. "Well what do you want?"

"I need a different look," I said. "Is that something you can help with?"

"Like what? A disguise?" she asked.

"Yeah."

A knowing look crossed her face. "Do you know how much that'll cost?" she asked, her hands moving to her hips.

"I have the money," I said, then motioned to Jennifer and Brandon. "And I'll need this for all of us."

Doll shook her head. "I don't think you have that kind of money."

I shook the sack which held my winnings.

Gangsta.

Doll ran a hand through my hair, then worked her fingers around my face. "We could go one of two directions," she said. "We could darken your skin, or we could make it lighter, as if you were a bunch of pale novatos coming out of the wormhole." She shifted my head side to side. "Since you guys are already so dark, that's probably what I'd recommend." Her eyes drifted to Brandon. "Except for him, maybe. He's still pale. We should probably turn him black."

"Sounds good," I said, "Let's do it."

I glanced up at Brandon who stood with his mouth open, shaking his head.

"She wants to paint my face black?" he asked.

I nodded. "Yeah."

"I can't do that," said Brandon.

"What are you talking about?" I asked. "Why not?

"Because of blackface," Brandon said.

"Who's blackface?"

Brandon shook his head. "It's not a person. It's entertainment based on racist black stereotypes."

He said it like he was reading from a piece of paper.

My eyes shifted to Jennifer, then back to Brandon. "What does that mean?"

"It means I can't paint my face black," he said.

"Why?"

"Because someone might find it hurtful," Brandon said.

"Would you rather die?" I said with a roll of my eyes.

"Yes," he said, nodding. "I would rather die than have my face painted black. It's bad enough that I have three K's on my arm."

I leaned back on the couch and sighed. "Doll, what can you do for him?"

She took a moment and studied him. "Well, I can't shave him because he doesn't have any facial hair," she said. "But I could color the hair on his head."

"What about that, Brandon? Can she at least make your

hair black?"

Under an overcast sky, we emerged from Doll's building. A cop stood at the end of the block, staring at a piece of parchment in his hands. He glanced up and his eyes quickly locked on us.

"We should walk on opposite sides of the street," Jennifer said. "Two men and a woman. They'll figure it out, even with the disguises."

The cop took a few steps in our direction.

"Yeah but stay where I can see you." I talked with my mouth cracked open, trying not to disrupt the makeup on my face.

I nudged them to cross the street, and then we began walking parallel. Brandon shot out in front, taking long, hurried steps.

"Slow down, Brandon," I called from across the street. "There's no reason to go fast. You're not doing anything wrong."

Despite what I had said, my pulse quickened. I was heading right for the cop, who drifted to my side of the street. His white eyes moved from me to the parchment. I squinted as I passed him. He was holding a sketch of a human, of me. But Doll had trimmed my beard, cut my hair, and lightened my face, arms, and legs. She also covered one of my brands. She recommended leaving the other two. "More authentic," she had said.

So I just smiled at the cop and continued casually down the road.

Before leaving the city, we found a human store and loaded up on supplies—food, backpacks, and water containers—for our trek through the desert. Unfortunately they didn't have bikes, so we'd have to walk it. I didn't want to risk going to a mop store.

We filled the water containers at a nearby stream, then pushed on.

We had been walking for about four hours when we spotted the checkpoint in the valley. Once we passed through, we'd be out of Central Bomba, leaving us with a three day walk through the desert.

I was optimistic that we'd be protected in North Bomba. Bob hadn't won the presidency, but he was still our region's leader. And I had campaigned for him. Hopefully that still meant something.

But I was also realistic. If Bob didn't think there was a need for me, he wouldn't lift one of his spongy fingers to help. And I had to keep reminding myself that we had stolen his car. Either way though, Mafa Fah had to be safer than Mafa Ahh or Mafa Bah.

A hundred yards from the checkpoint, I said, "Let's go through separately. You two first, then me."

I handed them fifteen coins each as a sprinkle of rain fell. There wasn't supposed to be a toll to leave Central Bomba, but it would depend on the guards. I stayed back, crouched behind a tree as Jennifer and Brandon approached the checkpoint. I could hear mop and human voices but couldn't make out what they were saying. When it looked like they had passed, I got to my feet.

The sky had darkened, and the rain had changed to a steady drizzle. I slung the sack of coins over my shoulder and hurried toward the gate. The guards had their heads tilted back, soaking up the rain, as I walked up.

They flinched when they saw me and reached for their clubs.

I pointed into the desert. "Huma Mafa Fah."

The guards took me in, looking me up and down. One guard glanced to his left, where two sketches hung from a post. The first was of Fof, the first human, and the other was of me. But the old me, not the huma with the trimmed beard and pale skin standing in front of them.

With the sack of coins clutched in my right hand, I started walking again. "Huma Mafa Fah."

The guard stopped me, setting his club against my chest. His eyes darted from the sketch to me. White residue washed off my arms and legs as the rain picked up. The guard lifted my chin, his eyes searching my face. He ran a finger across my cheek, wiping away the white base and revealing a dark streak—my natural skin color, at least on Bomba.

Taking a step back, the guard squeezed his hands together, soaking my forehead and cheeks. Then his eyes flickered wide.

"Huma ahhpp Aba," he said.

Human who won Aba.

I rushed through the checkpoint. Before I had even taken a dozen steps, a spongy arm collapsed around my shoulder. I went down in a pile of dust and dirt. The guard leaped on me, pinning me to the ground, his hand pressed against the back of my neck. Peeking out from under him, I saw the other guard run over. He raised his club as he reached us.

Tensing my body, I waited for the blow. But the guard's head jerked back, and he let out a long, throaty scream. Just inches from my face, lay the hammerhead snake, its mouth latched onto the guard's ankle. The snake was tan, blending in with the ground, and it had a triangle pattern along its back. The ends of its head were darker and curved toward its tail. It was a nasty fucking thing, seven or eight feet long and as wide as my foot. I held my breath as it slithered away.

The guard collapsed. He shrieked as pink blood oozed from his ankle. I never heard a mop yell so loud.

Craning my neck, I peeked at the guard on top of me. His knee had relaxed against my back. He stared at the other mop, his mouth hanging open. Slowly, I gripped the sack of coins. Then, shifting my body, I swung it up. As it whipped toward his face, I prayed that the coins would hit him and not the pot. It made a muffled clang as it struck his chin.

Gangsta.

As the guard's hands went to his face, I thrust upward, pushing him off and onto the ground. I whirled the sack around my head, and struck him again, this time against his temple. I stepped toward him as he fell to his side, then raised my right boot and stomped down on his face.

I could hear the other guard—the one who had been bitten by the hammerhead—continue to wail as I ran off.

CHAPTER 20

Jennifer, Brandon, and I hustled down the road, through the desert, heading for North Bomba. It had been three hours since we passed the guard gate, and the landscape had become less green and more barren.

"Can we take a break?" Brandon asked again.

"Soon," I said. "Let's go a little farther."

"It is hot, Dad," Jennifer said.

I stopped and glanced down the road. It was clear. "Fine," I said with a sigh. "Five minutes."

We moved a few feet off the road and set down our gear. "Be careful where you sit. There are some nasty critters out here."

After kicking at the ground, we plopped down and drank from our water containers. We wiped our faces and sat hunched over, taking long, deep breaths. A minute later, I heard an engine.

"Get up," I said. "We need to move."

We grabbed our packs and scurried farther off the road, our heads low. After a hundred yards, we dropped to our stomachs. Turning back, I peered at the car speeding toward us. It was packed with mops, probably a half dozen. Cops no doubt.

The car slowed as it got closer. I could see mop heads turning as it motored by.

"Don't move," I whispered.

Brandon shrugged. "I wanted a break anyway, so …"

As the car continued down the road, I got to a knee. "Let's stay off the road for a while." Squinting, I pointed up. "We can use the sun as our guide."

Jennifer and Brandon sat up and took another drink.

"Easy with your water," I said. "We have a lot, but it needs to last three days."

"I have some," a voice said.

I scrambled to my feet as a figure came from behind us. Stepping in front of Jennifer, I narrowed my eyes, and the person's face became clear.

It was Fof. He was holding a silver goblet. "We can pass it around if you like."

As before, he was barefoot with loose clothing.

We all looked at each other. Jennifer and Brandon's mouths hung open.

"Where did you come from?" Jennifer asked.

The old man pointed over his shoulder. "Back there. You?"

"Um … we came from Mafa Bah," she said.

"That's quite a walk," he said.

He handed the goblet to Jennifer, who took it, glanced inside, then looked at me. I shrugged, and a moment later nodded.

She took a reluctant sip.

"How is it?" the old man asked.

"*Good*," she said with wide eyes. "I don't know how you keep it so cold out here."

Jennifer passed the goblet to Brandon, who finished it.

"I'm fine, Brandon, thanks," I said.

"Oh ... sorry," Brandon said. "I couldn't help it. I don't think I've ever tasted water like that."

The old man smiled. "It's from Santuario." Then his droopy eyes shifted to me. "You came back," he said. "You must really like the desert."

I shrugged and rolled my eyes. "Yeah, I really missed the heat ... and the ants and the snakes and the scavengers ..."

"Don't forget about the tarantulas," he said.

My eyes moved to the scar on my arm. "You know, I don't think I ever thanked you for that, so ..."

"You're welcome," he said. "But it appears you handled the other predicament yourself."

I peeked at Jennifer. "I did what I needed to do."

The old man's eyes stayed on me. He never seemed to blink.

"You said there was a time for everything, right?" I said.

Then I heard the faint sounds of another engine. It was farther out, but I could see it moving toward us, coming from Central Bomba, a cloud of dust in its wake.

"You're very popular," the old man said. But he was

looking the other way, toward North Bomba. I whipped my head around and saw the car that had passed us moving in reverse.

"Shit." I turned to Jennifer and Brandon. "We're going to have to split up."

"What?" Jennifer said. "No way, Dad. Why?"

"It'll be safer for you—they'll come after me. And you have supplies," I said.

She clutched my hand. "No."

"They can come with me if they'd like," the old man said.

We all looked at him.

"What do you mean?" I asked. "Where?"

"Santuario," he said.

I stared at him, trying to gauge if he was serious. "That place actually exists?"

"Oh yes," he said.

"And everyone's allowed?" I asked.

His eyes shifted to Jennifer and Brandon. "These two are."

The engines grew louder; the cars were closer.

"And there are people there? Humans?" I asked.

"There are lots of people on Santuario now," he said. "Good people. Your daughter would be safe."

The cars squeaked to a stop, and mops climbed out in a swarm, pointing and shouting.

I took a step toward the old man, my mouth a hard line. "How do I know you're telling the truth? How do I know that Santuario is even real?"

"I don't lie, Norman."

"Uh huh," I said with a groan.

The old man stood there with his arms at his side, completely comfortable in the moment. "You don't always have to see something to believe in it," he said. "Sometimes you need to have faith."

I glanced at Jennifer and Brandon, then back to the old man. "And they'll be safe there?"

"There's no place safer than Santuario," he said.

I pulled off my watch and slid it over Brandon's hand. "Put this on."

"Why?" he asked.

"Because I want you to wear it," I said.

I secured the watch, which sat loosely on his thin wrist.

"And don't forget to wind it. It's mechanical."

The pounding of footsteps echoed across the desert as mops sprinted toward us.

"Here, take some money," I said to Jennifer, reaching into my sack.

"You don't need money on Santuario," the old man said.

"Okay, whatever," I said in a rushed voice. "Stay there for a few weeks, then come find me at my old house." I pointed at Brandon. "You remember where that was, right? House six?"

Before Brandon could answer, the old man said, "They can't leave Santuario."

"What do you mean?" Jennifer asked.

He stroked his long beard. "Once you arrive on

Santuario, you're there forever. It's not possible to leave."

I glared at him, growing angry. "You do. You leave and go back all the time."

The creases on his forehead deepened. "I'm a little different."

The mops were fifty feet out.

"Go with the old man," I said to Jennifer. "Go to Santuario."

Jennifer's face turned red. "Dad, no ..."

"Go. I'll find Santuario. I promise."

"Dad—"

"*I'll find it.*"

The old man nodded. "I think you will one day, Norman."

Shaking the sack of coins at the cops, I sprinted to my left. "Here! Here! Right here!"

As I had hoped, they all followed. Still running, I reached into the sack, grabbed a handful of coins and chucked them into the air. Half the cops stopped and scrambled for the money. The rest kept coming, gaining, taking long swift strides.

Then a line of figures emerged in front of me. I wiped sweat from my eyes and saw more cops. They had surrounded me. I slowed, turning in place. I hurled more coins into the air, but they didn't move, except to inch toward me, their gaze steady.

I looked passed them and saw Jennifer, who was hurrying away with Brandon and the old man. She looked back and our eyes met. Grief filled her face as the cops edged closer.

"Don't watch, honey," I whispered to myself. "Please don't watch."

Then I blinked hard, and she was gone. I don't know how he did it, but the old man had gotten them out of there. He was a goddamn magician.

Suddenly, there was a flash, and the cops scattered.

I began stumbling backwards and had to hunch over to slow myself down. What the hell was going on? I was on flat ground, but it felt like I was being pushed backwards down a hill. It was the same sensation I had experienced near the water treatment facility.

I jerked my head up and saw a mop pointing past me, his mouth hanging open. I looked over my shoulder and saw it—the giant bubble, as big as a house—floating there, twenty feet behind me. Dark clouds hovered above, but through the bubble, through the hole, I saw blue skies.

"No—no—wait."

I dropped to my hands and knees, clawing at the ground as the wormhole dragged me toward it like a vacuum.

"No—Jennifer—I have to get to Santu—."

I dug my heels, trying to slow myself down. But the drag was too strong. I barreled across the ground and then flipped, going into a full tumble. Curling into a ball, I squeezed my eyelids and held my breath as the wormhole sucked me in. A loud pulsing pierced my ears, echoing inside my head. Then came the moaning, and off I went, flying through space like a fucking missile.

CHAPTER 21

The man on the other side of the table flexes his hand. He's taken a lot of notes, and sheets of paper are scattered across the table and on the floor. The whole thing would have gone a lot quicker if he hadn't told me to stop every couple of minutes so he could catch up.

But he's kept me hydrated and fed. I've had so much that I feel bloated now, though you won't hear me complain.

The man scratches his cheek, which now holds a day's worth of stubble. "Is there anything else?"

"No," I say, shaking my head. I glance at his papers. "Why didn't you just record me? Why did you write everything by hand?"

"I prefer it," he says. "It helps me … remember, I guess. Plus, I'm not a fan of electronics."

He sets his pencil on the table and a grin spreads over his face. "I can't believe you won Aba. There was a gentleman a while back—this ex-special forces guy—that was able to defeat a Ba, but no human ever came close to actually winning."

I nod, having heard the story before. It was an Army Ranger, though I wished it had been a Navy guy.

Then a tingling fills my chest. I cross my arms and stare at the man. "How did you know that?"

"What?" he asks.

"The Ranger who took down the Ba during Aba? Where did you hear that?"

The man opens his mouth to say something, then stops.

"You sure as hell didn't hear it from me." I motion to his papers. "Go ahead and look. You won't see it in your notes."

He presses the tips of his fingers together and looks down.

My eyes move back to the tattoos peeking out from his sleeve. I scoot closer in my chair, studying his face and hands. He has sun spots, which is unusual for a man his age.

I tilt my head back and look up. The ceiling has a plywood covering, but the rest of the building is a framed wooden structure.

My heart begins to thump. "Am I on Bomba?"

The man looks at me, holding my gaze. "You're at an FBI training facility near Groom Lake." He clears his throat. "It's in southern Nevada. A couple hours' drive from your home."

My eyes stay on him. "I know where it is. But I don't

believe you."

"I don't lie, Norman," he says.

"You know, someone else said that to me recently."

He doesn't respond.

"But if you say I'm on Earth, prove it."

He raises his shoulders. "What do you want me to do?"

"Bring my wife in."

"I will, but after you've been inspected," he says.

"And I'm going to be inspected by guys in hazmat suits, right?"

The man nods. "Probably."

I motion to the door behind him. "Then let's see them. I want to see these guys. In their suits. Right now."

Stretching his neck, he looks at the door. "Okay," he says and stands. He straightens his tie, walks to the door, and peeks back at me. Then he opens it and leaves.

My chest rises and falls. I stare at the handle, waiting for it to turn.

Finally, the door creaks open and the man steps back inside. Behind him, come three people dressed in yellow body suits with green gloves and white head coverings.

I exhale, then nod slowly.

After they leave, the man closes the door and leans against it.

"You're on Earth, Norman."

"Maybe," I say, pointing at him. "But there's something about you. The tattoos, the sun spots, the way you talk about Bomba … you know stuff … more than you should."

The man gives me a long, careful look. He shifts his feet. "I was on Bomba."

My eyes search the room. "But we're not there now?"

"No. We're on Earth—exactly where I said we were."

I sink back into my chair, studying his face. "So you're *that* Joshua."

"What Joshua?"

"The old man's son. The one who came to Earth ... so others could enter Santuario." I point at him. "That's you."

He gives a reluctant nod.

Straightening in my chair, I say, "Then I guess I have you to thank for my daughter's safety. Right? Because if it wasn't for you, she would've never been allowed in."

The man walks over and sits back down. "If my Dad let your daughter in—which it sounds like he did—then he's the one you should thank. And he is right by the way—she'll be safe on Santuario."

I rub my chin. "Why do you think the wormhole brought me back?"

His eyes fall to the table and his shoulders slump. "So you could tell me what my father said."

The room is quiet for a minute.

"He wants you to go back," I finally say. "You know, he was just trying to protect you."

Joshua looks at me. "He should protect everyone. They all should be allowed into Santuario."

Again, the room falls quiet.

"Well ... considering my daughter's there," I say, "I'm not so sure I agree with you."

I hold his gaze for a moment, then glance around at the sheets of handwritten notes.

"Are you really with the FBI?" I ask. "It looks like you're writing scripture instead of an official report."

"Yes, I'm really with the FBI. And you're really at an FBI training facility." He glances up, taking in the room. "Of course, the location of this building isn't a coincidence. There's a lot of activity around here."

"With the wormhole?"

He nods, then loosens his tie. "I'm sure you've heard the stories of area fifty-one. That's been nothing but a help to us, really. With the wormhole popping up so randomly, it allows folks to pin the sighting on something. They just don't realize it's something else." He shrugs. "And the media, with their Heat Miser theories, has helped with all the missing people." He pauses. "And if you're wondering, yes, I feel responsible for all of them. Including your daughter."

I squeeze my hands into fists, then exhale. "What are you going to tell my wife?"

Joshua fidgets in his chair. "About your daughter?"

"About where I've been."

"I think we should be honest with her, but …" he sighs. "My boss insists we tell a different story."

I rest my arms on the table and lean forward. "Which is what?"

"That you spent the last several months searching for your daughter. You ended up in Death Valley, where you got lost and had to survive on bugs and insects and things like that ... which is why you're so thin. And your skin can be explained by the sun and heat."

"In Death Valley?"

"Right."

My eyes drop to the brands on my arms. "And how are you going to explain these?"

The man blows out another breath. "Infections. From spider bites."

"Spider bites?"

"Yes. But you'll need cosmetic surgery. We're going to try and make the brands look more like scars from an infected bite. We'll need to wrap your arms in bandages in the meantime. You're married, so it'll be harder for you to hide this." He peeks down at his bicep. "Of course, you could always go the tattoo route like I did."

"I'll pass."

The guys in the Hazmat suits poke and prod me. They look in my mouth, in my ears, up my ass—every damn orifice I have. They shine lights in my eyes, draw blood, and make me blow into a tube. I guess they're checking for the severity of my bad breath. I'll save you the suspense, it's horrible.

They dress me in FBI-issued sweat pants and a plain white t-shirt. It feels strange wearing a shirt and even stranger wearing one that's so clean. I can smell the detergent. Then they wrap my biceps in bandages to hide the brands.

After they leave, I sit on the table with my eyes half

open. I'm about to lie down when I hear a knock at the door. Joshua steps inside. He's holding something in his right hand, but my tired eyes can't make it out.

"We recovered this close to where we found you," he says, holding the object up. "Does it mean anything to you? Look familiar?"

The object comes into focus. It's the hand-carved trophy that Jennifer had made me for winning Aba. I nod and pull it from his hand. It was in my shorts when I went through.

He waits for me to explain, but I don't. I stay quiet and hold it against my chest.

"Your wife is here," he says.

My eyes drift past him and settle on the door. "She's right outside?" I ask, my voice cracking.

"Yes." Joshua pulls up my sleeves, revealing the fresh bandages. "Would you like to see her?"

I look down at myself. The trophy shakes against my chest. "Uhhh … of course. Do I …"

"Do you what?" he says.

"Is she just going to walk right in?" I ask.

He nods. "If you're ready for that."

I shift on the table. "Should I stand?"

"If you'd like to," he says.

Joshua helps me off the table. I set the trophy down and stand flatfooted as he walks out. I stare at the door. Then I look down at my feet, then my trembling hands.

I feel my face flush as the door pushes open. Amy runs to me. She comes so quickly that I barely have time to process what she looks like. Within seconds, her arms are around me. She tries to talk but can't stop crying. I can feel her trembling. Her grip is so tight that it actually hurts. My legs are still numb, but I'm certain Amy will keep me upright if they give out.

When she finally pulls back, her wide eyes search my sunken face. "Norman," she says, sobbing. "Oh my God." Her mouth hangs open as she takes me in—the weight loss, the sun damage, the dirt, the grime, the calluses. "Oh my God. What happened to you?"

I take her hands in mine. "I'm sorry."

"What?" Her arms continue to shake. "Why are you sorry?"

"Jennifer …"

"*What?*" she says.

My vision grows blurry with tears. "I'm sorry, Amy. I'm so sorry about Jennifer. I'm so …"

CHAPTER 22

I sit on Jennifer's bed, holding a framed picture of her. She looked so much older on Bomba, so much more mature. I wish Amy could have seen her—not the scars or the bony legs—but the woman she had become. I'm proud, and lucky, to have her as my daughter.

My eyes drift to the drawing Jennifer made when she was eight. In the picture, a boy and girl are holding hands, waving with their free hands to a figure in the distance. I had always thought of Frederick when I looked at the boy in the picture. But now it was Brandon I saw. The boy even had his thin, awkward frame.

I feel confident that Jennifer and Brandon made it to Santuario. I have no proof, but as the old man said, sometimes you need to have faith. And if I could pick one of Jennifer's friends to join her there, I would pick Brandon. He wouldn't be able to provide protection, not physically, but that didn't seem to matter on Santuario.

What Brandon would provide was friendship and respect, which is all a father could ever want.

I'm not in Jennifer's room for very long before Amy comes in. It's hard going anywhere without her these days. She doesn't like it when I leave the house, or even a room for that matter. She comes with me almost everywhere—to the store, to get my hair cut, to get the oil changed, even to work some days, where she helps Camila in the office. She also joins me for my evening walks.

Amy asks often about the time I spent looking for Jennifer and how I survived in Death Valley. I provide vague details and change the subject whenever possible. I'm not sure she believes me though. She probably believes I went looking for Jennifer, and in a way that's true, but she knows I'm hiding something, which is also true.

We sleep together every night now. It's an adjustment lying next to someone and having a full roof over my head, but slowly I grow accustomed to the luxuries of a first world country. I gain back all my weight, and then throw on ten more. I've never stacked my roast beef sandwiches so high.

I've been especially happy to see indoor plumbing. My first trip to the bathroom—sitting on that head with a bath rug under my feet—oh man. And I only had to walk ten feet to get there. And don't get me started about toilet paper.

My face and hands look strange to me now. They're so trim and clean. I stare at myself in the mirror for long periods of time, though the man I saw in Doll's mirror continues to flash in my head. I doubt that image will ever go away. Maybe I don't want it to.

The biggest challenge has been keeping the brands covered. I'm not sure how I'm going to get away from Amy long enough to have the surgeries. I don't know how the reconstructive surgery will work, but as long as my arms don't look like a scorching metal bar was pressed against them, I guess it'll be fine. An improvement at least.

Since my flip phone is still on Bomba, Amy and I go shopping for a new one. Though I object, she convinces me to buy a smartphone. It's too bright and feels awkward when I stick it in my pocket. But I'll admit, I don't hate it. I've even snapped a few pictures. No selfies though.

Although I don't download any social media apps, I do add a few songs, the first being *Should I Stay or Should I Go* by the Clash.

It takes me two hours to get to Mesquite. Camila helped me find the address online. Rodrigo had mentioned where his mother lived, and since she's the only Isabella Mateo in Mesquite, she wasn't terribly difficult to find.

As I pull up to her house, I see a woman sitting in a rocking chair on the front porch. She's heavier than I expected, but I guess that's naïve; I'm used to seeing Rodrigo, who would sweat out thousands of calories a day pushing a wheelbarrow full of stones. But I can tell from her face that she's his mother.

I grab the envelope, hop out of my truck, and amble up the walkway. Her head stays straight as I step onto the porch. It takes me a few seconds to realize she's sleeping.

I clear my throat, but she doesn't move.

"Excuse me," I say.

She flinches and thrusts her eyes open. "Didn't you see the sign?" she says. Her English is clear, but as with Rodrigo, she has a thick Spanish accent.

"What?" I say. "What sign?"

"No solicitors." She straightens in her chair, which begins to rock.

"I'm not selling anything," I say.

"What do you have in your hand?" she asks.

I can see where Rodrigo got his friendly personality.

"It's for you," I say.

She sighs and shakes her head. "I don't want any coupons. And I don't need my lawn fertilized or my driveway paved."

"I understand. I'm sorry to interrupt, Ma'am, but I have something to give you. Well, it's for Rodrigo …"

Her eyes narrow. She glances at my truck, then back at me.

"You knew my son?"

"Yes, Ma'am."

She crosses her arms over her chest. "Let me guess? You're here to give me a bill."

"No, Ma'am. But I do have money. I owed it to Rodrigo and wanted to pay it back."

Still rocking, she doesn't respond.

"You're Isabella, right? You're his mother?"

She nods.

I extend my hand, offering the envelope. "Can I give it to you?"

Isabella kicks against the porch, increasing the momentum of the chair. "You can, but I can't guarantee he'll get it."

"I understand."

She stops the chair. "So you're aware that Rodrigo went missing?"

Pulling the envelope back, I shuffle my feet. I'm not really sure what to say, so I nod.

"Did you work with him?" she asks as the chair begins to move again.

"I did."

Isabella peeks at my truck. "Why do you owe him money?"

"He uhhh … he lent it to me?" I say.

She laughs. "No way. If I taught my son anything, it's not to lend money."

Again, I nod.

She continues rocking as I stand there with the envelope clutched in my hand. There's eight-hundred dollars inside. Based on the likely exchange rate between the United States and Bomba, it's more than what I owe.

"Go ahead and set it on that table," she says, pointing to my right.

She doesn't trust me, but that's fine. I set it down and step off the porch.

"I just want to say that your son was a good man."

"*Was*," she says. "I guess you're not expecting him to

come back either, huh?"

I raise my shoulders.

"Well, I am." Her eyes return to the road, as if waiting for someone. "Rodrigo's tough. He'll make it back. So will Mateo."

I doubt Isabella leaves that chair very often. She probably spends many nights there rocking, waiting for her son and husband to come home.

She also has no idea that she'll be a grandmother soon. Of course, that's assuming the delivery goes well. On Bomba, the survival rate during birth isn't great, for the infant or the mother. And Shauna won't have any haba to help with the pain, because I never got it to her. It's one of many things that keep me up at night.

"Have a nice evening, Ma'am," I say to Isabella, and walk back to my truck.

The transition back to work is tough, but not for the reasons you might think. Being a hauler on Bomba left me in great shape, and I've been able to work straight through even on the hottest days. The problem I'm having is adjusting to a twenty-four-hour cycle. My sleep and wake times are off, and my work day seems incredibly short. It doesn't feel right to stop after a mere eight hours. When I hear guys from my crew complain about the heat or long hours, I just laugh.

I'm about to roll out of bed on Monday morning when Amy tugs on my shirt.

"No," she says. "Don't get up yet."

I had always gone to bed shirtless, even before Bomba, but I've worn one every night since I've been back. It's mostly because I'm cold; I haven't adjusted to the temperature, especially inside when the air-conditioning is running. Of course, the shirt also covers the bandages, which makes for less questions.

I turn and wrap my arms around her. Being intimate still feels awkward though, I think for both of us. "Are you going to come with me?" I ask. "To the office?"

"Yeah," Amy says. I can feel her breath against my neck.

"I like riding together in the morning," I say.

"Me too, honey."

She slides her hand up my shirt, running her fingers along my back. I flinch, and a shiver runs through me.

"But I've been thinking about going back to work," she says.

I pull back. "To New Horizons?"

"No. I had a different idea."

When Camila arrives later that morning, I ask her to join me in my office. Although I lost customers while I was away, Camila, with help from Amy, was able to keep the business running.

With a pen and paper clutched in her hands, she hurries to my desk. She sits down across from me and prepares to write. As usual, her eyes are puffy and her hair is pulled back in a ponytail. She reminds me of the women on Bomba.

"That new, Mr. Dohring?" Camila asks.

She motions to the trophy, the one Jennifer made me on Bomba. I keep it on my desk now.

"It looks like you," she says.

I pat my stomach. "In my youth maybe."

When Amy asked about the figurine, I told her Jennifer had made it for me before she went missing. A half truth I suppose. I'm starting to feel like a politician.

But I'm proud of the trophy. Lots of guys keep awards on their desk, but I'm pretty sure I'm the only one who earned theirs by winning a fight to the death on an alien planet.

"Anyway," I say, "we wanted to talk to you for a few minutes."

She peeks up at me. "We?"

With my thumb, I point to the corner of the room, where Amy stands with her arms folded. Her face is tan from our evening walks, and her clothes hang off her.

"Mrs. Dohring," Camila says. "I didn't see you there."

"Good morning, Camila," Amy says.

"Good morning, Mrs. Dohring. Good morning."

I interlock my fingers and set my hands on the desk. "We wanted to thank you for everything you did while I was away."

"Of course, Mr. Dohring," she says, nodding.

"Is everything okay with you?" I ask.

"Yes, Mr. Dohring. I entered new work orders into the system and printed out today's schedule."

"We didn't want to talk about work," I say, waiving off her comment. "We wanted to ask you about Leonardo."

Camila looks to Amy, then back to me.

"Mr. Dohring, Leonardo hasn't been in the office since you've been back, but ..." Her eyes fall to the ground. "I had to work lot of hours to keep business going ... I ... I couldn't."

"It's okay, Camila." I shift in my chair and blow out a breath. "The reason I was asking about Leonardo is because I wanted to see what you were doing for care?"

"My cousin watch sometime," she says with a shrug.

"So you don't have him in a facility or anything?" I ask.

"Care very expensive."

"Well, we'd like to help," Amy says.

"No, no, too expensive, Mrs. Dohring," Camila says. "Thank you, but no."

I lean back in my chair and clear my throat. "We're not giving you money."

Camila mentioned that Leonardo had grown, but my mouth still falls open when I see him standing at my front door the next morning. His clothes make him seem even bigger. His shirt is a size too small and his pants a few inches short. He stares down at me.

"How are you, Leonardo?" I ask.

His eyes drift to the ceiling and stay there.

Camila peeks out from behind Leonardo's broad shoulders. "He non-verbal, Mr. Dohring."

"Right ..."

Leonardo moans as Amy comes around the corner, and then he begins to rock on his heels.

"He's non-verbal," I say to Amy.

She holds back a smile. "I know, honey," she says. "But it doesn't mean you can't say good morning." Amy joins her hands behind her back and looks up at him. "Good morning."

Leonardo doesn't respond, but like they said, he doesn't speak.

We move to the kitchen where Camila spends the next five minutes thanking Amy. Leonardo has stopped rocking and is now facing Camila with his arm hooked around hers. I suspect it'll be challenging when she leaves. I wouldn't be surprised to find a few holes in the wall when I return.

Amy warned me that the first day would be rough.

Then Leonardo lets out a long, throaty moan. I stare at him. The hair on the back of my neck stands on end as I flash back to the wormhole—the pulsing, *the moaning*.

An eerie coincidence. I shake it off, grab my keys and slip my smartphone into my pocket. "I still expect you to be at work on time," I say to Camila.

"Yes, of course, Mr. Dohring," she says. "I allow extra time this morning."

"I have to meet with some clients in Vegas, so you'll need to give the guys their assignments," I say.

"Yes, Mr. Dohring, I know," she says.

I kiss Amy, then head for the door. "And if I find any holes in the wall when I get home, Camila, you'll have to patch them."

"I have spackle and a putty knife in my car, Mr. Dohring."

I turn to her. "Really?"

"Yes," she says.

"I was actually kidding, Camila."

She shakes her head. "I wasn't, Mr. Dohring."

With my windows down, I drive my truck east along State Route 583. I tap my hand against the wheel as my smartphone shuffles through its songs. It's only mid-afternoon, but I decide to head home instead of returning to the office. I have a quarter tank of gas and can probably make it back to Henderson but decide not to risk it and pull over.

As I stand at the pump, leaning against my truck, I hear *Should I Stay or Should I Go* come on. It's only one of a dozen songs on my smartphone, so it comes on often. But that doesn't stop the emotions from stirring inside me as it plays. My hands begin to shake, and I stuff them into my pockets. I glance at the cars and customers around me. Then I notice a missing person sign tacked to a telephone poll near the entrance to the station. The sheet is ripped and worn. Squinting, I can see a girl's face, and as I walk closer, the person becomes clear. It's Jennifer. She has her hair pulled back and she's wearing a nervous grin. It was her first day of work at Pasquale's.

I remember this gas station. This is where I hung my last flyer. After blotting my sweaty palm against my jeans, I dig a pen from my pocket. On the flyer, I cross out the word MISSING and above it, write LOVED.

Should I Stay or Should I Go is still playing when I hop

back into my truck. A wave of heat comes through the open window, and I wipe a film of perspiration from my forehead. I reach down, flip on the AC, and roll up the windows. The cool air feels refreshing against my face.

As I sit there with the engine running, my eyes wander back to Jennifer's picture. But it's the Bomba Jennifer I see, with streaks of dirt on her sunburned cheeks and dark circles under her eyes. I stare at it for a long moment. Then I shut down my phone which abruptly ends the song. I flip off the AC, roll down the windows, and decide to head to the office after all.

THE POWER OF A REVIEW

One of the most important things an independent author can receive is a review. It allows us to compete with large publishing companies and bring original works to the attention of other readers.

So if you've enjoyed this book, I would be grateful if you spent a minute writing a review (even a short one).

Thank you so much.

ABOUT THE AUTHOR

J.F. Wiegand is a software developer and the author of *I'm Not Weird, I'm Just Quiet* (yeah, he's an introvert) and *Race to the Edge of the World* (yeah, he likes to run). He lives in Mount Airy, MD with his wife, three children, and a Goldendoodle named Lucy.

He's currently working on his fourth book, the sequel to *The Curmudgeon and the Wormhole*.

You can find more about the author at jfwiegand.com.

Made in the USA
Middletown, DE
08 May 2020